BRASADA

by

Don Johnson

GoldenIsle Publishers, Inc.
Eastman, GA 31023

GoldenIsle Publishers, Inc.
2395 Hawkinsville Hwy
Eastman, GA 31023

Library of Congress Card Number: 98-73651

Don Johnson, 1927
  Brasada/Don Johnson

ISBN 0-9666721-2-7

1.   Civil War – Texas, 1860s – fiction. 2. Ranching, Texas Brasada
     Country – fiction. 3. Border outlaws – Texas & Mexico – fiction. 4.
     Commerce – gold & cotton – fiction. 5. Recovery, Texas – fiction
          I. Title
          II. Title: Brasada

Printed in the United States of America

Designed by Tena Ryals

First Edition

10 9 8 7 6 5 4 3 2 1

CHAPTER 1

He was trapped. Too late to turn back.

The prickly feeling at the nape of his neck told him so. He trusted that feeling. It had never failed him.

His eyes desperately searched the tangled thicket of mesquite and whitebrush. Something was there -- there must be some unusual sign — but he couldn't find it. He cursed the heavy brush as he pushed a thorn-studded mesquite limb out of his way, watching as it snapped back.

"Easy, boy." He patted the buckskin gelding on the neck. Fingering the leather satchel that hung over his shoulder, he murmured, "Colonel Ford wouldn't want us to lose this."

He remembered the words of Colonel Rip Ford. "There's a wagon train headed for the Eagle Pass Crossing. Take this dispatch to their commander. Tell him that Brownsville is in safe hands. He is to turn south and deliver the cotton directly to the merchants in Matamoros."

"Yessir, I'll leave right away."

"Watch yourself." Ford struggled to his feet and grasped the hand of Arthur Canton, his longtime scout. "These are hard times, and that cotton is worth a fortune. There is little some men wouldn't do to divert it to their own use."

The buckskin's ears came alert pointing straight ahead. Canton's hand darted to the .36 caliber Texas Paterson riding high on his right hip. But even as he made the move, he knew he was too late.

A fusillade ripped through the delicate green of the newly budded mesquite, and he twisted in the saddle under the impact of a heavy bullet slamming into his left shoulder. He spurred his animal straight ahead toward the source of the gunfire, firing the 5-shot Colt fast and accurately. Two men, caught trying to reload their muskets, sprawled awkwardly. Another turned to run but was knocked hard to the ground by the buckskin's surge through the brush.

Canton whirled his mount quickly toward the relative safety of heavier brush, but another volley crackled and three bullets ripped into his back slamming him from the saddle. He lay still, a trickle of blood dribbling from his mouth.

Excited voices shouted. First one then another swarthy face appeared, looking through the mesquite screen at the fallen Confederate scout. One stepped warily into the clearing and crossed to the body.

Looking over his shoulder, he shouted in Spanish, "He's dead."

He snatched the satchel from around Canton's shoulder and held it aloft. "And here's the packet."

A low moan came from the scout, and the man with the satchel whirled toward him just in time to see the revolver creep from under Canton's body. The bandit grabbed at his own pistol when Canton's last bullet tore his throat out.

The surviving bandits fired again and again into the dying trooper.

They gathered round the satchel, eight men dressed in typical loosely fitted garb of the Mexican peasant. One spoke, "Sanchez, you read the English."

Sanchez swaggered forward and snatched the document from inside the satchel, held it close to his face, and frowned.

"Aha!" he croaked. "The gringo spy was right. Even now the wagons move toward the Eagle Pass Crossing."

The men leaped on their short, stunted ponies, and with an exuberant yell, dodged out of the brushy motte and sped across the prairie. Behind them, the sharp-eyed buzzards began a long, circling descent into the mesquite grove.

The Spanish speaking inhabitants called it *la brasada*, a sweeping crescent of wilderness between the Nueces River and the Rio Grande in Southwest Texas. The land's rolling, rocky hills were gashed by numerous arroyos washed out through centuries of flood alternating with searing drought. On the flats, mottes of thick and wicked brush grew, tangled and thorn-studded.

Between these mottes and below them as an understory, nutritious grasses and forbes existed and flourished when the fickle climactic conditions were favorable. Vast herds of wild mustangs and wild cattle found the *brasada* an ideal breeding ground. With the formidable brush and distances as effective barriers against the intrusion of mankind, they had fattened and procreated undisturbed for many decades.

In the early spring of 1865, nature was in an especially benevolent mood in the *brasada*. A winter of generous rainfall had brought out a confusing abundance of plant life to flourish under the gentle March sunshine.

Guajillo waved its fern-like leaves with every breath of

4

wind, and the golden flowered huisache trailed its spiny branches almost to the ground. Grey leafed cenizo dressed the hillsides in lavender with a profusion of tiny blossoms. Wild vetches, mingled with buttercups and bluebonnets, together with dozens of unnamed forbes, had burst into fragrant bloom from seed that had lain dormant for decades awaiting such a season. Just four months of abundant rainfall had transformed the barren countryside into a multi-hued kaleidoscope.

The spectacular display was not wasted on the rider, who sat easily in his saddle as his blue roan gelding lunged scrambling up the bank of a small arroyo. He sniffed the air appreciatively, catching the heady scent of wild blossoms crushed beneath his horse's hooves.

Reining the blue to a halt on level ground, he watched as his companion scrambled up beside him. Both men were clad in Confederate grey, with Colt .44, 1860 Model Army revolvers holstered on their belts, and booted, breech-loading muskets hung from their saddles.

The first rider was of medium height, but stocky of build. His squinted eyes were bright blue in startling contrast to his sun-browned face. His features were regular, and his smooth unlined face was that of unstressed youth, convincing evidence that he had yet to reach his eighteenth birthday. As he tilted back his hat, a pale band was revealed above the tanned face, extending into the hairline. His light brown hair showed darker where the hat band had held the sweat.

Taller and thinner, the second rider was but three years older than the first – but looked much older. Unkempt black hair stuck out from under a hat which crowned thin, prominent features and a protruding Adam's apple. A heavy cud of tobacco bulged his right cheek.

Giving their horses a breather, they turned to watch a wagon train undulate toward them about a half a mile back. The first rider nudged his mount closer to his companion's blaze-faced chestnut. "Well, George, nice day for whatever we've got to do."

The other pushed his hat back from over his eyes before he responded, "You're dead right about that."

Lance squeezed his horse into a slow foxtrot up the rise ahead of them.

George turned to follow the other up the rise.

Captain Jess Waldrop sat his mount off to one side and watched the train move. The trail was a thin ribbon of dust. It rose in a choking cloud behind the wagons, each of which was loaded with sixteen 500-pound bales of cotton and pulled by

5

a team of twenty mules. They creaked their way along a pair of ruts cut so deeply in the Texas prairie that their outline would remain visible for more than a hundred years. Those dirt ruts had become the lifeline of the Confederacy.

Cut off from direct sea routes to European markets by the Union naval blockade, the cotton moved out of the South through its back door into Mexico. Transported from there by ships of foreign registry, the cotton fueled the hungry looms of Europe, kept the Confederate government solvent, and enriched the diligent merchants of Matamoros – Rebel, Yankee, Mexican and European alike. They all came together to bask in the warm glow of easy, bountiful, and devious profits.

Lately, the ebb and flow of opposing military armies had forced the cotton traffic northward to Eagle Pass, where the Rio Grande would be crossed and shipment continued down the river to Matamoros. Despite great efforts by the Yankees to stop it, the wagons kept coming, leaving little bits of white fluff hanging on the thorns of catclaw, mesquite, and tassajillo behind them.

The protection of one of these was Capt. Waldrop's assignment.

He had a dozen mounted troopers and the charge to escort the wagons to their destination, sell the cotton, and return the proceeds in gold to the Confederate government.

In spite of the long journey and its attendant fatigue, Waldrop sat his dappled grey tall and straight. He could no more permit himself to slump in the saddle than he could cheat at cards.

He glanced at the trooper with the sergeant's chevrons on his sleeve who reined up beside him. He shaded his eyes and peered ahead. "Who's scouting out front, Sergeant?"

"Morgan and Gibson, sir."

The captain mentally clicked through his roster. He not only knew the names of all his men but was quite familiar with their service records. Lance Morgan and George Gibson, good men, both of them. Both from Tennessee with little else in common.

Lance Morgan, eighteen years old, excellent rifle shot, probably grew up hunting squirrels, mediocre at best with a handgun. Farm boy from a prosperous, solid family. No combat as yet.

He was what the captain thought of as a "doer." He was confident and resourceful, an excellent combination. His lack of experience might make him do something the wrong way, but, by God, he'd get it done. There was something else about the boy -- an intangible quality that was hard to name. But it

6

drew others to him. Even some of the older veterans looked to the youngster when they had a problem. Had an open, honest look. Product of good parents. Sturdy, solid stock.

George Gibson was a different story. Just twenty-one, he had three years of combat experience and had been cited twice for valor. With only average military skills, Gibson achieved by sheer determination.

On the record where Father's Occupation was listed, George had written in "blacksmith." Technically, it was correct, but that had been a long time ago. Waldrop knew the boy lost his mother while quite young and had been reared by a father who, unable to cope with his young wife's death, became the town drunk.

To Waldrop, that made Gibson's accomplishments all the more remarkable.

He dabbed away beads of sweat that formed on his upper lip and turned to the sergeant. "Call in the scouts, Sergeant. We make camp early tonight."

"Yes sir," the sergeant replied as he reined his horse about.

CHAPTER 2

The market place of Matamoros, Mexico, was a maelstrom, sucking up cotton from any source. Buyers were little concerned as to the origin of the fiber – or even whether the sellers were the rightful owners of the cargo.

The price of cotton, which was sixteen cents a pound in 1862, had, by 1865, surged to $1.25 a pound. A wagon load of sixteen bales, weighing five hundred pounds each, would now fetch $5,000 in gold or hard foreign currency. Such possibilities for gain brought out brigands from both sides of the border.

Sergeant Tucker touched his wound tenderly as he recalled that the final leg of his last trip had been a virtual hundred-mile battle. All the wagons had gotten through, but the cost had been dear. Four troopers killed, three badly wounded, two drivers killed, and two others wounded. By the time the cotton was sold on the Mexican side of the river, half the escort had been incapacitated, but every bale had been delivered. Capt. Waldrop had a right to be proud.

He smiled at the captain. "Well, sir, old Rip Ford has been givin' them what-for around here since he took command. Maybe they've learned their lesson."

The captain returned the smile. "Let's hope so, Sergeant. I, for one, wish he'd been in command a long time ago."

Arrival of the scouts interrupted the talk. As they reported to the captain, he noticed that although he was younger and had less time in service than Gibson, Lance Morgan seemed to just naturally assume the role of spokesman.

"Nothing moving out there, Captain. No fresh tracks or sign of any kind."

"That's good, men. We're setting up camp in that clearing just ahead. You may consider yourselves relieved."

Jess Waldrop watched Lance Morgan ride away with a strange feeling. The boy reminded him of someone he'd never see again. The sight of young Lance Morgan twisted a sharp stick in the captain's old wounds.

8

The wagon camp was laid out in proper order. Fires were blazing nicely, and the cook had a goodly supply of red coals raked into a narrow trench. Jess Waldrop nodded with satisfaction as he retired to his tent. There was something about a well-organized camp that made him feel good.

He paced the distance to his tent with measured tread. However, once inside, the fiddle string tautness gave way, and he slumped into his chair in a state of near collapse. Tonight the relaxation was short-lived. Almost before he settled into the chair, he popped back on his feet at the sentry's shout.

"Rider coming."

Striding to the tent opening, Waldrop peered out to see a lone rider approaching from the east. He caught a glimpse of Segeant Tucker moving through the knot of men who had gathered to watch.

"Sergeant Tucker."

"Cap'n?"

"Offer that man some supper. Tell him he's welcome to camp here – then have someone keep an eye on him."

"Sir, you get a good look at that man?"

"What about him?"

"Cap'n, it's a nigger."

"A nigra? What would a nigra be doing way out here?"

"Hard to say, sir."

"Well, give him some supper anyway. Nigra's got to eat just like the rest of us."

"Yes sir." The sergeant touched his hat and smiled. He turned and strode purposefully toward the rider who had been challenged by the guard. "I'll take it from here, Corporal," he shouted at the sentry.

Tucker looked the rider over as he pulled his horse around to come nearer.

Big. That was the first impression. Six and a half feet at least. Brawny arms bulged out of cut-off sleeves. Pants tied up with a piece of plow line and well-worn boots stuck through the stirrups. Farm nigger likely. Sat a sure saddle though – and on a mighty fine animal.

"What's your name, boy?"

The horseman doffed his floppy hat. "Mike, sah – I belongs to the Morgan family."

"Lance Morgan? You Lance Morgan's nigger?"

"Yassuh. I come a far piece to find Massa Lance."

The sergeant smiled. "I guess you have at that. How'd you find us?"

"Well, suh, the major back home tole Massa Morgan where Massa Lance been sent. And you leaves a pretty big

9

trail."

The sergeant laughed. "We do at that. Come with me."

He led the big black man to one of the large, four-man tents and stuck his head in the opening. "Morgan, come on out. You got a visitor."

Lance stuck a puzzled face out the opening. "What?"

Then a big smile broke over his face as he saw the huge man standing behind Tucker. "Mike, you old rascal. What're you doing here?"

He rushed out of the tent, somewhat hampered by having one boot on and the other in his hand. The big Negro caught him by both upper arms and lifted the trooper into the air

"Massa Lance, lemme see if you've growed any."

Back on the ground, Lance hopped on one foot as he tugged on the other boot. One big black hand remained on him to steady him.

"Not much bigger, but harder. Massa Lance, you comin' a man now."

"Well, I'm bigger'n I was when you used to put me on your shoulder so I could pick a nice ripe one off old man Darcy's apple tree."

"That you is," the man chuckled quietly.

"But hey, Mike, what are you doing here? Is everything all right at the farm?"

The black face turned solemn. "No. No, it ain't, Massa Lance. It's yore momma."

Lance choked out the word, "Momma?"

"God rest her soul, she's gone."

Lance's face paled. His mouth worked twice before he could speak. "Not Momma, Mike."

Mike placed a gentle hand on Lance's shoulder. "It was a fever, Massa Lance. Come through the country this winter. Got lots of folks down our way -- yore momma, old Aunt Bessie, and lots more."

Captain Waldrop sat at a small table in his tent reading from a well-worn copy of *The Works of Shelley*. The remains of a half-eaten meal were pushed to one side to make room for the book. He glanced up in response to a scratching at his tent flap.

"Come in." He rose as Sgt. Tucker entered.

"It's Morgan, sir. He'd like to see you."

"Of course, Sergeant. Send him in."

Capt. Waldrop stepped around the table as Lance entered. "Ah yes, Morgan, I heard about your mother. Please accept my condolences. I'm very, very sorry."

"Thank you, sir." Morgan was solemn but composed.

10

Waldrop shook his head. "It's tough – damned tough. I know how much it must hurt."

"Yes sir. I'll miss her a lot."

"I know you will," Waldrop said.

"But right now, my daddy's gonna need me for a while. After we get this train through, I'd like to go home for a couple of weeks if I could get leave."

"I'm sure it can be arranged, Morgan. You'll be getting a new assignment anyway. Would you like to keep your servant with you for now, so he can go back with you?"

"Mike? Oh, yes, sir. That would be great."

"It's not unprecedented for a soldier to have his nigra with him on duty – although not usually a private. However, in this case, it seems appropriate.

"Your new assignment will probably be on the front lines. Tell me, Morgan, how do you feel about Union troops?"

"They killed my brother at the first of the war – now my mother's dead because of the Yankees. How should I feel? I hate 'em like poison."

"I was afraid you were feeling that way." Waldrop sighed. "Sit down, boy."

Lance dropped onto the stool, teeth clenched, arms folded tightly across his chest.

Jess Waldrop spoke gently. "Hate is a useful tool in war, boy. You use it like a drum to stir the troops into a fighting fever. Stronger than fear – more powerful than caution – hate makes men do things they could never do under normal conditions. But it's a dangerous tool – corrosive. Like strong acid in your veins, it eats you up from the inside. I don't know what you're feeling right now – but if it's hate for the Union soldier you've got it all wrong – and I wouldn't want to see you carry it around like that."

Lance started to stand but was restrained by the Captain's outstretched hand.

"Hear me out, boy. Your brother died in a war -- tragically, so did your mother, but in a different way. What I'm saying is that no Union soldier decided one day to go out and kill Lance Morgan's brother – nor cause his mother to die – nor to kill Jess Waldrop's son."

"Your son, Captain? I didn't know."

"He was my only son -- the wellspring for all future generations of Waldrops."

"Then – the Yankees killed him too."

"Not the way you're thinking. Likely it was some other scared youngster who may not have even seen who he was shooting at. Look, Morgan, the purpose of war is to destroy the enemy's ability to destroy you. And, as long as this war

11

lasts, we do what has to be done. But hate the Yankee soldier? I never have – and I don't to this day."

"Sir, how can you kill a man you don't hate?"

"That's a tough question, son. I'm not sure I can answer it for you, but I'll try. In a war, you do what you have to do. You take no pleasure in it – may even detest doing it – but, the point is, you do it. Because it has to be done – and you're man enough to do it. Do you understand what I'm saying?"

"I think so, sir."

The captain lit a cigar without taking his eyes off the boy. "War is a hateful thing – but it's just war. We'll never have peace between North and South as long as the hate goes on -- the personal hatred between the peoples. It'll destroy us all. The Yankees are just like us, Morgan. Some are good, some bad, but most are somewhere in the middle – just like us."

He regarded the puzzled face of the young man before him. "Just think about it. War is not a personal thing."

"Yessir."

Lance struggled to his feet. The captain placed a hand on his shoulder.

"I didn't really mean to unload on you like that, Morgan. But this is a bitter war, and it may be an even more bitter peace. No use to make it harder on us than it has to be. Consider leave granted just as soon as this detail is finished. Until then, your servant – Mike, is it? – will remain with our company. I'm sure he'll pull his own weight which, from what I've seen, should be enough for any man."

Captain Waldrop watched the young man go and shook his head sadly. He was so much like that other boy who was about his age – what was it? – four years ago? Doesn't seem like – but it was. No matter. They had the same look – the same mannerisms – and both too young for what one did and the other might have to do. Eighteen is much too young. Too young to charge the cannon. Too young to slump beneath an oak tree in the first major battle of the war, trying to hold back with your hands the blood seeping from a ragged hole in your stomach. But then, almost everyone at Bull Run was too young, and no one who was there would ever be young again.

A half-dozen fires punctured the darkness of the prairie night. Men gathered in small groups around them or strolled between them, singly or in pairs, just changing location. The group at the end fire shouted with laughter as one of the group drew a harmonica out of his tunic. Shortly, the melody of "Green Grow the Lilacs," piped single note at a time, wafted into the still air.

George Gibson poked idly at the fire with a green stick.

12

The fire felt good against the chill of the night air. He didn't feel like talking, and neither, it seemed, did anyone else. The group was unusually silent. George took the opportunity to size up those gathered around this fire.

Lance and Mike sat directly across from him bantering back and forth with easy familiarity. On his left was Roy O'Neil, thin and wiry, with a sharp ferret face and greasy black hair that tended to flop down over his eyes to be pushed back with big knuckled fingers. Mississippi white trash to George's way of thinking – the kind that licks the boots of any authority – but snake-mean when given the opportunity.

The Magruder twins, Jim and Joe, were on his right. Good enough sort. A little too stuck on themselves maybe. Hard to blame 'em though. The Magruder Plantation was one of the biggest and finest in Northern Alabama. Could have both been officers if they'd wanted to use their pull. Probably didn't want to go to the trouble. The whole war was just a big lark to them anyway.

Then, O'Neil's voice broke the silence. "Hey, nigger. Bring me some a' that hot coffee, willya?"

George took a quick look across the fire. Lance frowned and started to his feet until Mike placed a big hand on his shoulder.

"Yassuh," Mike said. He got quickly to his feet and brought the steaming pot around the fire.

"Hey, Lance," Roy yelled. "This is the life. Never had no nigger to bring my coffee to me before."

Mike filled the man's cup, and as he turned to walk away, O'Neil stuck his foot across his path. In the process, he jiggled his cup, spilling hot coffee down his arm. With a scream of rage and pain, Roy leaped to his feet.

"Clumsy nigger!" He lashed out with his booted foot, but Mike turned aside and the kick merely grazed his leg.

In a single bound, Lance was across the fire and right in the soldier's face. "What in the hell you think you're doing, O'Neil?"

The anger on O'Neil's face was replaced by uncertainty. "Hell, Lance, ain't no reason for you to get riled up. I was just gonna teach that nigger of yours to watch his step."

Fury stood out in Lance's face as he pushed it closer to the other man's. "O'Neil, Mike is my nigger. And if you so much as touch him again, I'll kill you."

As Lance started to walk away, O'Neil grabbed a small trenching shovel that lay nearby and swung it at Lance's head. But George had been expecting something of the sort. His heel lashed out against O'Neil's knee, throwing him off balance, and the shovel blow went awry.

O'Neil whirled toward the new threat but froze as a large form stepped into the light of the fire. "What the hell is going on here?" boomed the voice of Sgt. Tucker. "Dammit, O'Neil put that shovel down or you'll eat it. If the cap'n finds out . . ."

"Yes, Sergeant, what if I find out?" The captain's voice spoke dryly from the darkness outside the firelit area.

"Aw, it's nothing, sir," the sergeant said. "The boys having a little scuffle."

Waldrop stepped into the light. "Yes, Sergeant, I saw the scuffle."

"O'Neil, come here to me." The captain barked out the order.

The soldier stepped toward the captain and stiffened, arms straight down his sides.

"What's the meaning of this disturbance?"

O'Neil seemed to shrivel inside. "Wa'nt nothing, Cap'n. I was just playin' around with the nigger a little, and Morgan got kinda mean about it."

"Not nearly as mean as I'm going to get if there is any repetition of this foolishness. Does my meaning come clear, O'Neil."

"Yessir."

"O'Neil, you're confined to your tent for the rest of the evening. And, you can consider yourself fortunate to get off so lightly."

With that, Waldrop turned on his heel and strode off to his own quarters.

O'Neil waited until the captain was well out of hearing, then muttered, "That struttin' little bastard, I'll take . . ."

Sgt. Tucker interrupted. "Watch your mouth, O'Neil. And get back to your tent right now."

The trooper made a show out of shouldering George to one side as he lurched off to his tent. George made a move toward him but was stopped by Sgt. Tucker's heavy hand.

"Let it go, Gibson," the sergeant cautioned.

CHAPTER 3

The Rio Grande twisted through the semi-arid country like the path of a giant serpent. Where the soil was deep and the rocks small, it spread into a wide, slowly moving flow. But just below the bluff on which the wagon train had paused, hard, giant boulders forced the water into a narrow channel, leaping and surging through a constricted passageway, splashing foaming spray over volcanic rocks that had defied the abrasive scouring of the sand-laden water for thousands of years. Here and there, those massive stones thrust glistening peaks above the surface, so numerous that a casual observer might think one could cross by stepping from one to another.

Any who tried it, however, found themselves dead wrong. Gaps of up to twenty feet between these rocks were filled with a swift, tumultuous torrent of water often deeper than wide. The rocks were undercut by erosion to form treacherous whirlpools and underground currents that were often days giving up any debris that found its way into that maelstrom. Mexicans who lived, worked, and died along the river's banks long before the Americans came, called it *Rio Bravo,* "mean river" with good reason.

A few hundred yards upriver, it took on more docile characteristics. In a long, arcing bend, the river flattened out over a smooth, gravelled bottom, giving the appearance of a placid lake. Here, the loaded wagons would cross.

If they held the proper line, and if heavy rains upriver didn't suddenly engulf them in a flash flood, crossings were relatively uneventful. However, if a wagon strayed from the established pathway, there were potholes in the river bottom that could swallow it up, load and all.

But these drivers had been here before. With a great creaking of axles, shouting of mule skinners, and rasping of brake shoes held tight against the wheels, the wagon train began its descent into the river bed.

Varying flood levels through the centuries created a series of relatively flat benches, one just a few feet above the next, to

15

the top of the river canyon. Angling down these benches along a route of minimum steepness, the wagons strung along the edge of the water. Sgt. Tucker and three troopers crossed first and positioned themselves to serve as markers for the wagon drivers. Urged on by shouts and cracking of whips, the mules plunged into the water and on across.

Once on the other side, the wagons lined up again for the trail. Capt. Waldrop rode up to the head of the train where Sgt. Tucker had the platoon assembled.

"Men, we've had good luck so far, but we're not there yet. The ten miles to Rosita might be the longest ten miles you've ever seen. So, keep alert. Keep your eyes and ears open, and report anything -- anything unusual."

Sgt. Tucker rode up beside him.

The captain shouted, "Sgt. Tucker, post the scouts."

The sergeant turned back toward the men. "O'Neil and Jim Magruder forward. Keep your eyes open and your head on a swivel."

He turned to the captain.

"Our luck's still holding, Cap'n."

Jim Magruder sat his mount atop a high rise and stood in his stirrups to get a little extra height.

"Damn that Roy O'Neil. Where did that red-necked rooster go? The captain said plain that we was to stay in sight of one another, and he has to hightail it first off."

By mid-afternoon, he was really concerned about his fellow scout. He decided to make another sweep across to the left, where O'Neil was supposed to be. Topping a small ridge, he spotted him.

O'Neil was afoot, leading his horse.

"Where the hell you been?"

Roy's horse was wringing wet with sweat and the saddle girth hung loose. The man looked up in surprise. "Oh, Magruder. I'm just givin' my horse a little breather."

"Sure looks like it could use it. What happened?"

"Nothin'. Just been givin' this nag a little workout."

Magruder looked at him in disgust. "O'Neil, you're an idiot. Supposed to be scouting this area -- and you're out trying to run a good horse to death."

O'Neil blew his nose between is thumb and forefinger onto the ground. "Mind your own business, Magruder. I'll do as I please with my own horse."

Magruder rode to a position directly in front of the man, forcing him to stop. "O'Neil, this is my business, but I guess you ain't got enough sense to see that."

O'Neil looked at the ground and scuffed his toe against a

16

rock. "Hell, Jim, I ain't done nothin' wrong. Maybe got a little too far away, but I'd of seen if anything was wrong."

"Not true, O'Neil. You're not doing your job."

Roy's face began to show concern. "Yes, I am, Jim. Hey, you're not gonna say anything to the captain, are you? Rosita's just over that ridge up there. We've got it made."

"How do you -- oh yeah, you've been here before, haven't you?"

"Oh hell, yes. I know this country. Fact is, my horse is so sweaty 'cause I rode on up a ways to take a look. You can see the town from there."

Relief flooded Magruder's face. "Well, naw, I'm not gonna say anything. But tell you what let's do, O'Neil, when we get reassigned after this detail."

"What's that, old buddy."

"Let's get assigned to different units."

Jim Magruder started toward the distant ridge at a lope.

Except for the thriving business in cotton going in one direction, and guns and goods going the other, Rosita didn't have much to recommend it as a town. Once a pleasant, little village where a man could come for his winter supply of *frijoles* and to down a few bottles of *cerveza*, it had been drastically transformed by events not of its own making.

By mere accident of geography, it had become a world trade center -- a watering hole for weary soldiers, mule skinners, highwayman, swindlers, fortune hunters of every stripe, and assorted camp followers. Now the procession of wagons filled with cotton became the focal point of attention for the motley element lining its dusty streets.

A man in a derby hat, riding a high-stepping black horse, fell into step with the captain. He spoke with a French accent. "Good afternoon, Captain. May I presume that you already have a buyer for your cotton?"

Capt. Waldrop nodded a greeting. "You may, sir."

The man smiled broadly. "I thought as much. However, we live, my Captain, in a world of quick and sudden change. What is true one moment, may be much less so the next.

"I am Pierre Alvaròn, at your service, sir. I find myself in dire need of cotton to complete a shipment to Lyons. I am prepared to offer a premium price for your shipment."

Capt. Waldrop, for the first time, faced the man directly. "I'm sorry, Mr. Alvaròn, but as I said, this shipment is contracted to the firm of Gates & Gates of Liverpool."

"And as I said, Captain, my need is urgent. The premium of which I spoke would be in the amount of five cents a pound, in gold coin." The man glanced furtively to all sides.

17

"The papers would be left open to be filled in for any amount you wish. Is my meaning clear, Captain?"

Jess Waldrop pulled his mount to a stop, his gaze level and cold. "Because you are a stranger and don't know me, and because I understand your situation, I am extending you the courtesy of saying your meaning is not clear. For, if it were, I'm afraid I would be forced to kill you."

The other man paled under the captain's steady stare but recovered enough to show a thin smile. "Your meaning, unlike mine, is perfectly clear, Captain. I salute you."

He touched hand to his derby hat and turned his horse back into the crowd.

The *cantina* was obviously a former residence, converted to its present usage with a maximum economy of effort and expense. Crumbling adobe walls held up a roof of carrizo cane cut by hand from the river bottom and hauled to the site by burro. A faded sign featured a painting of a Mexican fighting bull of unlikely proportions and the hand-lettered name: *El Toro Bravo*.

The inside was no more pretentious than the outside. Some of the interior walls had been removed, which necessitated the addition of several strategically located poles and beams for support. A hand-hewn bar extended the length of the room with only a small opening at one end for passageway behind it. Crude wooden tables and wood and rawhide chairs were the only furnishings.

A half-dozen teamsters from the wagon train had a card game going at the back table. Two bottles of fiery *mescal* on the table were quickly being emptied into the glasses clutched in the fists of men intent on serious drinking.

In the corner, a Mexican boy in white cotton trousers and straw sandals, played *flamenco* on a battered guitar while a couple of overweight, flat-faced women in long skirts stomped the floor and wiggled their hips at a level of enthusiasm on a par with their dancing proficiency.

Pierre Alvaròn stood at the bar, dulling his disappointment at not obtaining the cotton, through the obscuring haze induced by Mexican brandy. Two other patrons had the look of cutthroats. They occasionally glanced down the bar at Alvaròn's fine boots, balancing their value against the risk involved in obtaining them.

This was the scene that greeted Lance Morgan, George Gibson, and the Magruder twins as they entered the bar. Joe Magruder leaned out to look down the bar at Lance. "Lance, we appreciate your nigra looking after our horses. Gives us a head start on the others."

Lance waved an acknowledgement.

Pierre Alvaròn had watched quietly as the group entered the *cantina*, but now moved closer. "You gentlemen came in with the wagon train of cotton today." It was not a question.

"Permit me to buy you a round of drinks."

He nodded to the bartender, who filled each of the glasses.

Lance turned and extended his hand. "Thank you, sir. I am Lance Morgan of Tennessee."

"And I, sir, am Pierre Alvaròn, recently of Paris, but for now an inhabitant of this lovely city of Rosita."

It was apparent that Alvaròn's stay at the bar had been lengthy judging from his unsteady motion as he bowed.

"Could you tell me, sir, if there is another train of cotton due here in the near future?"

Lance paused in lifting his glass. "I wouldn't have that information, Mr. Alvaròn. And if I did, I wouldn't be privileged to discuss it."

"Ah, but of course, the security. I understand."

The Frenchman turned his attention back to his half-empty glass, paying no more attention to the soldiers.

Their own attention was drawn to the door as it swung open to admit another Confederate soldier. On his head was a large, white Mexican *sombrero*.

George Gibson approached the newcomer slowly, stooping to peer under the hat.

"Roy? Roy O'Neil?"

O'Neil seemed to take in the identity of the patrons and hesitated at the door. George grabbed him by the arm. "Come on in, Roy. I'll buy you a drink."

Convinced the others seemed to be in a good humor, O'Neil quickly made his way to the bar and tossed down the drink he was handed. He turned uneasily toward Lance.

"Oh, Morgan, I didn't mean any harm the other night. You know – with your nigger and all. Just a little joke."

Lance looked at the man carefully. He seemed to be sincere. "Let's just forget it, okay?"

"Yeah, that's great, Lance. We ought not to be fightin' amongst our ownselves." He stuck out a grimy paw which Lance reluctantly took.

Joe Magruder asked, "Roy, you seen any of the others?"

"Yeah. Most of 'em are over to *Papagallo's* across the street. Them the captain didn't take with him."

"Well, does anybody know when we're supposed to get out of here?"

Roy poured himself another from the community bottle. "All I heard is that Cap'n Waldrop is meetin' tonight with them men from Gates & Gates. Headin' to San Antone tomorrow with a wagon load of gold."

George put his hand roughly on O'Neil's arm. "Dammit, O'Neil, keep your voice down."

"Can't nobody else hear me."

George glanced uneasily at the two hard-looking men. "I hope the hell not."

The last word of George's statement was lost in the loud rattle of gunfire from down the street. The troopers all bolted for the door.

"Uh oh," George muttered. "We got trouble for sure."

Joe Magruder hit the door first and staggered backward into the room, a spreading flow of blood pouring from his chest. His brother knelt beside him, tearing at the buttons on the fallen man's tunic.

Lance stumbled into the street, shaking his head violently to clear the cobwebs left by a large dose of spirits. The stillness of the quiet night had exploded in the fury of gunfire, galloping horses, and shouting of riders. The doors of *Papagallo's* swung open and the other Confederates poured out, only to be driven back by a murderous volley.

Lance cursed his own clumsiness as he tugged at his revolver and swung it to line up on the flashes of light coming from down the street. He emptied his pistol at them without being able to tell if he'd hit anything.

As he was reloading, a form rushed up beside him, and he recognized George's voice. "Lance – our horses!"

"Oh, damn." He hadn't even thought about them.

He and George had just started up the street, when a dark form appeared from the side of the *cantina*. Lance strained to pierce the darkness with his eyes as the *cantina* door swung open again, and a shaft of light fell across the man – dark and swarthy with bandoleers across his chest. And Lance was looking down the muzzle of his aimed musket.

Lance's movements seemed painfully slow as he desperately tried to pull his revolver up into firing position, knowing he'd never make it.

Then, the man just rose into the air as though levitated. Another form materialized in the darkness, a giant man holding the bandit high above his head before slamming him hard against the adobe wall.

"Mike! Mike! Over here," Lance cried.

"I sees you, Massa Lance. I'm coming."

Looking even bigger in the dark than he really was, Mike stumbled to where Lance and George were crouched.

George reached out to support him as he stumbled. Pulling back his hand, he examined it by the small ray of light that came from the bar's window.

20

"Lance, he's been hit. He's bleeding."

"It's not bad, Massa Lance. But they got the horses. I tried to stop 'em, but I couldn't. I'm very sorry," Mike mumbled and slipped to the ground.

Immediately, a new outbreak of shooting erupted as a wagon, drawn by two horses, careened down the street. The driver rolled drunkenly in the seat. Four mounted bandits pursued the wagon, firing frantically at the driver.

Lance stepped quickly into the wagon's path and caught the horses' bridles. As he struggled to get the horses under control, he saw the driver, now lying on his side in the driver's seat, was Capt. Waldrop.

The four bandits reined their horses up to where they could fire point blank at the wagon's occupants. Suddenly, the *cantina's* doors burst open, and Pierre Alvaròn lurched into the fray.

"Alors!" he shouted, leaping into the middle of the street. "To the barricades."

The four riders, startled by this unexpected development, seemed uncertain of which way to direct their fire.

Positioning himself in classic dueling stance, Pierre shot one of the riders dead. Then, without hurrying, he shifted his position, fired, and another toppled from his horse.

A bullet fired by one of the horsemen spun him around.

But that gave George time to draw a bead and fire directly into the gunman's face, toppling him backward, as Pierre sank slowly to the ground.

The last rider turned to gallop away, but a volley from *Papagallo's* dropped him from his horse.

"Comrades," Pierre was on both knees, hands clutched over his chest. Bloody froth showed on his lips. "Tell your captain -- that while the circumstances -- the unsettled times -- have not permitted me -- to live always a noble life -- they have at least afforded me -- an honorable way to die."

Blood gushed from his mouth, and Pierre Alvaròn, late of Paris, pitched on his face into the dusty street of Rosita.

The bandits at the far end of the street were regrouping for another attack. Hearing a noise behind him, Lance jerked around, George and Jim Magruder were half-dragging Mike toward the wagon.

"Jim," Lance called, "how about Joe?"

"He's gone. I can't help him now."

There was another rush of footsteps, and Roy O'Neil appeared by the wagon. "Let's get outa here."

"Take it easy, Roy." George's voice was calm. "We've got wounded here."

"We can't help 'em. They'll just get us all killed."

21

O'Neil's voice was that of a man on the verge of hysteria.

"Shut up, O'Neil." Jim Magruder's voice cut like a knife. "We take them with us, or we don't go."

The second attack came with a thunder of hooves. It was met by flashes of fire from *Papagallo's.*

Lance said. "We've still got help across the street."

"Yep," George agreed. "Three of 'em."

The oncoming horde split around the wagon, driving their fire home from both sides. Jim Magruder went down, firing his revolver as he sank to his knees. Lance bent over the fallen Magruder just in time to hear his last words, "That son-of-a-bitch -- that sorry bastard."

O'Neil's big *sombrero* sailed off his head and rolled down the street like an erratic wheel.

"My hat!" he screamed, and chased after it.

"You damn fool, forget the stupid hat," yelled George.

Just as Roy caught up with his hat, a Mexican turned his horse and leveled his rifle on the trooper at point blank range. Then, he hesitated for a moment, giving George a chance to steady his gun hand with the other and squeeze the trigger. The bandit was knocked backward off his horse.

O'Neil grabbed the hat and retreated to the wagon. Lance had put the captain and Mike in the back and was in the driver's seat holding back the fear crazed team when the soldiers from the *Papagallo* made a break for the wagon.

The bandits, who had made a whirling turn after passing the wagon, filled the air with bullets. Two troopers were cut down before reaching the wagon. The other, a man Lance recognized as Tip Ryan, a Virginia storekeeper's son, leaped to the wagon seat just before the back of his head exploded. He fell backward into the darkness of the street.

George and Roy scurried up beside the wagon, slipped under the tarp, landing beside the two wounded men in back.

"Get us the hell outa here, Lance," George yelled as he flipped up the tarp so he could shoot out the side.

Lance relaxed his hold on the reins, and the horses bolted up the street at a mad gallop. The sight and sound of the wagon coming straight at them, with flapping tarp, unnerved the bandit's mounts, and they reared and plunged uncontrollably. One of the men, who seemed to be the leader, shouted orders in Spanish to his men. George shot at him as the wagon passed, but the bandit's horse reared at that moment, and the bullet whizzed past his head.

A couple of miles out of town, George and Roy, white *sombrero* still clamped firmly on his head, climbed onto the seat with Lance. There was no sound of pursuit.

In the wagon Mike was sitting up holding his left side.

Jess Waldrop still lay on his back.

"I don't think they're close," Lance said pulling up the sweat-lathered horses that were champing hard at the bits. "We'd best see about the captain."

"You all right, Mike?" Lance asked.

"Yassuh. Just a little weak and dizzy. But I be all right. The cap'n though, he hurt bad."

Lance carefully opened the captain's tunic to expose a wound in his chest. Blood oozed from the hole, and Lance could feel a smashed rib where the bullet had entered.

He turned to George. "Not much bleeding."

George shook his head. "He's bleeding inside, Lance."

Capt. Waldrop opened his eyes, now cloudy with pain, and started to speak. "Morgan — thank God you're . . ."

Lance interrupted. "Don't try to talk, sir. It just . . ."

He stopped at the captain's impatient gesture.

"I've seen this kind of wound before, boy. It doesn't matter whether I talk or not, and I've got something to say. How many of the men . . ?"

Lance shook his head. "Just us. Gibson, O'Neil, Mike and I – we're all that's left. What about Sgt. Tucker?"

"He was wounded but holding them off while I got the wagon away. Then, I saw their leader, they called him 'Santiago,' stand over him and fire three shots into his head."

"And the gold?" Lance asked.

"We've still got it – under the wagon seat. Get it back to San Antonio, Confederate Headquarters, Morgan. I'm counting on you, boy."

"I'll do my best, Captain."

Lance told the captain about Pierre Alvaròn.

Capt. Waldrop smiled. "An honorable man – during a hard time to be such."

He took a deep breath, let it out, and never drew it again.

George crawled out of the wagon, while Roy sat and stared at the dead captain. Lance turned his attention to Mike. His wound, while painful, didn't appear to be dangerous.

"More bad news, boys," George said as he stuck his head back in the wagon. "Left front wheel's just about gone. Won't last another quarter mile. I don't think the horses will either. And in case nobody's noticed, we were pointin' the wrong way in town when we took off. We been going deeper into Mexico all the time."

CHAPTER 4

Near its spring-fed source, the Sweetwater River bubbled crystal clear and shallow over an outcropping of rock worn smooth and flat through the centuries. Here, Scotty MacDuff and his son, Bain, stretched out stark naked in the shallows letting the sun-warmed water course over their bodies stripping away the heat, sweat, and grime of a hard day's work.

Bain had recently discovered the location of little outlets through which the icy spring water fed into the river. With a minimum of effort, he could enjoy a treatment of soothing warmth alternating with invigorating cold.

Scotty climbed to his feet, and with a mighty roar, plunged into the deeper water up to his chest. He thrust against the current with arms outspread as though to hold back the rushing river.

"Aaah, my lad, Ponce de Leon didn't come far enough. It's surely that Fountain of Youth that flows right here through our own property."

A fine trace of the burr lingered in the man's speech, one more appropriate to the lochs and glens of Scotland than to the brush country of South Texas.

Bain, a strapping young man of seventeen years, propped himself on one elbow to watch his father's antics. "If true, father, I'm afraid we'd both be back to creeping on our knees by now."

"Not so, son. This is no fountain to take you backward -- but powerful waters that eternally preserve you at the prime of life. Do you not see what they've done for your own father who, after fifty summers, retains the body of a callow youth – but the mind of an ancient sage?"

Whooping with laughter, Bain leaped to his feet and joined his father in holding back the surging Sweetwater. "Perhaps I will do even better. After all, I started at a younger age."

MacDuff stood upright and gazed fondly at his son. His face grew more serious, but the twinkle never faded from his eye. "I pray that will be the case, my son."

Slightly embarrassed at the serious bent the conversation had taken, Bain plunged beneath the water, struggling mightily against the current. He reappeared moments later no more than thirty feet upriver from where he'd gone under.

Shortly thereafter, the two lay on the rocks along the bank while the sinking sun dried them off before dressing.

Bain looked with distaste at the small heap made by his sweaty shirt and grimy trousers. "Hate to put my nice clean body back into those grubby clothes."

Scotty rolled over to take a look. "Don't blame you, boy. Only a moment ago, I spotted a couple of buzzards circling that pile like it was a dead horse.

"Speaking of which, I suppose you checked on the mares down by Big Frog Spring."

"Of course. They're all fine. Four new foals already -- three colts and a filly."

Scotty's face brightened. "Good. Very good indeed. With those mares, and Old Dusty as the sire, this should be the best crop of foals we've ever had."

"You think so? We already have the best in the country."

"Bite your tongue, boy. Sounds like the haughty spirit that comes before a fall."

"It's only what everyone says."

"It's very well to have others say it, but unbecoming for us to say it even between us."

Bain chuckled. "You're right, of course, father. But I still say we have some mighty fine horses."

"That we do, and we'll have even better if the Lord is willing and grants us time."

Bain slipped on his trousers, boots and hat, but eschewed the sweaty underwear, shirt and socks, tying them into a small bundle behind his saddle.

Scotty watched in amusement. "Your mother and sister will think I've captured myself a Comanche and am bringing him home for supper. They're likely to run us off with a broom."

The MacDuff Ranch bespoke the owner's penchant for tidiness and order. It was laid out with an eye for both the practical and the aesthetic. Set in a high valley, with hills behind to block out cold north winds, it was open to the cooling southerly breezes of summer. A whispering spring danced down the rocks from the hills and cut across in front of the house, presenting the appearance of a medieval moat encircling a European castle.

Mesquite logs, seasoned to rock-like hardness, had been

joined together with precise workmanship to create a simple but sturdy house, tight against all elements. Outbuildings of similar construction included a combination bunkhouse/tack room, a log corral with attached shelter for the horses, and a smokehouse. A cooling shed straddled the icy spring and served as repository for milk, butter, eggs and garden vegetables. Food placed in metal buckets and lowered into the cooling stream was kept fresh for many days.

A sturdy log bridge lay across the stream in front of the house, leading to a broad road that ended at a hitching post just out from the front door.

A small cultivated orchard of peach, apple, and plum trees was dwarfed by towering native pecan, oak, and cottonwood trees that hugged the perimeter of the stream, sending probing taproots down into the perennially moist substructure.

Supper was on the table by the time the men put their horses away and entered the house where they were greeted first by a slim and attractive woman in her late forties. There was much about Erin MacDuff to back up her husband's claim that she had been "the bonniest lass in all of Scotland."

Erase the few touches of grey from her hair, add a little fullness to her figure, remove all the lines from her face, and she could have been an identical twin to her daughter who stood just behind her.

The young girl giggled, green eyes dancing with amusement. "Bain, you'll never know how funny you looked riding up like that."

She dodged the half-hearted swipe taken at her by her brother, tossed her long auburn hair and scooted for her place at the table.

"Colleen, stop your teasing," said her mother, who then turned her attention to the men.

"You two have certainly taken your time about getting home today."

Scotty draped an arm around her affectionately. "Erin, my love, any time away from you seems so long, I sometimes lose track of it."

The color rising to her cheeks seemed to wipe away the years. "Scotty, you're such a scoundrel."

"If I may be excused, mother and father," said Bain with a little comic bow, "I'll put on attire suitable for our evening meal."

He was gone only a couple of minutes. When he returned, they all took their places at the oilcloth-covered table, Scotty offered thanks, and they began their meal.

Bain glanced up from his heaping plate. "I forgot to mention, there was a mule with the mares down at Big Frog

26

Spring. Couldn't make out the brand."

Scotty looked concerned. "We'd better get him out of there. He just might get to chasing those new foals. Guess he got away from that cotton train that passed the other day. We'll go over there tomorrow and take a look."

Bain didn't look up. "A lot of cotton moving through here lately."

Scotty reached for the potatoes. "Confederacy needs to sell it. I hear supplies are low on the battlefields."

"That's where I should be, father, with the army. Every boy I know that's my age has gone."

Erin quickly interjected, "And some of those boys won't be coming home."

Scotty held up both hands. "You all know my feelings on this matter. There is no need for discussion."

Erin said, "War is a foolish thing."

"Now, Erin," Scotty said, "I believe in war when there's something worth fighting for."

The woman sniffed in disagreement. "Nothing is worth the killing."

Scotty frowned and tilted his head up. "Sometimes, you have no choice."

Erin's lips grew thin. "There is always a choice."

Scotty put down his knife and fork. "This very land was given me for my services in war."

Erin got up abruptly and stalked to the stove. "I wish we'd gotten it some other way."

Scotty shook his head in exasperation. "I fought in a war of freedom for all Texians. It came to a time when any freedom-loving person had to fight."

Bain interjected, "Then, why can't I fight for what I believe in?"

"Not the same thing at all, Bain. I fought against tyrants who had taken control of the government by force. They suspended our rights -- plundered our property. Then, I worked with San Houston for annexation to the United States – a rightful government for a free people. No son of mine will ever take arms against that country."

"There are those who say such talk is treason."

Scotty's face turned hard. "My views are well-known to all our neighbors. And I know theirs. Those who support secession have what they think is good reason. And I have mine. But we don't shoot at one another."

"But the Yankees have . . ."

Scotty cut him off with a wave of his hand. "I know – I know the South has grievances, and that some northern politicians have been guilty of excesses. But our differences

27

could have been resolved -- without bloodshed. Now, it's gone too far. We will both be the losers."

Erin resumed her seat with a determined look on her face. She spoke softly but firmly. "Enough. We will enjoy our supper with no more talk of war at my table."

The family finished its meal with only polite conversation, but Colleen smiled and winked her support to her brother.

The brush country, especially on the Mexican side of the Rio Grande, is no place for a man on foot. Darkness magnifies the difficulties many fold. An ordinary arroyo, relatively easy to cross in daylight, becomes a bottomless gorge with uncertain and treacherous footing. Thousands of thorny plants, from the flattened devil's pincushion to the spindly chollo, or "jumping cactus," await the touch of an unwary traveler.

Roy O'Neil's boot banged against a rock, and the heavily loaded saddlebags thrown over his shoulders brought him to the ground on one knee.

"These bags weigh a ton. Lance, you sure these ain't heavier than the others?"

"You took first pick." Lance reminded him.

"Yeah, but I think I made a mistake. Lemme trade with you a while."

Lance handed over the bags he'd been carrying without a word and shouldered those of Roy's.

O'Neil continued to whine. "How about the nigger? Can't he carry something?"

"No, he can't," Lance responded. "Mike can barely walk as it is."

"Dammit, O'Neil," George said, "if you'd keep your mouth shut, you wouldn't run out of wind so quick."

Keeping their general direction by the stars, the men had blundered through the darkness for two hours since leaving the disabled wagon. The gold, loaded into saddlebags, which were slung over their shoulders, grew heavier with each step.

Straining muscles became weary and sore. Cactus spines injected their venom into aching joints, while barbed thorns tore at both clothing and skin. While no sounds of pursuit had yet been heard, the men knew the bandits had not given up the chase.

"We'd best pick up the pace, men," George muttered. "Some of them Mex trackers are good as injuns. When the sun comes up, they're likely to be all over us like stink on manure."

By dawn, the men had traveled a semi-circle down river

from Rosita. Guided by converging trails that signified they were approaching a settlement, they made their way to a rocky ridge where a small village spread out below them.

They let the heavy bags slip off their shoulders onto the ground, then sprawled out in utter exhaustion.

George crawled to a spot where he could get a good look. "I think it's Pata Chica. If so, the Rio Grande should be just a few miles more."

Lance spoke from flat on his back. "We ain't gonna make it a few more miles in the shape we're in. Mike's weak and bleeding again."

George shifted his cud of tobacco. "What you think we oughta do?"

Roy spoke up. "Hell, we got gold. Let's just walk right into town, get some horses, whatever else we need."

Lance's look expressed disgust. "O'Neil, you're so dumb, you don't know 'come here' from 'sic 'em'." There's at least a dozen people down there who'd kill you just for your ratty boots. What do you think they'd do for $120,000 in gold?"

"Hey, Lance," George interrupted. "See that little place over there?" He indicated a small *cantina* set on the edge of the village. With several houses clustered nearby, it looked almost like a separate town.

"Might be all right," Lance agreed. "Maybe we could hole up there for a while. But, we gotta do something about this gold. We can't carry it down there."

"Well, I can carry some of it," Roy said. He had one bag open and was filling his pockets.

Lance was furious. "Dammit, Roy, put that gold back."

"What you talking about?"

"That's not our gold," Lance said. "It belongs to the Confederacy, and you can just keep your hands out of it."

"That's crazy!" Roy shouted. "We almost got killed over that gold. I say it's ours. What about it, George?"

George squirted a stream of tobacco juice from his lips. "Dunno about that. If gettin' nearly killed over somethin' makes it yours, I reckon I own half of Georgia by now. I figure we're soldiers, still under orders, and those orders were to get this gold back to the Confederacy. I guess we're entitled to take out enough for expenses, but that's all."

"You're both crazy," Roy snapped, but he put the gold back in the bag. "Now what?"

The men decided on the remnants of a past rock slide as a suitable hiding place, gouged out a hole for the bags, and covered them with rocks. Brushing out their tracks as best they could, they returned to the ridge.

29

"That takes care of that," Lance said. "Now, let's see if we can get into town quietly."

A clap of thunder almost drowned out his words. The men looked behind them to see a heavy bank of clouds building up rapidly into a sudden thunderstorm so common in the region.

"Let's get a roof over our heads," George shouted.

That early in the morning, the *cantina* was virtually deserted. An old withered man, bald on top with long grey hair around the edges, lethargically stroked the earthen floor with a homemade broom. At the back of the room, a leftover drunk slumped at a table.

At the sight of three white men in dirty and torn Confederate uniforms and a huge Negro apparently drunk, ill or wounded, the little old man scurried behind the bar.

"*Buenos dias, señores,*" he piped.

While Lance helped Mike to a chair at a front table, and Roy swept the room with his eyes, George walked straight to the bar.

"Do you speak English?" he asked.

"*No, señor.*"

"We need some help. Do you understand?"

"*No inglés, señor.*" He turned to the back of the room and shouted, "*Arabela! Por favór.*"

The door opened and a woman entered the room. Dressed in the style of a traditional Mexican dancer, she stood as in a pose, face uplifted, jet-black hair pulled back severely into a knot at the back of her head which was tilted with a dancer's grace. Her skin was smooth and the color of ivory, her finely chiseled features without flaw.

"*Que pasó,* Pablo?" she asked.

Then, she looked about the room and understood. "I am Arabela Cruz, the owner. How may we help you?"

Lance stood transfixed, his mouth agape. Of all the sights he might have expected to greet him in that adobe building, this was to him one of the least likely.

George stepped forward. "You speak English?"

She smiled and tossed her head. "Of course."

"We have a man who's been hurt. He needs a place to rest. We can pay; we have money."

With a fluid movement, she stepped to the middle of the room and smiled wryly. "Confederate money, *señor?*"

"Mexican gold."

Her smile brightened. "My house is yours, *señores.*"

Lance abruptly came to himself. "Cut the damn talk. Mike is bad off."

30

Her brown eyes softened. "Of course. Follow me,"

She led the men out the back door to a small one-room house adjacent to the *cantina*. She helped them get Mike into a small bed in a corner.

"This house is yours for as long as you like."

George grinned skeptically. "How much?"

"For each day, five dollars."

George roared. "Five dol . . ."

Lance cut him off. "We'll take it."

The girl turned to George and shrugged apologetically. "The price includes my silence, *señor*. And that of my helpers. I will have certain expenses."

Lance stammered, "But — where will you — uh . . ."

She laughed. I have a room also in the back of the *cantina*. I will stay there. You will not be disturbed."

"We're grateful," Lance said.

The rain came down in a torrent, wiping out every trace of the men's passage through the wilderness.

CHAPTER 5

With the coming of evening, the *cantina* took on new life. Music of the Spanish guitar hung on the night air, and laughter wafted across to the little house where the troopers waited with restless impatience.

Only Mike, with his wound tended and freshly bandaged, was resting easily in bed. The others alternately sat against the wall, stretched out on blankets provided by Arabela, and paced the floor.

"The hell with this," Roy grunted. "I'm gettin' myself a drink."

George pulled himself up to a sitting position. "Maybe not a good idea. We don't wanta attract any attention."

Lance scratched his head. "You're probably right, but I figger the whole town knows we're here by now. And I can't stand being cooped up any longer myself."

George grinned. "Well, if one goes, we might as well all go. You be all right, Mike?"

Mike clasped his hands behind his head. "I'm fine Mistuh George. This nigger ain't goin' nowhere."

Arabela's eyes widened at the sight of the three troopers; otherwise, she made no sign of recognition. As they seated themselves at an empty table, she brought a bottle of tequila and three glasses.

Behind the bar, Pablo was serving an assortment of customers, mostly *vaqueros* from surrounding ranches and a sprinkling of river-bottom farmers. Some were astonished at the presence of Confederate gringos, but the Texas/Mexican border of 1865 was not considered a healthy time and place for undue curiosity. Therefore, the entrance of these unexpected guests was noted – but unremarked.

Two grey-haired ranchers sat at one of the tables discussing a trade involving a Barb stallion and four black bulls. At another table, a guitarist tuned his instrument.

By the time the men had opened their bottle and poured a

round of drinks, the guitarist was ready. Arabela twirled across the room. Castanets, appearing on her fingers as if by magic, began their rhythmic clatter. From the back two other girls joined in a gypsy dance, frenzied yet stylized, unchanged for more than two hundred years.

Abruptly the music and dancers stopped. The guitarist started again, slowly. He slapped the sides of his instrument, then plucking one string at a time, he started a slow, measured beat. Arabela stood as though frozen in time, face uplifted, eyes half closed, then stamped her tiny foot forward and back in time to the music.

She leaned forward until her face was almost on the floor, twisted her body, and rose slowly in a swooping motion. The guitarist hit a rapid tempo, fingers flashing in the intricate pattern of *flamenco*. Heads held high in traditional Spanish arrogance, the three dancers stamped and twirled in precise patterns, castanets chattering a response to the beat of the guitar.

The other girls were highly skilled at their art -- but it was Arabela that held the eye of the audience. Incredibly graceful, her movements were alternately coy then deliberately, tantalizingly sensual.

Lance was thunderstruck. His glass sat untouched. Only his eyes seemed alive, eagerly drinking in every movement as the dance ascended to its climax.

The end was a crescendo of music and movement. Abrupt silence followed -- not a movement in the room. Then, the regulars, for whom the performance lacked the thrill of surprise, offered warm but routine applause. George and Roy whooped and clapped their hands enthusiastically, with Roy occasionally putting his fingers to his mouth for an earsplitting whistle. Lance sat entranced, silent and still. Nothing in his few years had prepared him for the sight of such grace and beauty.

With a perfunctory bow of acknowledgement, the girls retired to the end of the bar where their brandy glasses awaited. Roy, who had not slacked off his drinking since he'd hit the door, made his way unsteadily to Arabela's side.

"Hot damn, that was good," he slurred, lurching against her, letting a hand slip down to squeeze her buttocks.

Arabela moved adroitly to one side, leaving him hanging on the bar.

"I'm glad you and your friends liked it," she said.

He reached across and angrily grabbed her arm. "Whatza matter? Think I'm not good enough for you?"

She pried his fingers from her arm. "No one touches me unless I say so."

34

Roy fumbled in his pocket. "How much before I'm good enough?"

Her eyes flashed anger. "Your money buys nothing but a drink in this *cantina, cabrón.*"

"You whore!" His open hand lashed out in a slap across the woman's face.

Suddenly, he was propelled back against the bar. He looked around into Lance's furious face. "Get your filthy hands off her," Lance hissed.

"The hell with you," Roy shouted. "You got no say-so over me."

The fury in Lance's face belied the calmness of his voice. "Boy, I think the time has come to whip your tail."

Every head in the *cantina* had turned their way. Those in close proximity to the two men began to edge away.

Arabela stepped toward the two. "There is no need for fighting. I can take care of myself. Do you hear . . ?"

She stopped as George lay a hand on her arm. "Let them be, ma'am. This has been festerin' a long time. Might as well let 'em get it outa their systems."

Roy stood in a slight crouch, clenching and unclenching his fists. A slight smile tugged at the corners of his mouth. "Well, the little rich boy's gonna fight. I been waitin' for this, Morgan."

He suddenly lunged forward and jammed a bony fist into Lance's face. Caught off balance, Lance staggered backward with the salty taste of blood in his mouth. He stepped forward too quickly and took a right to his stomach, then a left to the side of his head, and his knees buckled.

As he went to the ground, Roy aimed a kick at his head.

Lance saw it coming, and fighting off the fog in his vision, rolled over just as the kick went high over his head. Roy pressed the advantage, moving in quickly. But Lance struggled to his feet and grabbed his opponent in a bear hug, holding him tightly while the senses ebbed back into his throbbing head.

Roy lifted his knee, aimed at Lance's groin, and pushed hard with both hands. Lance's grip loosened, and the two staggered apart. Eager to renew his attack, Roy moved forward carelessly. This time, Lance was ready and caught him with a hard right to the chin. Roy's eyes turned glassy, arms dropping to his side. Lance threw another right into the other's midsection and had the satisfaction of hearing the air go out in a choking gasp.

But the wiry sharecropper snapped back quickly. He circled Lance more cautiously now. Lance stood upright, turning to face O'Neil as he moved. Then, both lunged forward in a flurry of fists. Lance shifted his shoulders, throwing his full weight behind a hard blow to the ferret face in front of him. There was a sharp crack, and Roy staggered backward, holding hands over his face. Blood streamed from his nose and trickled between his fingers.

"That's enough. I've had enough, Morgan."

He lowered himself into a chair and sat there moaning. "Broke my nose. Dammit all. He broke my nose."

George pulled Roy's hands away and took a look. "Won't hurt your looks none, that's for sure."

He turned his attention to Lance. "Yours ain't gonna be improved none though."

Lance felt a large swelling just in front of his left ear, his left eye was swollen and probably turning black, and there was a long, tender abrasion on his right cheek.

George spoke to Arabela. "I'm sorry for this little fracas in your place of business, ma'am. We'll pay for any damage done. But right now, I'm takin' these two outa here. They can say their regrets in the morning."

He then addressed the entire room. *"Caballeros! Muy buen gusto en conocerle* – it's been a real pleasure."

The *vaqueros* roared with laughter at his heavily accented Spanish and cheered him through the door with a chorus of *"Buenos noches, Señor Gringo."*

Lance rolled off his blanket onto the bare floor. His head throbbed, and a tight sensation told him his face was swollen. Various abrasions greeted the movement with stinging pain. As he pulled himself up, his head banged against the bottom of a chair. Stiffly, he got to his feet.

Roy O'Neil was curled up in a ball at the other end of the room. Mike was fully awake and sitting up. George squatted by the side of Mike's bed regaling the black man with tales of his childhood in Tennessee.

Lance smiled in spite of the pain shooting through his body. It was a little strange, he thought, how much at ease George was with Mike. Most white men, if they didn't have orders to give or something like that, didn't much know what to say to niggers. Of course, with himself, it was different. After all, he'd practically been raised by Mike. Mike was like part of the family. But Mike was nothing to George – just a big nigger – that belonged to someone else.

George watched Lance struggle to his feet. Seeing him take a tentative step and stagger a little, he grinned widely. "Looks like you win again. Old Roy's still out cold."

Lance grimaced. "If this is winning, I'd sure as hell hate to lose."

36

The door opened, admitting a bright shaft of sunshine along with a young Mexican boy of about fourteen. *"Buenos dias, señores.* I have brought you some food -- some breakfast."

His burden consisted of a pot of beans, in which floated several chunks of unidentifiable meat, a platter of tortillas, and a cup of freshly diced onion and green chili peppers.

The boy swept his hat off in a grand gesture. "I am Leon Cruz, brother of Arabela, and at your service *caballeros."*

George tossed the boy a coin which he deftly snatched from the air, then backed quickly out the door.

Striding across the room, George nudged the motionless Roy with his toe. "Get up, Roy, or we'll eat without you."

It was a more subdued group that entered the *cantina* next evening. Mike, while still weak, had accepted Lance's invitation to go with them. Roy remained morose and silent. Lance tried, with limited success, to present a cheerful front.

Arabela served the men herself, bringing them steaming bowls of pungent stew with hot chilies and beans. Lance's eyes followed her every movement. And when she accidentally brushed up against him while serving, she drew away quickly in flustered confusion.

After the evening's entertainment, the men rose to return to their hut. Arabela was serving drinks to a table of *vaqueros* toward the back of the room while the other two girls flirted outrageously with a couple of men at the bar.

Lance dawdled while leaving and glanced back over his shoulder at Arabela who excused herself and hurried to the door. She took a deep breath and planted her feet directly in his path. George took one look and hustled Roy and Mike toward their hut.

The small room had an iron bedstead in one corner, a small table on which sat a basin and pitcher of water, a wall lamp with metal crucifix hung underneath, and a single chair.

Arabela's hand trembled slightly as she lit the lamp. She stood still for a moment before turning to face Lance who waited hesitantly near the doorway.

She made a small gesture with her hand. "My room."

"Yes," he said.

"This was my room for — my room for work. Do you understand?"

His mouth was dry, making the words come hard. "Yes, I understand. But you said 'was'?"

She stood close to him, her gaze lowered. "No more. Not for more than a year now."

37

He opened his arms, and she stepped into them silently. Her face pressed hard against his chest slightly muffling her words. "I am the *dueña* now – the owner. I no longer . . ."

He put his fingers against her lips. "It's all right."

She lifted her face for his kiss – gentle, tentative. Then another -- eager and searching while he clutched her body close to his. The stiffness between two bodies unfamiliar with one another quickly melted under the fire of passion.

He let out a groan and pulled her closer. His kisses covered her face, and he nipped gently at her lips, her ears, and her neck as he lowered her to the bed. Resting his weight on his elbows, he caught her head between his hands. His fingers entwined in her hair as he moved over her. She gasped, caught in a wave of unexpected pleasure.

He was moving now with more confidence in the role of the dominant male.

She closed her eyes concentrating on a pleasure she'd not known up to now. But even with the passion burning inside her with almost unbearable intensity, she still focused her entire being on giving pleasure to this man/boy she hardly knew. And in the giving, the pleasure washed back over her with a terrible sweetness. As she abandoned herself completely to his ardor, a whirlpool swept her down into a vortex of scalding emotion – to a rapture she'd never known before.

CHAPTER 6

The four men sat at a table in the *cantina* washing down their breakfast with warm mugs of beer. Knowing there was now no way to keep their presence a secret, they moved openly in the area around their own hut and the *cantina*. Lance spent his days with the other men, but his nights belonged to Arabela.

She passed behind him, bringing them a fresh pitcher of beer, reached down and touched the hair at the nape of his neck. He rolled his shoulders in appreciation of the gesture and tilted his head back against her arm.

George squinted. "Boys, we gotta get outa here."

Roy O'Neil shoveled in a mouthful of beans. "What's the hurry, George? Hell, we doin' all right here."

"You think ever'body in town don't know we're here," George snapped. "And if anybody's tryin' to find us, and you know they are, they'll do it. Just a matter of time."

Lance was still frowning but nodded his head in agreement. "You're right, George. We been lucky so far. But the luck won't hold forever. Arabela's got a nag -- probably can get more – but it'll take a couple of days."

Roy looked up from his plate. "Somebody better scout out the area first. I'll do it."

Lance looked at him in surprise. "Good idea, Roy, but we oughta draw straws or something."

O'Neil shook his head. "I'll go. Nothin' else to do."

The short, heavy-set Mexican squatted on top of a large outcropping of rock and spat through crooked teeth. Short rawhide leggings covered dirty white trousers. Heavy roweled spurs, looped over straw sandals, plowed two little furrows behind him when he walked. A pair of bandoleers crossed his chest and twin Colt Navy revolvers hung low on his hips.

He snarled in Spanish at a collection of similar figures grouped in a clearing beneath the overhanging rocks. "I had as well have had a band of women with me. You call yourselves men? I think not. Twenty-three men do not let four gringos and a wagon load of gold just walk away in the night. A week has passed and still we look – as the coyote sniffs the brush after a sick rabbit.

"*Madre mia!* We had the gold right in our hands!" He held a closed hand over his head, lowered it to eye level, and opened it.

"Nothing! Are we to content ourselves with rustling a few cattle and horses from the gringos? Are we to always leave the big prize to others?"

Pulling himself to his feet, he placed his hands on hips. "Do you know that eighteen of our comrades died on the streets of Rosita? Yes, you know that. Do you know why they died? I'll tell you. They died for gold -- gold for you and me. That we might have good whiskey to warm us inside -- and the women to warm us outside."

He scrambled down from his perch on the rock and strolled among the men. "I tell you, one might say they have died for nothing. But we will have that gold. And those gringos. I, Santiago, say it is so. Do I not always keep my promises? You have always had easy money in your pockets – easy plunder of the *norteamericanos*. I say we will have the gold – and our revenge on those gringos who would cheat us of our rightful plunder."

One of the men was a little slow making way for the bandit leader. Quick as a striking rattler, a revolver flashed against the side of his head, and he slumped to the ground, blood pouring from a deep cut.

The bandit leader dropped it in his holster.

As he swaggered through the band berating them for stupidity, cowardice, and their questionable ancestry, the surging exultation dimmed his disappointment at not already having the gold. The feeling of great power swelled his chest and flared his nostrils. A tingling sensation stirred in his loins. He lapsed into silence, then strode purposefully to a crude, temporary shelter erected under some large cottonwood trees.

Standing in the makeshift doorway, he blinked his eyes against the semi-darkness of the interior. Constructed of mesquite and carrizo cane, the shelter was little more than a brush pile. Huddled against the far wall were three girls, the eldest of whom was just eighteen years of age.

He snarled into the shelter. "Get out. Now!"

The three scuttled toward the opening, but just as they reached it, his voice boomed again. "Stop!"

The youngest, a slender girl of about fifteen, started to whimper. This brought a humorless grin to the man's face. "Not you, *chica*. You need another lesson in womanliness."

He caught her by the arm and tossed her against the back wall where she collapsed into a small bundle. The others hurried out into the sunlight.

The young girl raised a tear-stained face. "No," she pleaded. "Please, Santiago, no more — please!"

Three men dragging in wood for the evening fire heard the screaming start.

"Aha," one laughed, "Santiago is at it again."

"Maybe we can walk now with not so much caution around here." said the other.

The third chuckled. "That is a certainty. Better one of them than us."

In the early evening, the bandits gathered around a fire that had burned down to glowing coals. These fires held an assortment of pots and pans, the contents of which bubbled up an aroma that made obvious why the bandits' tastes ran to heavy seasoning both in and on their food.

Santiago sat apart from the others with his needs and desires carefully anticipated by his companions. He looked up from his plate, a trickle of gravy coursing down his chin.

The sentry shouted, *"Cuidado.* Someone approaches."

Although the men stopped eating for the moment, they showed little overt reaction to the news. They shifted positions slightly so they could keep their eyes on the stranger as he rode in, but only as reasonably cautious men who have nothing really to fear. The man rode to the clearing and stepped down. One of the bandits recognized him. *"Es el hombre del sombrero blanco!"*

Santiago, still chewing on a chunk of meat, walked up to the newcomer. *"Señor* O'Neil. I expected you sooner."

"Couldn't get away no sooner," Roy muttered. "Got anything to drink around here?"

The bandit leader tossed him a half-full bottle of *mescal.* O'Neil twisted off the top, drank greedily, and wiped his mouth on the back of his hand.

"Your men sure played hell at Rosita," he grumbled. "Damn near killed me, let the gold get away and then lost our trail. I thought you was supposed to be fightin' men."

"Careful with your tongue, gringo. You carelessly lost the white *sombrero* – you should have been killed." The bandit chuckled. "With the bare head, all you gringos look alike."

Roy squinted at the man. "Don't be smart, Santiago, I ain't in the mood."

"Take care with your mood – that it don't get you dead, *amigo,*" the bandit snarled. "But enough. Where is the gold? And where are your gringo friends?"

41

Roy squatted on his heels. "Think I'm a fool? I'll show you where the others are – and the gold. Then, we split it just like we agreed on my last trip through here."

Santiago spread his hands in mock dismay. "You don't trust me, *amigo?* And I gave you my word."

Roy just grunted.

About two-hundred yards from the bandit camp, a small figure crawled unseen between the trunks of two small mesquite trees bordering a long and steep arroyo. Two brown eyes studied the scene carefully. Ear low to the ground, Leon Cruz struggled to hear what was being said, but the distance was too great. He pondered the possibility of getting closer, but the ground was barren for at least another hundred yards past the mesquite trees. The bandits had chosen their spot with care.

He quickly decided that it wasn't worth the risk. What he'd already seen was enough and had to be reported immediately. Picking his way carefully to where he'd tied his small mule, he climbed into the saddle and turned the animal back down the canyon floor, keeping well away from the skyline.

George slammed his fist hard down on the table. "That sorry little bastard!"

Lance tilted his chair and pushed his hat back on his head. "So that's who Jim Magruder was cussin' so."

"What you talkin' about, Lance?"

"Before he died Jim was lettin' somebody have it — Roy."

George muttered. "We shoulda known. Wish you'da killed him the day you had that fight. Hell, wished I'da killed him just about anytime."

Leon Cruz stood by the table shifting his weight from one foot to the other. Arabela stood beside him, one arm over his shoulders. She spoke hesitantly. "He is a very bad man. A man with the mean eyes is never to be trusted."

"It's good you didn't trust him, Arabela," George said.

"Yes," said Lance. "We thank you." He looked at the boy. "Leon, you saved our lives -- and a lot of gold that belongs to our country."

Leon ducked his head in embarrassment . "I did not like that man, *señores*. I did not like his look– I did not like his talk. He had no respect."

"Well, we gotta have some horses," Lance said. "Arabela, can you get us five horses?"

The girl shook her head. "I will get you three horses."

42

Lance said, "But you and Leon will have to come with us."

She smiled sadly. "This is our home."

"But, he'll kill you — this Santiago?"

"No. You will take away the gold, and he will have no reason to hurt us."

Lance's chin jutted stubbornly. "I won't go without you."

"You will," she smiled, "because you must – just as Leon and I must stay."

She turned quickly, pulling her shawl over her head and hurried into the dark.

It was early morning before she returned with three horses and a small bag filled with jerky and dry corn.

"It's not much," she said, "but it will stop the hunger for a while. Go with God, *mi amór.*"

Lance caught her in his arms and held her close. "I'll come back just as soon as I can."

She brushed the moisture from her eyes. "Yes. If you can, return to me, my love."

She dropped her arms to her side, and he stepped into the saddle. As the trio rode away, only Mike looked back to lift a hand in farewell.

The outlaw band thundered over the hill just outside Pata Chica. Santiago rode in the lead with Roy O'Neil by his side. O'Neil nudged his mount a little closer and shouted, "Just a little farther."

Santiago nodded. *"Bueno!* You better be right, gringo."

Roy leaned closer. "We split the gold first, right? Then, you go after the others – I go on my way."

Santiago's face split in a toothy grin. "You don't wish to say goodbye to your friends? No matter. You go where you like – once we get the gold."

"Up on the ridge over there." Roy pointed to the left.

"Mas rápido, muchachos!" Santiago yelled.

They galloped quickly to the location O'Neil had indicated. He was quickly off his mount and stumbled to the spot where he'd helped hide the gold.

He stopped, mouth open in disbelief. Many tracks and the overturned stone told the story. Someone had been there -- and recently. The gold was gone.

"Dammit! They dug it up."

Santiago's face grew dark. "Where is the gold?"

"Hell, I don't know. I guess they dug it up already." His face suddenly brightened. "Sure. They dug it up and are

43

waiting for me in Pata Chica. They'll have it with them."

Santiago shoved his face close to the other man's. "I don't like this, gringo. You said the gold would be here. Now you say it is there."

Roy wiped his face with a bandana. "It's gotta be there. They wouldn't go off and leave me."

Santiago smiled coldly. "You are right, gringo. You wouldn't lie to your good *amigo*. It would be very bad for your health."

The *cantina* was quiet. A number of *vaqueros* quenched their thirst at the bar and carried on a conversation with Pablo. Arabela sat at a table with her two dancers. Her hands fluttered nervously as the girls chattered incessantly.

Leon appeared in the doorway, stood silently, and nodded.

The girls lapsed into sudden silence. Arabela rose and spoke sharply to them. They disappeared quickly out the back door. The two *vaqueros* scurried quickly out the front door without finishing their drinks.

Pablo looked questioningly at Arabela. She shook her head. "Be still, Pablo. It's all right."

Roy O'Neil strode into the room rubbing his hands together nervously. Dust powdered his clothing and clung to his face. His eyes darted around the room.

"Arabela, where's Lance and George at?"

She spoke flatly. "Gone."

The man's face contorted. "Gone?" Frantically, he lurched across the room and clutched her arm. "What do you mean gone? Gone where?"

She smiled. "Gone. Back to Texas — to Matamoros — to Mexico City. I don't know where. They've gone."

O'Neil's face flushed with anger. "Liar! They wouldn't have gone without me." His fingers bit into her skin.

She tried to pull her arm free. Anger showed on her face. "You coyote! They know about you and your bandits."

His face paled. "But how? What are you . . ."

"I saw you." Leon stepped forward, puffing out his chest in excitement.

"Saw me what?"

The door banged open, and Santiago stepped through flanked by two of his bandits. "So, stupid gringo. You let this boy – this puppy follow you."

Roy mopped the bandana over his face. "No matter. They can't be very far. We'll catch 'em."

Santiago grinned sardonically. "No, my friend. We will catch them – but you will not be with us."

"Whatta ya mean by that?" Roy faced the bandit in a

44

semi-crouch.

"You are no longer of any use to us. You are . . ."

The bandit's words were cut off in mid-sentence. Knowing he had little chance to outdraw the bandit, O'Neil unleashed his body in a savage rush, head down, straight into the Mexican's face. Caught off balance, Santiago fell backwards, his gun spinning across the floor. His two startled companions stumbled back out of the line of attack.

Rather than try for the horses, he chose to press his advantage over the fallen bandit. As Santiago tried to pull himself up, O'Neil swung his boot crashing into his face.

By then, other outlaws had entered and fired frantically in O'Neil's direction. Bullets thudded into the floor as Roy rolled across the room. He managed to draw his revolver as he reached the far wall. Raising himself on an elbow, he fired and one of the bandits went down, dead before he hit the floor with a bullet through his heart. Several shots rang out, and O'Neil jerked with the impact and slumped to the floor.

Santiago regained his feet and staggered across the room. Standing over O'Neil, he emptied his revolver into the body.

Swinging around, his eyes blazed in a murderous rage. Blood trickled from his lips and nostrils. He worked his mouth, spit out a broken tooth. His breathing was deep and measured, eyes darted from side to side.

The band melted back toward the walls. None looked directly at their leader. Silence hung in the air.

Then, an explosion of laughter came from Santiago. "Come *muchachos,* we drink."

He swaggered to the bar, his men crowding in behind him.

He pointed to Pablo. "Bring me a bottle."

Filling his mouth with the clear *tequila,* he swished it and spat, then another big gulp which he swallowed.

"Bring me the girl!"

Two men grabbed Arabela and dragged her to him. His gaze swept over her.

"So, you are friend to the gringos, no?"

She stood silently.

"Hah! You look like a gringa yourself."

Without warning, his hand flashed across her face in a backhand motion.

"*Puta!* Whore! Where is the gold?"

"I know of no gold, *señor.* Only these few coins they paid me -- and they are yours." She pulled herself free, tugged a small leather bag from the front of her dress and held it out to the bandit.

He roared with anger and slapped the bag from her hand. Coins scattered across the room.

45

"You know of the gold. Where is it?"

"I know nothing of gold -- only what they pay me."

He drove his fist into her stomach, and she doubled up between her captors, retching at the pain.

He caught the top of her dress and ripped it off her shoulders down the front to her waist. Stepping back, he reached into his vest pocket pulling out a long, thin cheroot. "The gold?"

She shook her head frantically. "They must have taken it with them. If I knew, I'd tell you. I just don't know."

He scratched a match with his thumbnail, put the cheroot in his mouth, and lit it, puffing out a cloud of smoke.

"You know - and you will tell me."

Her eyes widened, riveted on the tip of his cigar as he puffed it into a gleaming orb.

"*Si*. You will tell me."

Still puffing on the cigar, he bent over to thrust it toward her bared breast.

"No!" The sound came from Leon who hurtled through the crowd of men to stand between Santiago and Arabela.

Santiago stepped back in surprise. "So! Is the puppy to show his teeth?"

With a swing of his hand, he sent Leon sprawling to the floor. But the boy bounced up immediately, grabbing a revolver from the holster of one of the bandits. At point blank range he stabbed the pistol toward Santiago's chest and pulled the trigger.

The quick hand of one of Santiago's men deflected the gun, and the bullet plowed harmlessly into the ceiling.

Another outlaw pushed his revolver into Leon's back and fired. The boy crumpled instantly.

Arabela screamed and kicked out with both feet in an effort to free herself. She stamped the heel of her shoe down on one man's instep and jerked her arm loose. With the one free hand, she clawed at the other man's eyes.

The powerful hand of Santiago closed on her throat. He held her against the wall and methodically beat her into unconsciousness.

CHAPTER 7

Knowing the Mexican trackers would try to trail them, the three Confederates followed a zigzag route through the rocky ground toward the Rio Grande. Their progress was at best steady.

Lance reined up as he reached the top of a small ridge. A couple of miles ahead, he could see the breaks leading down into the river.

As the others pulled up beside him, he asked, "George, what do you think?"

The older man looked back behind them. "Don't know. Haven't seen any sign all the way."

Lance frowned and shook his head. "I don't like it. We couldn't have gotten more than an hour or so start on 'em. Maybe less."

"They should have been right on our tails," George agreed. "We're not gonna run off from them on these nags."

They were brought up short by a shout from Mike. "Something's comin'."

A wisp of dust appeared on the horizon behind them.

George squinted his eyes, "No more'n seven or eight I'd say from the dust they're kickin' up."

Lance looked puzzled. "Something's wrong, George. Oughta be a least two – maybe three times that many."

George scratched his chin. "Maybe some of 'em dropped out — nah. Boys, we'd better get outa here."

The three struck a long, easy lope down the ridge toward the river *vega* below. Lined with carrizo cane and scattered brush, the river was shallow and slow moving, as it was at most crossings. But just below, it narrowed into a swift and turbulent current.

The men spurred down the slope and hit the first water in a rocky bed twisting away from the main channel. From a clump of carrizo to their right, came the roaring of gunfire.

Lance, riding in the lead, felt his horse die between his knees. He kicked free of the stirrups and hit the ground rolling. As he came to a stop, he saw George swaying in the saddle, both hands clasped to his slowly coloring chest. As he watched, George's mount buckled at the knees and went down.

A noise to his left whirled him around, but it was just Mike leading his horse at a run. "Massa, you all right?"

"I'm not hit, Mike. See about George."

Lance checked his position and found that a log of driftwood offered him some protection from the source of gunfire. He checked his various aches and pains. All seemed to be superficial. In a crouching run, he hurried to where Mike was bending over George, who lay crumpled on the rocky ground.

Mike rolled him onto his back and tore back the tunic to expose a gaping wound in the left side of his chest.

Large caliber, Lance thought. Probably a .50 Sharps. He stuck a hand under George's back. Clear through just under the left shoulder.

Mike shook his head. "He hit bad, Massa Lance."

Lance wadded his neckerchief and stuffed it in the hole in the man's chest and strapped it tight with his belt.

A bullet whined off a rock near George's head.

Lance fired three times into the clump and was rewarded by a cry of pain.

"Damn, Mike, we're caught in the middle now. Those bastards behind us will be all over us in a few minutes."

"Yassuh. I see 'em coming mighty fast."

"We gotta get George outa here."

"We only got one horse, Massa Lance."

Lance crawled to the edge of the water and looked down river. "Can you get George up on that horse, Mike?"

"Yassuh. Easy."

Once George was draped over the horse's back, the two men leaped to their feet and raced for the river, emptying their revolvers at the bandits in the brush.

An angry buzzing of bullets filled the air around them.

Just before they reached the river, the horse stumbled and died. Mike slipped the ropes and had George on his shoulder almost before the horse hit the ground.

Lance ran directly to a large log hung up in the boulders along the river's edge. He lunged against it with all his strength, but it didn't move. Suddenly, Mike was at his side. He gently placed George in the water, back up against a boulder, and put his massive shoulder to the log.

The veins stood out on his neck, and his back muscles rippled as he threw himself against the timber. With a loud creaking groan, the log turned and floated free of the rocks.

Both men hoisted George against the log and tied him securely with the rope from Mike's saddle.

Lance guided the log out to the swift current, and with the three men clinging to its stubby branches, it hurtled into the rapids below the crossing.

Scotty MacDuff liked his breakfast early. The sun was just beginning to spread a soft glow over the eastern horizon when he pushed back his chair and rose from the table. He fished into his pockets for the stump of a clay pipe and a small leather bag of twisted tobacco.

As he tamped the tobacco into the bowl, he motioned to his son. "Bain, I'm still worried about those mares down at Big Frog Spring. Wish you'd ride down there and take another look at 'em today."

Bain stared out the window at nothing in particular. "All right, father, but I'm sure nothing's wrong. We were down there getting that mule out just a few days ago."

Scotty put a match to the pipe and puffed to get it going. "Those 'few days' are almost two weeks now. Besides, we've got a lot at stake in those mares."

"I know, father. You've mentioned it before."

"And I'll probably mention it again. It doesn't seem to stick with you."

"Sorry, father. I'm on my way."

George's breathing came heavy and irregular. His skin felt hot and dry to the touch. Mike raised his hand off the injured man's head and turned to Lance who was trying to start a fire with powder from a cartridge dried in the sun after being soaked by the river.

"Massa Lance, he gonna die less'n we do somethin'."

Lance spread his hands helplessly. "I know, Mike. I just don't know what to do."

"I knows some things that maybe might work."

Lance shrugged. "Do whatever you can, Mike."

"I'll see what I can find."

The huge Negro eased off into the brush heading down toward the edge of a small stream that emptied into the river. Lance watched for a moment, then turned back to chipping two rocks together over a smear of powder and small pile of tinder.

By the time Mike returned, Lance was nursing a small fire, feeding twigs into the tiny flame. Mike was carrying a couple of brush stems and a handful of weeds and herbs.

"Mike, what is all that stuff?"

"It's a potion, Massa Lance."

Lance scowled. "Think it'll do George any good?"

"Sometimes it work."

"Might as well try it. Can't do him much hurt."

Mike slipped a long-bladed knife out of his boot and started shaving slivers of bark from the bush limbs into a canteen of water. When he had finished, he dropped the canteen into the edge of the fire.

Searching through the river rubble, Mike found a large rock with a slightly dished face, and placing the herbs and weeds in a small pile on it, began pounding them into a wet pulp with another flat rock. Scooping up the mass, he carried it to where George lay. He pulled back the rag from over the wound to reveal purplish, puffy flesh around an almost black center. Angry red streaks radiated out from the wound. Mike plopped the sticky, wet pulp down over the area, replaced the soggy bandana, and returned to where the canteen was beginning to simmer. With a pair of sticks, he pulled it from the fire.

"We got no cup, Massa. We best let this cool a while, then we'll see if we can get some down him."

Bain MacDuff pushed a springy mesquite limb to the side. The mares hadn't been where he thought they'd be. Now he'd have to search out the lower flats downstream.

He idly leaned forward and swatted a deerfly on his horse's neck. Unexpectedly, his mount froze in place, its ears pointed straight ahead, and it let out a low nicker.

Bain went instantly alert. He backed the horse a few steps then circled to the side to see what might lie ahead. There were two men in the clearing ahead, lifting another from a prone position and putting a canteen to his lips.

He moved closer, slipped the Colt .44 out of its holster and nudged his horse into the clearing.

"Sit still – right where you are," he ordered.

The two men looked up in surprise; now he could see that the larger one was definitely black. The white man stood, hands slightly raised in front of him.

"We need help."

By then Bain could see that the man was only slightly, if any, older than himself.

"Who are you? And what are you doing here?"

"We're what's left of an army detail guarding a cotton train after the Mexican bandits got through with us."

Bain cautiously swung down from his horse. "You came by here about two weeks ago?"

"That's right, with Captain Jess Waldrop commanding. I"m Private Lance Morgan, the hurt man is Private George

Gibson, and this here's my servant, Mike. We need your help if you're a mind to give it."

Bain saw that the ragged tunic had once been part of a Confederate uniform. He holstered his revolver and stuck out his hand. "I'm Bain MacDuff, and you'll have whatever help I can give." He glanced down at George. "How bad is he?"

Lance shook his head. "Bad. He needs a doctor."

"Can't help you there," Bain said. "But our ranch is just a couple of hours away. We might get a doc out from Terwilliger later."

The men quickly constructed a travois from a pair of saplings, gently placed George on it, and strapped it to Bain's horse. With Bain leading the way, the group plodded up the trail toward the MacDuff Ranch.

George was taken directly to the main house and bedded down in Bain's room. Bain moved his gear into the bunkhouse where Lance and Mike were to stay.

Erin MacDuff, clearing the men from her way with a sweep of her arm, moved in to take a look at George's wound. His breathing was now much easier, and he seemed to have no fever. She pulled back the stained neckerchief and made a face at the terrible stench of the pulpy mass Mike had put on the wound. She stripped it off and threw it into a pan.

She looked up at Lance, and a smile touched her lips. "I don't know what that gosh-awful stuff was – but it seems to have helped."

Lance raised his hands. "I don't know either, ma'am. Something Mike here made up."

Mike grinned and bobbed his head as all eyes turned toward him. "Jes' somethin' an ole lady showed me once. Think she was my granmammy. Don't know if it was exactly right – but was close as I could come."

George stirred and opened his eyes for the first time since Lance and Mike had pulled him from the river.

Erin exerted her authority. "All right, all you men, out! This man needs a bath." She looked around sternly. "And, it appears, he's not the only one."

Lance flushed. He heard a quiet giggle behind him and turned to see Colleen bringing in a bucket of water. He stumbled out the door, Bain and Mike right behind him. He could feel his ears burning – and he wasn't quite sure why.

After a bath in the cool stream, Lance slipped into the clean clothes Bain had brought him and headed for the bunkhouse. A real bed! With real sheets! Lance was asleep before his head hit the pillow.

The dark of night still lingered when Lance awakened to the sound of a voice. "Hey, Lance. Lance Morgan."

He raised his head to see Bain, fully dressed, holding a lamp over his bed. The boy reached down and gently shook his shoulder. "Mother waits breakfast for no man," he said with a smile. "And your nigger's been up for an hour. Already split a big load of wood I been supposed to do for more'n a week now."

Lance peered out the window. There, in the first streaks of sunlight, stood Mike out by the woodpile, a sheet pinned on him like a long flowing robe. Lance looked questioningly at Bain.

"The sheet? Mother's idea. We didn't have any clothes big enough for him and his aren't dry yet."

Lance choked on a cut-off chortle. "Damn! He looks like a big, white buffalo, don't he?"

Bain laughed. "That would about cover it."

Old Doc Marshall was the best horse doctor in that part of the country. He was the only doctor of any kind around, and this wasn't the first time he'd treated a human patient.

His sensitive hands probed and prodded as he explored the upper body of the man on the bed. He stepped back and nodded with satisfaction.

"No sign of infection. No fever. Don't see much to do right now but keep him rested and the wound clean."

Lance looked anxious. "Is he gonna be all right?"

Doc paused in the polishing of his glasses. "No guarantees in this business – but I see no reason he shouldn't make a reasonable recovery."

"How long?"

Doc put on his glasses and squinted through them. "Now you've asked me a question I can't answer. No way to tell. Gunshot wounds are tricky. You never know exactly what damage has been done inside the body. Could be a couple of weeks — months — or even years."

Lance let out a slow sigh. "We appreciate what you've done, Doc. But we were hoping to be moving on in two or three days."

Doc chuckled. "You did, did you? Your friend here has a hole in him, and he's lost a lot of blood. He's lucky to be alive, and you expect him to travel in just a few days. Not likely. He won't be going anywhere for a while."

"But, we've got to get to San Antonio."

"Then you'll have to go without him. That's the one thing I am sure about."

Lance walked to the window, a frown on his face. Erin

stepped up beside him.

"Mr. Morgan, you do what you have to do. I'll see to it that Mr. Gibson is cared for."

"Thank you, ma'am. I just don't know exactly what to do right now."

It was two days before George fully regained consciousness. Lance sat by the bed in a cane chair .

George weakly raised his head. "You look kinda bad, Lance. You really oughta see a doc."

"George!" Lance's face brightened. "You're awake."

"Yep. And things look mighty improved over when I went to sleep."

Lance was chattering excitedly. "We got found. This is the MacDuff Ranch. They been ... ."

George lifted a hand. "Hold it, Lance. I know most of that. I been kinda driftin' in and out. Jus' been too weak to do anything about it. Tell me about before. I remember gettin' shot. After that it's a little hazy."

"You was hit awful bad. And Mike mixed up some stuff that seemed to fix you up pretty good."

George smiled and leaned back on the pillow. "Mike's a good friend."

Lance smiled uncertainly. "A friend? George, I think of Mike like one of my own family, and I like him a lot. But I don't understand you calling him your friend. Makes it seem like you're equals."

George raised himself on his elbow. "Yep, you're right about that. Anybody that's my friend, I figger's gotta be at least my equal."

"But, George, Mike's still a nigger."

"That he is, Lance, but what the hell? So am I."

Lance looked shocked. "What do you mean, George? You're as white as I am -- or anyone else. You sayin' you got mixed blood -- are you, George?"

George gave off a short laugh and paid for it with a wracking cough. He caught his breath and waved the concerned Lance back to his seat.

"Naw, Lance, nothing like that. To you I'm white as a lily. But let me tell you what it was like back home."

He pulled the pillow up behind his back and sat up in the bed.

"My daddy was the town drunk. But he was my daddy. And at one time, he was as good as anybody -- better'n most. Least, he was always good to me.

"I couldn't stand it when the kids made fun of him. They used to sing, 'George's daddy's acting dumb, 'cause his

53

belly's full of rum.' Seems like most of my days was spent bustin' somebody's head — or gettin' mine busted."

Lance interrupted, "But what's that got to do with . . ."

"I'm gettin' to that. 'Bout the only kind that didn't give me no trouble 'bout my daddy was the nigger kids. Mostly they was my playmates.

"Seems like at home, everybody was standin' on somebody else or gettin' stood on. At the top was them that owned land. Right under them was the lawyers, doctors, preachers, teachers, and the like. Then, you had your folks with money — store owners, cotton brokers, and traders. Under them was them that worked for wages — and then, them that didn't work much at all — white trash.

"Now, white trash ain't got no land, no money — no nothin' 'cept their white skins and each other. They had to have somebody to look down on — and that was the Gibsons and the niggers. Seems like everybody had to be in some group — and since I didn't seem to fit anywhere else — I sorta thought of myself as a nigger. I lived with the niggers and lived like a nigger. First white friends I ever had was when I joined up with the army."

Lance had a bewildered look on his face. "George, I didn't know. I'm sorry."

George slumped down on the pillow. "It's all right. Reckon it don't matter much any more. Well, guess I'm a little tired right now. Can't talk no more."

Lance took his hand and squeezed. "I understand — I guess a little more than I expected to — or wanted to ."

Mike sat by a little stream, idly skipping pebbles across its surface. Lance stepped up beside him as Mike raised his head. "How is Mistah George, Massa?"

"He's awake, Mike, but he's awfully tired right now. Thought maybe later, after he rests, you might want to go in for a little visit."

The black man's eyes widened. "You think that'd be all right, Massa?"

"I don't think there's anyone he'd rather see."

Lance turned at the sound of footsteps. Colleen carried a small bundle in her hand. She held it out to Lance. "It's your uniform, Mr. Morgan."

He unfolded the bundle to see his old uniform cleaned, expertly mended and freshly pressed. "Why, Miss Colleen, who did all this?"

"Who indeed! I did it with my own fingers. Did you think me completely unskilled, Mr. Morgan?"

"Of course not. But, the — uh . . ."

She laughed. "Why, Mr. Morgan, washing and mending a man's undergarments is nothing strange for a woman with a father and brother to see after."

Lance grinned at her words. "A woman?"

She drew herself up. "I'm seventeen years old."

He was still smiling as he bowed. "I thank you, ma'am, for this fine job you've done. You sew a mighty fine seam."

She clenched both fists. "Lance Morgan, you half-grown men are all the same — dumb."

She turned quickly and ran toward the house.

Lance watched her go, a perplexed look on his face. "Now, what did I say to bring that on?"

Mike shook his head, a broad grin on his face. "Massa Lance, ain't nobody ever gonna answer that question."

The row of spindly saplings growing along the bank of the stream had been turned into stick figure people with tin cans for heads. Lance stepped back to survey his handiwork. He nodded with satisfaction, then checked the location of the holstered .44 on his hip.

He turned and with measured tread stepped off ten paces, whirled and slapped at his holster. With only a slight hitch in his movement, he drew the revolver. However, his thumb slipped off the hammer as he cocked it, and the bullet slammed into the ground just a few feet in front of him. He tried it again, this time in slow motion. The movement was smooth and true.

He carefully thumbed back the hammer and squeezed off a shot.

A clean miss.

He moved forward a couple of steps, steadied his right hand with his left, and fired again. The can danced with the bullet's impact.

At a movement behind him, he twisted quickly, bringing the revolver into firing position.

"Hold it, lad." Scotty stepped out of the brush into full view. His stumpy pipe was going full blast from the corner of his mouth. "Although, from what I've seen, I doubt I'm in real danger – that is if you're actually shooting at me."

Lance grinned ruefully. "I'm afraid you're right, sir. I can't seem to do much with a handgun."

Scotty puffed on his pipe. "Favor the rifle, do you?"

"Yes sir. With a rifle the bullet goes where I point it. With a revolver, it goes wherever it wants."

"Well, maybe I've got a shortcut for you." Scotty held out a short, double-barreled shotgun. "T'was once a fine fowling piece – made by one of Scotland's finest weapons makers."

Lance gazed at the firearm. The receiver was beautifully engraved with a hunting scene and inlaid with silver. The highly polished stock was clear walnut with ebony inserts.

Scotty tossed it to him. "Had it specially shortened by an old German gunsmith in San Antonio. Now, you can handle it fast as a handgun – and inside fifty feet it'll cut a sizable hole through anything in front of it."

Lance handled the weapon reverently. "I'd love to have one like it."

Scotty chuckled. "Give it a try."

Lance spun toward the stick figures, cocking the hammers as he turned. The two blasts were almost simultaneous. Two cans took to the air, both demolished.

Scotty laughed out loud. "Well, my boy, you seem to have gotten the hang of it rather quickly."

Lance held the shotgun in front of him in awe. "What I wouldn't give for one like it."

"You don't need one 'like it'; this one's yours."

"But, sir, " Lance stammered, "I don't understand."

"It's not important that you understand, Lance. It's only important that I understand. Accept it from a friend."

"I don't know what to say. My thanks seem so small."

"No such thing. True thankfulness is never small. I just want you protected, and I hope this weapon will do that. However, there is a condition that goes with it – one you might not be able to accept."

"A condition? What condition, sir?"

"You probably don't know, son, but I'm not in sympathy with the Confederate cause in this war."

Lance looked puzzled. "But you're no Yankee."

"No, I'm not. But I support the union of all states -- North and South alike. I could never accept the breaking apart of this country."

"But, Mr. MacDuff, the North tried to . . ."

"I know — I know. The politicians and other trouble makers have come up with plenty of reasons for both sides to fight. But this nation's been good to me. And my condition is that this weapon never be used in this War Between the States. I could never live with that."

Lance nodded. "I can understand your position, Mr. MacDuff, even though I don't agree with it. I accept your gift and its condition."

CHAPTER 8

Lance felt awkward and clumsy. He stood on the porch of the MacDuff ranch house and shifted his weight from one foot to the other. The first light was beginning to streak the eastern sky, and Mike was strapping saddlebags full of provisions and supplies onto two horses tied at the hitching post a few feet from the front porch.

"Well, son," Scotty said. "Do you think of anything else you might need? You won't find much between here and San Antonio if you run short."

"No sir." Lance spoke hastily. "You and your family have done enough already."

Erin took his face in both hands. "Nonsense. I feel — we all feel — like you're family now. And we'll miss you – and Mike too – while you're gone."

"Yes, ma'am," Lance stuttered. "I feel the same way. But you've done so much – the shotgun – horses – supplies. Someday, I'll try to repay you. Somehow."

Scotty wrung his hand. "Just keep yourself safe and well, lad. This stallion of yours will do the job for you. He's a son of Apollo, the best horse this country ever saw.

Lance glanced over his shoulder at the magnificent blood bay pawing at the ground by the hitching rail. "I think he's the best horse I ever saw. I named him Captain Jess."

Scotty smiled. "That was your captain?"

"Captain Jess Waldrop, fine an officer as a soldier could ever want."

"I'm sure he was," Scotty said.

Lance peered over Scotty's shoulder to where Colleen stood in the doorway. "Miss Colleen, I want to thank . . ."

The words came to a stop as the girl dashed forward, put both arms around his neck, and kissed him on the mouth. Lance flushed deeply and looked first at Erin then at the grinning Scotty.

He gently disengaged himself from the girl's arms. "I have to go now." He looked around once more. "Where's

Bain?"

"He's saddling his horse," Scotty answered. "He's going to ride with you for a way. He can check the cattle in the east pasture on his way back. Have a good journey, and don't worry about George. He's in good hands and looks as though he'll be up and around in no time."

Colleen looked into Lance's eyes. "You'll come back?"

A few minutes later, Scotty stood with his arm around Erin, watching the men ride over the horizon. He felt a hand slip through his arm on the other side.

"He'll — they'll be back, won't they, father?"

"Of course he — they will." Scotty laughed and put his arm around his daughter's shoulder. "After all, we have George as a hostage."

A few miles from the ranch, Lance and Mike hit the main trail leading into San Antonio. The heat by now was unrelenting, pressing down on them like a tangible weight. Lance tipped half a cup of water from his canteen into his hat and slapped it back on his head.

"Mike, let's find a place to wait that sun out for a while."

Mike paused in wetting down his own hat. "Yassuh. Some trees over yonder – mebbe a spring or somethin'."

Lance shaded his eyes to take a look. "Somebody's moving in down there. Looks like they beat us to it."

Their approach to the glen was cautious. A large body of men was moving around among the trees. Muscles taut and eyes alert, Lance and Mike reined in about a hundred yards from the motte.

"Hello, there," Lance called out.

One of the men separated himself from the others and stepped into the clearing. "Hullo, yourself. Come on in. We got coffee brewin'."

Lance nudged the bay forward. "Who are you?"·

"Mississippi cavalry. Who are you?"

Lance could see the men were in Confederate uniforms. "Cotton train detail -- or what's left of it. And we're mighty glad to see you."

The two were quickly surrounded by the soldiers.

Lance dismounted. "What's the Mississippi cavalry doing 'way out here?"

The man smiled. "Headed for Mexico, that's what."

"Mexico? What the hell for?"

The man tilted his head questioningly. "Just how long you boys been out of touch with the world?"

Lance accepted a cup of coffee offered by one of the men. "Oh — don't exactly know. Maybe several weeks I guess."

The man shook his head sadly. "This here your nigger?"

"Yes. Mike belongs to me. Why?"

A bitter laugh forced its way out of the man's mouth. "Oh no, he don't. You just think he does."

"Whatta you mean?"

The man sank down on his haunches. "You'd better find a place to sit. That Mike don't belong to nobody. He's his own man now."

Irritation showed in Lance's voice. "I think you'd better tell what you're talking about."

"War's over, boy. We got whupped good. All the darkies is free men now. Lee surrendered. Everybody else is turnin' in their arms."

Lance froze in shock. "But you've still got your guns."

"Yep. And we aim to keep 'em. But we gotta go to Mexico to do it. We're joinin' up with Maximilian. No oath of loyalty for us."

Lance shook his head. "I just can't believe it."

"You'd better believe it, boy. Be Yankee patrols all over this place in a few days. You'll have to take the oath or they'll throw your butt in jail. Or, you can go with us. Join up with Maximilian."

"Why Maximilian?"

"Hell, I don't know. I just know the Yankees don't like him, so I figger we can get in one more lick at 'em before we go down. So, how about it, boy? Come on with us. Be better'n kissin' Yankee boots the rest of your life."

"Boys, it's mighty tempting. But I got business at home in Tennessee right now. I'll have to take my chances."

"Suit yourself. Either way, you're welcome to rest here with us outa the sun. We figger night travel is safer -- and more comfortable."

Lance started loosening the cinch on Captain Jess. "Mike, I expect you and I have got some talking to do."

Mike was making an effort to keep his eyes down as he always did when speaking to a white man, but in spite of himself, they kept shifting up to look at his former master's face.

"Massa Lance, you mean I don't belong to you no more? I don't belong to nobody?"

"That's right, Mike." Lance sat on a fallen log with his legs stretched out in front of him. "You're a free man."

Tears streaked the big black face. "A free man! Lordy!"

Lance was surprised. "Mike, you wanted to be free?"

Mike shook his head slowly. "Massa Lance, everybody

wants to be free. I'm not quite sure I knows how."

"I don't understand, Mike," Lance said irritably. "You said you wanted to be free – and now you are free. What's knowing got to do with it?"

"I jus' never been free, Massa Lance. From when I was a little sprout there was always somebody to tell me what to do.

"You was born free, Massa Lance. You always knows you is free – knows what you can do and can't do. Me? I always had to have somebody to tell me."

The irritation melted from Lance's face and was replaced with a look of remorse. "I'm sorry, Mike. I just never really knew how you felt."

"No, sah. Guess you never had no reason to know."

Lance flushed. "No. I guess I didn't."

He hesitated, then stuck out his hand. "I guess this is goodbye."

Mike took his hand. "Yassah, Massa Lance."

"Mike, what you gonna do now, you think?"

"You say I'm a free man, now? Go wherever I want?"

"That's right."

"Then I knows exactly what I'm gonna do."

"What's that, Mike?"

A big grin split Mike's face. "I'm goin' back home to Tennessee jus' like we planned."

In a much shorter time than they would have ever guessed, Lance and Mike rode back away from Alba, Tennessee. His father dead of the fever, farm sold to a Carpetbagger for taxes, the local population helpless under the heavy hand of a corrupt government imposed by an unsympathetic federal authority. Nothing remained for them at home.

Lance shifted around to look back. "Well, Mike, it was a short homecoming."

"Yessuh. Mighty short."

"They just had to steal our one little dinky farm, Mike. But I tell you right now, I'm gonna have so much more than that it'd make their heads swim to think about it. I can outdo every damn, stinkin' carpetbagger that can swarm into the South. They'll all see."

As his voice trailed off, Lance resolutely turned his face to the west and didn't look back again.

CHAPTER 9

Arabela sat apart from the other women under the watchful eye of Santiago. She forced herself to take a bite of the pungent stew from a cracked bowl held in her lap. She turned aside quickly, upsetting the bowl and spilling the contents at her feet. Lurching to a nearby tree, and holding onto the trunk for support, the woman emptied her protesting stomach on the ground.

Santiago sprang immediately to her side. He drew back his hand, and she cringed against the tree awaiting the blow that never fell. Instead, he slowly lowered his hand.

"*Que cabrona!* Woman, you must eat for the little one. The son of Santiago will not be a weakling."

She pulled herself upright and faced the bandit leader. Her face and upper body were discolored in many places by deep bruises – and scars from the burning.

"Will you beat me some more, Santiago? Will you beat me because I can't hold down the food?"

He struck quickly with his open hand, knocking her sprawling on the ground. She stared up at him, naked hatred written on her face. "Will you keep beating until you beat the child out of my body?"

Just as quickly as he had struck out, he knelt by her side and gently helped her to her feet. "Why do you provoke me, woman? If you cause harm to come to the son of Santiago, you will regret it deeply I promise you."

She shook her head slowly. "Why must you think everything that happens is because of you? I do not fail to hold down my food because I wish it. I carry the sickness of many who are with child. It is nothing. It will pass."

He scowled down at her. "It had better pass."

Dragging Arabela behind him, he strutted to the center of the outlaw band. "Hear me, *muchachos*! This woman who carries the son of Santiago is to do no more work in this camp. She will be allowed to rest when she wishes.

"You," Santiago pointed to the man in charge of

61

cooking, "You will find special food for her – food she can hold on her stomach. If she continues with this sickness, you will answer to me. Do you understand?"

"*Si, patrón.*"

From that time, Santiago no longer beat Arabela, nor did he force himself on her sexually. But he devised a new tactic that was fully as effective in deterring the young woman from incurring his wrath.

When he was displeased with her, he would grab one of the other women and beat her brutally in front of the horrified Arabela, then turn with a leer and say, "That's what you'll get after the baby is born – but doubled."

The sickness proved to be temporary, much to the relief of the bandit cook, and Arabela went to her full term with no further complications. When time came for her to be delivered of her baby, the camp was in turmoil.

Santiago paced through the camp nervously, shouting out contradictory orders to everyone within earshot. One of the bandits had a wife with experience in such matters, and she was immediately designated midwife with dire warnings of her fate should anything go amiss with the baby's arrival.

The woman disappeared into the small rustic shelter where Arabela lay at her labor. Eventually Arabela's muffled cries were punctuated by a shrill, more demanding wail. Shortly, the woman scurried out and placed a squirming infant boy in the waiting hands of Santiago.

The bandit chief swaggered into the opening before which the band had assembled. Holding the baby aloft, he cried, "Observe, *muchachos*, the first boy child of Santiago, your leader! Take notice that he is perfect and unblemished, one who will lead your sons even as I have led you."

The bandits cheered wildly, with many emptying their revolvers into the air. The baby, startled by the noise, let out a scream. Santiago quickly lowered the child and gave him back to the woman to be returned to his mother.

For more than a month, Santiago savored the role of proud parent. He announced that Arabela was henceforth exempt from all work around the camp. Her sole duty was to be the proper care and rearing of her infant son.

Then, the whispering began.

It started with Carlos, husband of the midwife, and quickly spread throughout the group. It always ceased when Santiago came within earshot but recommenced quickly as soon as he was gone.

Then, late one evening, one group failed to spot the bandit

chief in time. He saw them whisper together, laugh, and then fall silent as he approached.

He whirled on the group in a rage. "What passes here, *cabrones*? Inform your leader of this funny thing, and we will all laugh together, no?

"Carlos! Tell me why you whisper and laugh."

No sign of fear crossed the man's face which wore an expression of amused contempt. He lithely uncoiled from his sitting position to an upright stance. He stood indolently and pushed his hat over his head to fall to his back where it hung by the chin strap.

"Yes, wise and brave leader. What would you know of your servants? Why we laugh? We laugh because our leader, before whom we trembled and cringed, has become a chattering monkey."

Silence fell over the camp. Men held their breath waiting for the explosion sure to come. Santiago turned a purplish hue and spittle formed on his lips. Yet, his voice was a forced calm. "Explain yourself, Carlos, before you die."

"The great stallion prancing before us has said much of his son who is to lead our sons even as he has led us. But we find that the great leader is nothing but a fool. He has sired nothing. The beloved first man child of the great Santiago is nothing but the son of a gringo."

Carlos anticipated Santiago's draw and went for his own weapon a split-second before his leader, but it wasn't enough. Santiago's revolver barked before that of Carlos's cleared its holster. Carlos died on his feet, an ugly, blue-ringed hole through the center of his forehead.

Santiago turned to the others who had gathered around him. "The man lied about my son. I had to kill him. You heard him lie." He turned to those to whom Carlos had been whispering. "You heard."

One of the men rose to his feet. "Yes, Santiago. We heard. But Carlos spoke the truth. The child is no Mexican. If your eyes were not blinded for your desire for a son, you would have seen for yourself."

Santiago growled in anger, "You lie too!"

The man shrugged his shoulders. "No. I speak the truth as we all know the truth. Will you kill us all?"

Santiago whirled, turning his back to the group, and slipped his revolver back into its holster. Slowly, he staggered into the darkness away from the fires.

A few minutes later, he returned, his eyes two black pits of fury. He squatted by the fire and motioned with his hand. "We will know this thing. Bring the woman and the baby."

Within a minute one of the men came into the firelight

carrying the baby and dragging Arabela. He pushed the woman to her knees before the bandit leader. Santiago snatched the baby and held it close to the firelight. Dipping a finger in water in a nearby bucket, he swabbed at the infant's skin. It was unmistakable. Fair hair, light skin, blue eyes. The baby gurgled up at the bandit and arched his back. Santiago's eyes widened in recognition of the truth.

He hurled the infant to the ground from which Arabela immediately scooped him into her arms and held the screaming baby to her breast.

"It's true," Santiago hissed. "He is gringo."

"No, Santiago! He's your son," Arabela screamed as she prostrated herself at the bandit's feet.

Santiago stared down with utter hatred in his eyes. "The devil child will die. And you will die – but not until you have prayed and begged for it many times will death come. That I promise you. The child will be placed in a den of the red ants. You will watch. Then, what I have in store for you will make the child's death seem pleasant in comparison."

He turned his face from them. "Take them away – until tomorrow," he shouted.

The night passed the midpoint, but there was no rest for Arabela. From the time she had been kidnapped, she had accepted the fact of her own death. She knew it would come – and better sooner than later. But the birth of her child, the love child of her union with the young American, had changed her entire outlook.

She was startled by a sound at the entry.

"*Quien es?* Who is it?" she called.

"Quiet, please. It is *El Cojo,* the crippled one."

"What do you want? It is not yet morning."

"No. It is not morning. You must be gone from here before morning. Come."

"I don't understand."

"Woman, I am an old man— a cripple — and I have done many bad things for which I must answer to my God. But the torture and murder of an innocent baby and his mother will not be one of them. The guard is unconscious. Now go! Once you get out of the camp, you will be on your own. I can be of no more use to you."

Arabela crawled quickly to the opening. The guard lay still on the ground. She turned to the old man who sat watching her. "God be with you, *El Cojo.*"

She clutched the baby tightly to her breast, hurried across the clearing and into the woods. The wilderness of the mountains was her first goal.

Juanita Cruz attacked the dust that collected inside her small cabin with the vigor of an ancient warrior slaying a dangerous dragon. With all the dust on the outside, she coexisted with an easy tolerance, but once it intruded on her own special territory, she declared a war of no quarter.

Today she pursued her enemy beyond the normal bounds and flailed him where he lurked on the small portico outside her door. Just as she was administering the *coup de grace* to a pocket of resistance at the end of the porch, her eye caught a movement out toward the distant mountains.

She shaded her eyes against the brightness of the midmorning sun and searched the area. Something or someone was moving toward her house.

Her first thought was to call for the *patrón*, Don Miguel de la Garza. But she didn't want to disturb the *patrón* over something she was sure she could handle herself.

As the figure came closer, Juanita could see it was a woman carrying something. And she appeared to be in very poor condition, falling every few steps. Juanita stepped back inside and filled a canteen with water before she stepped out to meet her visitor.

Arabela's head was beginning to clear. The oppressive heat of the sun was gone, and to replace it was a cool, damp cloth on her forehead. She was inside a house -- then remembrance brought her up with a start. "My baby! Where is my baby?"

She sat upright. A woman stood over her.

"Rest easy, *señora*. I have your baby right here. He's quite well – better shape than you. Here, I'll put him down beside you."

Arabela gratefully held out her arms and received the infant. Then recognition came in a rush. She had reached her destination.

She looked more closely at the woman who made no sign of recognition.

"Juanita! Don't you know me?"

"No, *señora*. I've never seen you before."

"Juanita, it's me, Arabela."

Juanita looked at the woman in disbelief. This woman was old looking -- scarred and haggard. Arabela was young, poised, and beautiful.

"Arabela?" she murmured. "My little sister, Arabela?"

"Yes, Juanita, your sister."

Juanita stepped back from the bed, concern in her face changing to a stern look of disapproval. "Arabela! How dare you come here? What do you want from me?"

"Juanita, please. For me, I wouldn't have come. It's for the baby. They would have killed him."

"What are you talking about? Who would have killed him? Has one of your lovers turned on you? Have you caught some terrible disease?"

"No, no, for God's sake, listen to me. I'm not like you think I am."

"All I know is you're a whore – *una puta* – who gives yourself to men for money."

Pain showed in Arabela's face. "Yes, I was all that. But not for myself. Please believe me."

"What do you mean?"

"The last year that mama lived; who paid for the doctor?"

"Why, no one. He gave us his services out of kindness."

Arabela shook her head. "Is that what he told you? That greedy-handed leech lied. He was paid all right. A sweaty, fat pig of a man with the odor of a body unwashed for months paid for one visit. A thin reed of a goat with rotten teeth paid for another. The medicine was bought with money from a greasy coyote who took pleasure from a woman's pain."

Juanita put both hands over her ears. "No, I don't want to hear this."

Arabela swung her legs over the edge of the bed and got to her feet. "You don't want to hear it. You think I wanted to do it? You think I wanted the money for pretty dresses and silver jewelry?"

Arabela swept her hand down her scarred body and ragged dress. "See my pretty dresses, my silver jewelry."

Juanita slumped in a chair crying. "I didn't know. I just didn't know."

Much later, Arabela stood with her hands in a pan of soapy water which held the supper dishes. Juanita fought a pitched battle with a thin coat of dust which had sneaked in under the edge of the table top. The young infant lay on the floor playing with his bare toes.

"Juanita," I am so happy here. I'm grateful that you took me and my baby in."

Juanita pushed hair back from her face. "It is nothing. Our family owes you much for what you went through. Maybe if I had known, we could have done something."

"Done what? Conjured up the money? No, it was the only way."

"But your life has been ruined."

"How so, my sister? I have had the love of a wonderful man. I have his son to cherish. And I have regained my place

66

in your eyes. What more could a woman want?"

Don Miguel de la Garza listened with astonishment to the story brought to him by his cook and head maid. When she had finished, he rose and paced across the room.

"Yes. I have heard of this Santiago – a cruel and savage brigand. But I wouldn't have thought even he would dare attack a Confederate army detail – and right in the streets of Rosita. This outlaw must have friends in very high places. This makes him a dangerous enemy. However, I've never heard of his crossing to this side of the mountain.

"Hopefully, we will be spared a violent encounter with the man, and your sister any further contact with him. If you would feel more comfortable, you may move with your sister and the baby into the *hacienda*, Juanita.

The woman ducked her head in humble acknowledgement. "Thank you, *patrón*. But as you say, he has not been seen to cross the mountains, and we are content in my small house."

Don Miguel turned to leave the room, then paused and spoke over his shoulder. "If you'd like to bring little Gabriel to work with you sometimes, he would be more than welcome in my house."

Juanita nodded again. "I thank you, *patrón*. That is a thing I will do with much pleasure."

CHAPTER 10

There was little resemblance between the Lance Morgan who looked down on the outskirts of San Antonio and the fresh-faced boy who had ridden guard on a wagon train of cotton through this same area slightly more than a year ago. His once clean-shaven face was covered with a two-week stubble. His eyes seemed harder, with more steel than sky in the blue of them.

The trek from Tennessee had been hard and long. With no money, the men were forced to stop periodically to work at what odd jobs they could find to buy provisions for the next leg of the journey. They had also found that night travel, while slower, kept them out of sight of the Yankee patrols that frequently swept the roads looking for unreconstructed Rebels.

But the only thing on their minds right now was refreshing themselves at the first *cantina* they could find. Lance nudged the big blood-bay with his heels, and they moved down the long slope toward town at a trot.

In the *cantina*, they watched the waiter, a young Mexican boy about fourteen, dodging tables, outstretched legs, and staggering drunks with a practiced air.

Mike nodded toward the boy. "Looks kinda like Leon Cruz, don't he?"

Lance looked again. "Yeah. I think he does some."

Mike chuckled. "You got that same far away look in your eye you used to get when you was a sprout. You miss her, don't you?"

"Yeah, Mike. I do. It's kinda hard to think about anything else lately."

"Yassuh. I been noticin' the closer we gets to Mexico, the farther away from here and now you gets."

Lance laughed. "Well, here and now, that cool beer goes down pretty good."

He let his mind drift, filling with the lovely Arabela. The way her nose crinkled when he held her in his arms. The soft touch of her fingers at the nape of his neck. The searching eyes that drank in every detail of his features.

Only then he noticed. Mike had spoken to him.

"I'm sorry, Mike. What were you saying?"

"I was askin' 'bout the gold. We got a passel of gold hid away over in Mexico. Somethin's gotta be did with it."

"Reckon we need to go get it."

"Then, what we goin' do with it?"

"I guess we'll turn it over to some authority. If we can find the right one. We'll talk to George about it."

The road from San Antonio to the MacDuff Ranch seemed twice as long as it did going the other way. Each mile was an exercise in tedium. The same countryside which had dazzled Lance with its splendid beauty and fragrance was burned harsh and dry by the summer sun.

Brittle stems of what had been lush grasses and forbes of early spring now crunched to powder beneath the hooves of the horses. The small, pale sun washed all vivid color from the landscape leaving only a monotonous grey-dun hue that stretched to the horizon in every direction.

The first glimpse of Scotty's ranch house caressed the men's eyes like a cool compress. They heard the gurgling of the spring gushing down the rocks behind the house and saw a small ditch Scotty had cut from the stream to run across one end of the garden. Small eyelets cut in its bank allowed trickles of water to course down the garden rows to the thirsting summer vegetables flourishing in soil kept fertile through liberal applications from the MacDuff stables.

The two paused, then dismounted, and led the horses toward the house, allowing them to cool slowly under the shade of the wide branching cottonwood and pecan trees.

They hadn't covered half the distance when the front door burst open and a flying figure set sail across the yard toward them – and another just behind the first. Colleen MacDuff was followed closely by her brother, Bain. Scotty and Erin waited in the cool sanctuary of the front porch. George Gibson was nowhere to be seen.

"So, George has his own place now."

Lance stretched his legs out over the edge of the porch. Gathered where they could catch the cooling breeze filtering through the leaves of the trees growing along the stream, the group sat basking in the pleasure of good company too long apart. Colleen stayed tenaciously within an arm's length of Lance – where she'd been ever since their arrival.

Scotty puffed reflectively on his pipe. "George was on

his feet prancing around like a newborn foal within two weeks after you left. Had a strong mind to get something of his own around here. Said he had no interest in going back to Tennessee."

Lance nodded. "I kinda thought that. Wish I'd done the same. Where'd he locate?"

Scotty pointed with his pipe. "Found himself a little spread just north of here. Caught a few unbranded cattle and built himself a shack. Seems contented as a pup with a full belly."

"You can do that here? Just start with nothing?"

Scotty laughed. "That's the *usual* way it's done here."

Lance looked toward the horizon.

Erin leaned over and touched him on the arm. "You look to be deep in thought, Mr. Morgan."

The young man flushed. "I'm sorry, I was just sorta wondering if I could see my own future out there."

Scotty pulled Erin back beside him. "Nothing wrong with that, lad. A man needs to find something to put his life into. George seems to have found what makes him happy."

A fleeting frown came over Lance's face. "And I'm glad he has. But I don't think I can be content with just a small place and a few cows."

"Dream your dreams as grand as you like, my lad. But don't stake your soul on them." Scotty tapped the spent contents of his pipe on the edge of the porch and brushed them onto the ground.

Lance's jaw took on a hard set. "I guess I don't know exactly what I'm gonna do right now. But it's gotta be something big. It's just got to."

"But how are things going with your ranch, Mr. MacDuff?"

"Call me Scotty, lad. Everyone does. But to answer your question, we've had a few problems. The country's full of federal troops and state militia – yet the bandits are worse than ever. Troopers seem more interested in bringing down federal wrath on any unrepentant Texas Rebels than in keeping law and order in the country. State militia – nothin but a band of thieves and cutthroats."

"Have you lost stock Mr. Mac — ah — Scotty?"

"Aye, that I have, lad. At least half my cattle are gone – most into Mexico. Several of my best mares and a couple of breeding stallions."

"And the troops do nothing?"

"Hardly anything but protect the thieving carpetbaggers in town who are engaged in quasi-legal pillage and plunder.

"Gabe Leming, a good friend and neighbor, was

slaughtered with his whole family just ten miles southwest of here. Tortured, killed, and the ranch looted of anything of value. We found a couple of dead Mexicans and a lot of tracks. The troopers showed up four days later. Nothing to do by then, of course."

Lance looked puzzled. "But you were loyal to the Union. Seems they would at least protect your place."

"Things like that don't matter to 'Little Phil' Sheridan. His people don't know -- or care. I'm a Texian, therefore assumed to be a Reb."

"Damyankees!" Lance exploded in anger, then realized the company present. He rose and bowed toward Mrs. MacDuff. "I beg your pardon, ma'am. I forgot myself."

Erin nodded. "Perfectly understandable, Mr. Morgan, or may I call you, Lance?"

"Please. I would like that very much."

Scotty spoke softly. "There is far too much stupidity and avarice on both sides, lad. And I don't excuse it in anyone. But let me tell you one on the other side. I don't suppose you've heard of the Fredericksburg Massacre?"

"No, I haven't."

"A German settlement. Good, hard-working people. Only asked to be left alone to raise their crops and animals. But they were loyal to the United States Government which had provided sanctuary for them when they needed it.

"Well, a group of hell raisers, who considered themselves volunteer Confederates, rounded them up and placed them under arrest. When a few tried to escape, they wiped out the whole group, Shot them down without a chance. They weren't fighters − not even armed."

Bain spoke for the first time. "I wouldn't want to contradict my father, but that one incident hardly balances out the killing and looting going on now."

Scotty looked quickly at his son. "Do you forget, Bain, that these killers are not Yankee soldiers? Some of them are even native Texians."

"The soldiers allow it to happen, and that's just as bad in my book."

"I'm not defending Yankee arrogance, son. I'm just pointing out that Southern self righteousness is hardly justified by the facts."

Bain rose to his feet and stalked to the stream where he stood looking out across the pasture.

Erin gently chided her husband. "Now, Scotty, there's no use getting an argument started the first day Lance and Mike have come back to us."

Scotty nodded and paused to relight his pipe. "You're

71

right, my dear. Lance, please excuse a crusty old man's unasked-for observations, but this country's in a boil right now. We've got Yankees and Rebels, gringos and greasers, Negro troops and Southern whites -- plus a mixture of all kinds of outlaws. We're lucky that, so far, our home hasn't been attacked. But right now, that's very much a possibility at any time."

"Oh, father." Colleen was frowning. "Things aren't that bad around here. I declare, you'll have young Mr. Morgan leaving again no sooner than he's come."

Lance leaned over and touched her sleeve. "Lance. Please, my name is Lance."

"Very well. Lance it is." She wrinkled her nose at him.

The young man's eyes widened and his mouth popped open. Just for an instant. No. Not at all. She was not like Arabela in any way.

As usual, morning came early at the MacDuff household. After a hearty breakfast, the men hurried through the dim morning light to the horse corral where Bain was putting the finish on one of the promising young horses from the MacDuff remuda.

Scotty led them to the stable where they saddled their mounts for a wide-ranging tour of the MacDuff Ranch. It was plain to Lance that Scotty was a man who left little to chance.

His holdings were carefully selected to offer choice grazing. They were well watered and convenient for working stock with a minimum of manpower. His livestock were well nourished and gave evidence of careful selection by someone familiar with the basics of good breeding practices.

Bain rode ahead as they started up a small ridge in the southernmost pasture. He stopped abruptly as he reached the summit and waved his hat in the air. The others quickened their pace.

The boy was pointing straight ahead. "Buzzards! Circling the motte just across the flats."

The group clattered over the ridge in a hard lope. Reaching a clearing, Lance could see a horse laying on its side. It had been skinned. Standing beside it, confused and nickering softly, was a foal no more than three weeks old.

"One of my best mares," Scotty moaned.

Mike, who had entered the brush, turned in his saddle. "Here's another one, Mistuh MacDuff." He looked again. "Oh Lordy, it has a baby too."

They found two more -- all hamstrung then throats cut.

Bain turned away in disgust. *"La luna media."*

Mike looked to Lance. "What did he say?"

"I don't know, Mike. Scotty?"

The Scot turned his head toward Lance. *"Luna media --* the half moon. It's a long knife shaped in an arc -- razor sharp. The Mexicans used it when they hunted wild cattle for their hides. Now, it's obviously being used on horses too. Beastly practice – used by barbarians."

Mike tugged at Lance's sleeve. "Sounds like Santiago."

"Maybe so." The boy's face clouded. "Could well be."

Scotty murmured. "The mares with new foals couldn't keep up when they stole the rest of the herd. And the half-moon makes no noise."

The evening meal was glum at the MacDuff household. Even the normally effervescent Colleen was grave and solemn. Scotty excused himself early and retired to his bedroom. Mike and Bain found themselves a spot on the front porch where Mike was showing Bain the fine points of making a flute out of a willow branch. Erin and Colleen washed the supper dishes and Erin, at the pleading look on her daughter's face, allowed it was her bedtime as well.

Once her parent's bedroom door had closed behind the woman, Colleen bounced out of her chair, her face miraculously brightened. "I feel like a walk."

She glanced over her shoulder at Lance who was standing across the room by the water bucket. "Would you care to come along. The stream is lovely by starlight."

He hesitated, then drained the glass of water he'd been holding. "Sure. Why not? Maybe the night air will do me some good."

Each ripple in the stream caught a reflection of starlight that streaked the water with silver. The stars burned with such brilliance against the pitch black sky there was hardly the trace of a twinkle.

Lance stared in awe at the spectacle. He had never lost his wonder at this country where the stars seemed so much lower than back home -- almost reachable -- and were displayed all the way down to the horizon. As he watched, a falling star sparked a long arc across the blackness.

"When I was a young girl," Colleen murmured, "I thought you could catch them like fireflies. I used to reach up and run to where I thought they'd be. But they always burned up before I could catch up to them."

"Yes." Lance nodded. "A lot of things do that."

They stepped down to the rocky shoreline, and Colleen knelt down to dip her hand in the water and create a double streak of reflected silver as she split the surface current. "Lance, tell me about the girl in Mexico who helped you.

73

What was she like?"

Lance could feel his face flush uncomfortably. "She was the owner of the *cantina* where we stayed. And a performer – a wonderful dancer."

"What's her name?"

"Arabela."

Colleen rose to her feet and shook the water from her hand. "Are you in love with her?"

Lance felt confusion making it hard to breath. Why not just give her a straight answer? Still he hesitated.

"Well — I knew her for such a short time -- just a few days. But yes, I think I am."

"Will you go back there?"

"I have to, Colleen. There's a lot of gold there, and I have to bring it back. It's my – our responsibility."

"What are you going to do then? After you get the gold, I mean."

"Colleen, I don't know what I'll do." His irritation showed in his voice. "I'll just have to decide when it happens. I just don't know . . ." His voice trailed off.

She put her hand on his arm. "I'm sorry, Lance. I didn't mean to upset you with all these questions. I just hope it works out well for you. I truly do."

He smiled down at her. "Thank you, Colleen. I know you do. I'm very grateful for all you and your family have done for us. You've been like my own family to me."

She frowned slightly. "Lance, I have a brother. I'm not looking for another."

She left him then, skipping over the rocks back toward the house. He leaned against a tree trunk and silently watched her go.

CHAPTER 11

Juanita Cruz placed the young Gabriel in a crude, handmade cradle in the corner of Don Miguel's kitchen. She was pleased because the *patrón* had seemed entirely enchanted with the infant that morning. He had chucked the baby under the chin and been rewarded with a gurgle and a smile. Don Miguel, a long time widower with no children of his own, had again expressed delight at having the child in his home whenever Juanita wanted to bring him.

As she worked, she sent up a few words of thanks to her God who had brought her sister and her nephew to the door of her little house. She could see it only as a small miracle requiring at least a portion of Divine Providence. This was part of her reward for attendance at mass whenever possible, her daily prayers, and the overall chastity of her life which she considered to be without spot or blemish. The Lord was surely expressing his approval of her purity and piety with this great blessing.

It was a busy day for Arabela. The weekly washing had to be done, tortillas prepared, plus the unceasing warfare against the ubiquitous dust layer that Juanita viewed with such horror. Arabela, herself, saw little harm in a few dust particles, but to please her sister, she had vowed diligence to see that none remained to plague her sister upon her return from the *hacienda*.

She was just finishing a good scrubbing of the wooden table when she heard a slight noise at the door. She looked over her shoulder and froze. There, almost filling the doorway, was the one person she hated and feared above all others – Santiago.

He entered the house with his usual swagger and stood with arms folded across his chest, a mocking grin on his face. "So the soiled dove has been preparing for my visit, no? There was no need to clean so vigorously." He looked around appreciatively. "Who else lives here?"

"No one. I live alone." Arabela's eyes were wide and staring.

"How do you live? Who provides your food? Don't lie to me, woman."

"I work," she said, trying desperately to remain calm, "at the *hacienda* of Don Miguel de la Garza."

"Then, why are you not now at work?"

"Don Miguel is a kindly man. He gives me one day of each week. This is that day."

She quickly tried to change the line of questioning. "Santiago, how did you find this place?"

He scratched a match across the stove and lit his cheroot. "This is my land," he snarled. "I find what I want to find."

Once again, Arabela accepted her death as an accomplished fact. The acceptance brought a measure of peace to her. She sneered at the bandit. "Then you have, no doubt, found the gold you looked for."

Santiago's face clouded. "I will find it! Whether you tell me where it is or not. But I warn you − it will go easier on you if you tell me now."

Three of the bandits came quietly through the open door. Beyond them the other members of the band waited outside.

She faced Santiago, arms hanging limply at her side. "I've told you before -- and I say once more -- I know nothing of any gold carried by the Americans."

"Then you will die hard, *puta!* And the baby. Where is that devil child?"

Arabela's heart thumped hard, but she made a tremendous effort to keep herself calm as she replied, "You ask me that? He is dead. You killed him."

"You lie, woman. The baby was alive when you slipped away into the night."

"Yes, but he was injured when you threw him to the ground. It died the next night, and I buried him in the mountains."

One of the bandits limped forward. "This might be true, Santiago. I, El Cojo, saw blood on the baby's lips. I think maybe he was broken inside."

Santiago scowled. "Then I have been cheated out of killing the devil child the way I had intended. But I will deal with the whore mother right now."

He stepped forward and smashed his right fist into the woman's face. Her lips, compressed back against her front teeth, burst as the pressure on them became too great. The teeth bent backwards, splintering the bone that held them in place. Blood gushed from her broken teeth, filling her mouth and trickling down her chin.

76

Santiago stood panting with emotion, looking down at the woman on the floor. He motioned with his head. "Take her outside."

Two men dragged the half-conscious woman to the door and pushed her to the ground outside.

Santiago stood over her, reached out with a foot, hooked the hem of the woman's skirt and pulled it high above her waist. Except for the white underwear, she was exposed from the waist down. He stooped and caught the waistband of her undergarment and ripped it off.

"You like what you see, *muchachos?*"

The outlaws responded with a chorus of cheers.

"There is enough woman here for all of us. We will share, *amigos!*"

Arabela stirred and tried to get to her feet, but the bandit put a booted foot in her swollen and bleeding face and pushed her back to the ground.

"First, we remove the rest of these rags, and I will show you how it's done. Then, we will share the woman in turn."

He leaned down and reached for her blouse. She stirred again, touching her swollen face. A startling roar sounded from the doorway, and Arabela's chest blossomed with a gush of blood.

Santiago whirled in a rage. El Cojo lowered his rifle.

"You fool! What have you done?"

A flash of fear showed in the cripple's face, but he stood his ground. "But Santiago, the woman was reaching for something – maybe a knife. She could have killed you."

One bandit spoke. "She reached for something, Santiago. The whore may have hidden a weapon."

Santiago reached down and ripped the remaining clothing from the woman's body. He held it up. It was empty.

He bounded across the yard to confront El Cojo with the crumpled cloth. He shook it in front of the crippled man's face. "Nothing, you fool! She had nothing!"

He crashed a heavy blow to the side of El Cojo's head. He slumped to the ground, the rifle dropping from his hand.

Juanita hummed a happy song as she walked the well-worn trail toward her house. Little Gabriel snoozed contentedly on her back in a small, leather harness.

The day had gone well. Gabriel had been playful and Don Miguel had been very complimentary both of the meals she had cooked and of the baby he found so charming.

The sun dimmed behind the distant peaks, and she hurried around a small hillock just in back of her house. She could hardly wait to tell Arabela of the day's happenings. Then, she saw the pathetic bundle that was her baby sister.

Juanita paced mechanically to the scene of the tragedy. She placed the baby on a blanket under a mesquite tree and handed him a small gourd rattle which he shook happily.

Then, she turned to her grisly task. She caught the body under both arms and dragged it into the house. Placing it on the bed, she folded the arms and covered the body with a worn blanket. Kneeling at the bedside, she spoke a short prayer for the soul of her departed sister.

Still moving as in a trance, she walked to the yard carrying a torch kindled from the cooking stove. She heaved the torch to the thatched roof of her tiny house, picked up the baby, and started back down the trail to the *hacienda*.

She never looked back.

CHAPTER 12

Millions of years ago, violent earthquakes and erupting volcanoes had dramatically rearranged the structure of what now lay beneath the surface of the *brasada*. Permeable soil and gravel lay over layers of hard volcanic rock. When rain fell, it percolated through the porous layer only to be stopped by the strata of solid rock below.

Slowly moving toward the sea, it trickled through layers of sand and limestone until faced by an occasional uplifted intrusion of solid igneous rock. As pressure built up behind it, there was only one way for the water to go – up toward the surface.

At many locations near the head waters of the Nueces River, this underground flow burst to the surface in a gushing stream which, following the path of least resistance, eventually merged with other similar springs to form the river itself.

The triangle formed by one of these larger springs and the Nueces River into which it fed had been appropriated by George Gibson for his own use. He stood now with a satisfied look on his face, checking the strength of a small corral made of upright stakes of mesquite and cedar, bound together with rawhide and the bottom buried some fourteen inches in a trench painstakingly dug in the rocky soil.

A wooden frame across the stream was constructed so that, with the additions of a few planks across it, water was diverted across the corner of the corral so stock could be watered without moving them from the enclosure.

He wiped sweat from his face with the back of a callused hand as he surveyed his handiwork. A lot of effort – but that oughta hold 'em.

Just up the stream about a hundred yards was his home. A half-dugout with mesquite timbers, mud, and carrizo cane making up the top half. He laughed softly to himself. He was now a man of property. Well, technically, maybe the land didn't quite belong to him yet. But the corral and house were products of his own hard work. And the small herd – that was all his – carrying his own Big G brand.

The soft nicker of a horse was the first sign that he was having unexpected company. He faded quickly into the underbrush between the corral and his dugout. He could hear the rustling of brush and the clink of hooves against the rocks. Shod horses pretty well ruled out Comanches, but there were always bandits, thieves, and the Texas Militia.

When the riders rode into the clearing, George leaped from his hiding spot with a whoop. "Lance, Mike, over here! Thought you'd be farmin' in Tennessee by now."

The three men alternately sat and sprawled on their bedrolls spread near a crackling fire just outside George's dugout. Darkness crept up from the low areas and touched even the peaks of the hills as the sun plummeted quickly below the horizon. Lance told George about their unfortunate trip back home.

"I'm really sorry, Lance, about your dad and the land. But from what I've seen around here, it's not too unusual."

"Yeah, that's kinda what Scotty was saying. How about bandits? They botherin' you any?"

"Nah. I just got a few head – prob'ly not worth messin' with for 'em. And I stay pretty close to everything I own.

George reached over and punched Mike's arm. "How 'bout you, Mike? How's freedom goin' down with you?"

"Well, Mistuh George, ain't been much different on the outside – but it feels mighty good on the inside."

"Still hangin' 'round with your old master. Guess you don't carry no grudge."

Mike grinned as though embarrassed. "Nawsuh. Mistah Lance, he always treat me right enough."

Lance tossed a small rock in George's direction. "Dammit, George. You make it sound like Mike oughta cut my throat or something."

George chuckled. "Well, never bein' no slave owner myself, I thought maybe they'd all wanta do that."

Mike broke in. "I jus' like bein' free -- even if I don't quite have the hang of it yet."

George opened a small bag and pulled out a wad of tobacco which he jammed into his jaw. "Gotta start goin' easy on this stuff. No mercantile around here to get more.

"But say Lance, what about our business in Mexico?"

"Reckon we better go back and get that gold."

"Then what? I don't reckon it's ours."

"I don't figger it is either. Guess we oughta turn it over to somebody -- maybe the state of Texas."

"Not a chance! Lance, you ain't been here in a while.

80

This government is just as raunchy as the one you told me about in Tennessee. I don't see that them damn carpetbaggers is entitled to one little solitary flake of it."

"I agree. But then, who the hell is? You wouldn't think of givin' it to the Yankees."

"No, Lance. I don't know who oughta get it – but ain't nobody gonna get it as long as it stays where it is."

"Except maybe that Santiago — if he finds it."

"Hell with that meskin. If you wanta go get it, Lance, I'm with you – but not to turn it over to no government."

Lance reflected a moment. "Let's get the stuff on this side of the river – then we can decide who it belongs to."

George squirted a stream of juice into the fire. "When do we leave?"

Lance could feel the excitement building inside him as they neared the village of Pata Chica. They rode cautiously, well aware of the likely proximity of their old adversary. First glimpse of the village indicated everything normal. An old man plodded purposefully down the dusty street with a fighting rooster nestled securely under his arm. Two small boys at one end of the street alternated in pouring dirt through their hands onto the top of the other's head.

Past the end of the street proper, they could see the small *cantina* where they'd spent such a short time – that seemed so very long.

They skirted the main part of town to circle in directly to the *cantina* and tied their horses in front.

Lance rushed ahead into the semi-darkness. He blinked his eyes and squinted in an effort to see more clearly. The place looked much the same as it had when they first saw it. Little Pablo's face, at first uncertain, lit up with recognition as George and Mike followed Lance inside.

"Buenos dias, señores. Bienvenido!" He hustled from behind the bar to shake hands with each of the men and bestow the *abrazo* on each.

Lance spoke slowly, uncertain of his grasp of the language. *"Donde esta la madama -- Arebela?"*

Pablo backed away looking from one man to the other. *"Pobre Arabela. Yo crio es muerto. Se fue con Santiago."*

Lance was bewildered. He could make out the words "Arabela" and "Santiago" and *"muerto,"* which he knew to mean dead.

George, who understood the language better, stepped in front of Lance and put his hand on the other man's chest. "Take it easy, Lance."

"What did he say, George? Something about Arabela and

Santiago?"

"Just a minute, I'll see."

He turned and conversed slowly with the diminutive bartender in halting and heavily accented Spanish. Then, he led Lance and Mike to a nearby table. Pablo rushed over with a bottle and three glasses.

"Better sit down, Lance. This won't go down too easy."

"What, George? What did he say?"

"Well, it seems Santiago came just like we figgered he would. But he didn't buy that story about her not knowing where the gold was. They killed Leon and took Arabela with them. Pablo is sure she's dead."

"Dead? How does he know she's dead?"

"Pablo says that Santiago don't keep prisoners very long. He says she's dead for sure by now."

Lance sat stunned. "I should have made her come with us. I could have forced her to come."

"You wouldn't have done that, and you know it. Besides she's not likely to have made it through that ambush on the river if she had been with us. There's nothing more you could have done."

"She should have told 'em where it was."

"Hell, Lance, now you're not even thinkin' at all. You know he wouldn't have let her go even if she told him what he wanted to know. She knew that, and so do you."

Lance felt cold anger stir in him. "And that bastard, Roy O'Neil — was he with 'em?"

"Yeah. But I guess he'd served his purpose for Santiago. They killed him right here."

Mike spoke for the first time. "You wanta go after 'em, Mistah Lance? You wanta go after 'em — I goes with you."

Lance didn't raise his head. "Too late for that, Mike. No use to get somebody else killed. Let's do what we came for and get back to where we belong."

George summoned Pablo and told him to close the bar for the rest of the day. Pablo looked bewildered but did as he was told. The few patrons had known something unusual was up when they saw the men come in. Some recognized them from before. All left the *cantina* quickly.

Another exchange between George and Pablo, and George turned to Lance. "Pablo wants to know what to do about the bar. He's been keeping it open and running it just like before. He's been paying himself and the girls and holding Arabela's share. He doesn't know of any relatives she might have."

"Hell, I don't know. I guess he might as well keep running it. If any relatives show up, then he can settle with them. I think Arabela would have wanted him to have it."

The three men caught hold of one end of the bar and lifted it over a few feet. Mike dropped to his knees and pulled out a large rock which had covered a sizable hole in the floor. George reached in with one hand and swung out the first saddlebag, heavy with gold coin.

"Madre mia! Que tal oro abajo mis zapatas!"

George laughed. "Pablo can't believe that gold was right there under his feet all this time."

Lance withdrew a handful of shiny coins and handed them to Pablo. He put a finger to his lips to indicate silence.

Pablo nodded vigorously. *"Si, señor. Mis labios son cerrados!"*

George explained. "Pablo's lips are sealed."

With the gold loaded onto two extra horses, the men made their way back in the direction they had come.

The familiar sight of the MacDuff Ranch lay before them. Lance, who was in the lead, stopped the horses a moment. "That place sure looks good to me."

"Something about carrying a fortune in gold through bandit country makes a friendly place mighty welcome," George agreed.

"Oh, God!" Mike's voice cut through their casual conversation. "Look there!"

Lance shaded his eyes peering past the pointing finger. "Where, Mike?"

"That mound next to the garden."

George raised himself in his stirrups. "I see it. Oh no! Looks like a fresh grave."

This time, no friendly figures came out the door to greet them. A foreboding silence hung over the MacDuff ranchstead, broken only by the monotonous hum of a locust. The men tied their horses in front and slowly approached the black ribbon-draped front door.

Erin opened the door and greeted them solemnly. "Gentlemen, it's good to have you here. Please come in."

Lance stepped through the door, his eyes desperately searching for other members of the family. Bain, face white and drawn, stood right behind his mother. The door to Colleen's bedroom opened and the girl rushed through straight into Lance's arms.

Only Scotty was missing!

Erin MacDuff, her voice shaky with shock and grief, told the story.

The MacDuff's had settled in for the night. Scotty had

83

taken down a book for the evening, Erin was finishing up a new dress for Colleen, and Bain and Colleen were engrossed in a chess game in the corner.

Moving suddenly, Scotty put down his book and came up from the chair. "Someone's out there."

Quickly, he jumped up and extinguished the lamp. He felt his way to the gun rack and removed two rifles, handing one of them to Bain.

A voice shouted from the darkness. "There in the house! This is Captain Masters, state militia. Do you surrender?"

Scotty opened the door a crack. "Come up here and identify yourself."

"And give you a chance to get the drop on me? Come out with your hands above your head."

Scotty shouted again. "No shooting! There are women in here."

The voice sounded shrill. "Then come on out with hands up! We're takin' you in, Reb – dead or alive."

Scotty tried once more. "Captain, you're making a mistake. Neither my family nor I have ever lifted a hand against the Union."

"You have ten seconds to come out."

Scotty glanced at Bain. "Stay right there, lad. I'm going out. They'll see it's all a mistake."

He opened the door and stepped through, hands raised high above his head.

A new voice sounded. "There he is."

A single shot and a blaze of light from the darkness. Scotty crumpled where he stood, shot through the heart. Bain was the first to reach him. He cradled his head to his breast, but Scotty never drew another breath.

"They shot him down without giving him a chance. My husband loved the Union – accepted the disapproval of his friends and neighbors because he loved this country and didn't want it broken in two.

"You know what the captain said? 'Boys, looks like we made a mistake. This ain't the Reb we lookin' for.'

"That's all he said. Then, they rode away. The only man I ever loved is gone. Uselessly. A good man – dead because they made a mistake."

Erin broke down and sobbed until Bain led her away to her room. Colleen sat silently, holding Lance's arm.

Next morning was filled by visits from neighbors who drove in on wagons, in buggies, or rode up on horseback. Each brought some token of esteem for the MacDuff family –

84

food items or a few flowers to place on the grave. All offered labor for any job to be done now – or in the future.

The inner steel around which the seemingly frail Erin MacDuff was wound became evident. She calmly assumed complete control over the situation. Although she'd never taken an active role in the ranch management outside the immediate area of the house and garden, it was clear that she had an intimate understanding of its various functions.

She assigned tasks to each volunteer that would assure the continued efficiency of operation that had marked Scotty's methods. She accepted condolences with grace and poise. Each visitor was made to feel that his or her visit was especially important and needed.

Shortly after the noon meal had been completed, a clatter of hoof beats announced the arrival of a new set of visitors. Everyone stopped what they were doing and watched a detail of federal cavalry pull up at the house.

The leader, in a faded and dusty blue uniform, dismounted and walked quickly to the door. As Erin appeared, he swept off his hat.

"Major Robert Mahaffey, ma'am. I'm terribly sorry about your husband. I have been instructed to express the sympathy and regret of the United States Government."

Erin's face was expressionless. "Would you care to come in, Major?"

He flushed. "Yes, please."

Inside the house, he politely declined Erin's offer to sit down and stood stiffly, hat in hand. "Ma'am, I can understand that this is a bad time for you, but I've been ordered to investigate your husband's death and to determine who or what was at fault in this terrible tragedy."

"I can assure you, Major, that I will . . ."

"What's that bluebelly doing in our house?" Erin was interrupted by Bain who stalked through the doorway, eyes flashing with anger. He stood beside his mother facing the major. "What are you doing here?"

Erin placed a small hand on her son's arm. "This is my son, Bain — Major Mahaffey."

Bain glared at the officer and ignored the outstretched hand. "I say again, Major. What do you want here?"

Erin frowned her disapproval. "Major Mahaffey is here to investigate your father's death, Bain. I was just about to offer our cooperation."

"Our what? Mother, I don't see how you can even be civil to this Yankee after what's happened."

Erin spoke sharply. "Major Mahaffey was not present at your father's murder. He's here to investigate and punish the guilty. I'm sure you'll do credit to the memory of your father who would never be rude to a guest in his house."

"In that case, mother, please excuse me. I prefer not to be present while you cooperate with this Yankee."

He walked stiffly out the door.

Erin's expression remained cool. "Please forgive my son, Major Mahaffey. He has had a terrible shock."

Relief showed in the major's eyes. "Perfectly understandable, ma'am. But please, let me make something clear. The group who killed your husband was not regular army. It was an element of the state militia."

"I'm familiar with the scum you call 'state militia'."

He flushed. "The recruitment of that group is out of my province."

Erin nodded. "Of course it is. But tell me, Major, how may I help in this matter?"

Supper was a gloomy one at the MacDuff table. Everyone ate perfunctorily with no real taste for the food. Bain was still sullen but superficially polite.

Lance was moody and silent. The sudden fear that had come over him when he'd first seen the grave disturbed him deeply. So did the realization that his first feeling on learning it was Scotty in that grave was a quick flood of relief. The guilt of that feeling gnawed at him. He didn't want to understand why he felt relief – but he knew why.

He pushed back his plate which had hardly been touched. Colleen instantly did the same.

Erin let a faint smile touch her lips. "I'm afraid Mrs. Putnam's excellent cooking has gone for naught tonight."

As the group left the table, Lance caught Bain by the arm. "Bain, we gotta do something with those saddlebags in your bunkhouse. Having all that gold right here makes me kinda nervous."

"Yeah, you're right, Lance. If word got out, we couldn't fight the bandits off with an army."

The four men rode out before dawn the next day. Across the ridge from ranch headquarters was a small cave hidden by brush and boulders that Bain had discovered as a child. There, under the gaze of four witnesses, the gold went back into hiding -- this time on the MacDuff Ranch.

CHAPTER 13

Erin MacDuff was worried. She paced the floor in agitation as the men she'd summoned to her house sat quietly. They knew she would speak when she was ready. Finally she whirled and directed a question to her son.

"Bain, how much have you been offered for those five geldings you just finished training?"

"Well, Mr. Rankin said he'd give us $10 a head."

"Ten dollars?" Lance jumped up in surprise. "I woulda thought those horses woulda brought $40 or even more."

"I agree," Erin said, "but every sale needs a buyer. We have no real buyers."

"But everyone needs good horses," Lance objected. "And yours are the very best."

Erin shrugged her shoulders. "My father used to say that need without the ability to pay doesn't constitute a market. And we need a market. We need to raise some money."

"What about cattle?" George asked. "Even with your losses to bandits, you've still got lots of cattle in your pastures."

Bain answered. "Yes, we do. And so does everyone else. We all have lots of cattle. They'll bring maybe five dollars a head – if you find somebody with five dollars."

"My son is correct -- but only if we're speaking of the local market. I have something else in mind. Mr. Taylor just returned from the North, and he says there's a shortage of beef in the Northeast. Cattle delivered to the railheads in Missouri and Kansas are bringing $20 a head and more."

Bain looked thoughtful. "I could get a herd together in a week or so, and we could take it right on up."

"It's a long trip," Erin cautioned. "And a dangerous one. But since there's no market here, I'm proposing that we take our cattle to where there is one."

Bain jumped to his feet, excitement shining in his face. "I'll start getting things ready tomorrow."

Erin shook her head. "Not you, Bain. I propose that Mr.

Morgan make the trip to see after our interests. I'll need you here at the ranch."

Lance stammered slightly. "I'm really flattered, Mrs. MacDuff, but I have no experience handling a herd that large on a trip that long."

"No one has experience on that trail, Lance. However, I know of a man who has trailed some herds before. He's resourceful and able, but most of all, he knows cattle and how to handle them. His name is Guy Madden, and I think he would make you an excellent trail boss.

"As we're low on cash right now, I can only spare enough for bare expenses. However, I'm prepared to make you an offer of a percentage of the profit -- if you're agreeable to such."

Bain objected. "Why can't Lance stay here while I take the herd through?"

"Because there will be legal matters that will require your presence, Bain. I'm sorry, but this is the only practical solution. More than likely you can go on the next drive. Does my proposition interest you, Lance?"

"It's a generous offer, Mrs. MacDuff. I'll do my best."

As the men left the room, Lance drew Bain aside. "I'm sorry, Bain. I know you'd like to go on this drive."

Bain grinned weakly. "I seem to remember you tellin' me once that we all do what we have to do."

"By the way, Bain, I noticed you've been practicing with your gun up in the hills quite a bit lately."

Bain looked surprised. "I've practiced a little. Why?"

"I've seen you handle your gun. You really think you need more practice?"

"Never can tell; might come in handy some day."

"You don't have anything special in mind do you?"

"Lance, I'm not goin' looking for trouble, if that's what you mean. But I tell you this, no bluebelly soldier -- no so-called militia man – is ever gonna push up against this family again and live to tell about it."

"Just be careful, Bain. Your family needs you very much. If anything happened to you . . ."

"I can take care of myself, Lance."

"I know, but I've seen situations get out of control – even for people who can take care of themselves."

The last sentence was wasted as Bain had already walked out the door.

Guy Madden put down his mug of beer and gazed at the earnest young man sitting across from him. "Don't know if I'm interested or not. No offense meant, but I don't know you. I don't know who you're workin' with. I don't know whose cattle you'll be drivin'. You're wearin' grey britches -- and that's a mark in your favor -- but not quite enough to make me jump into the saddle for no cattle drive to Kansas."

Lance laughed heartily. "You speak plainly, Mr. Madden, and that's in your favor. I don't know if I can answer all those questions, but I'll try.

"My name is Lance Morgan, which don't mean doodle-de-squat to you. I don't know any more'n you do about who we'll be workin' with, but -- as for the cattle we'll be drivin' -- they're Erin MacDuff's."

Guy looked up with sudden interest. "If you're talkin' about Scotty's widow, you just said the magic words."

"That's the one, Mr. Madden."

He stuck out his hand. "Call me Guy since we're gonna be workin' together. When do we start?"

The holding grounds on the flats teemed with bawling cattle, their numbers being steadily increased by small bunches brought in by shouting riders who dropped them off and rode back into the hills for more.

Guy Madden squinted his eyes against the sun. "Looks like this pasture's about gathered. When's your friend due in with his herd?"

Lance pulled Captain Jess up against Guy's big dun. "Said he'd be here this afternoon. I'm guessin' a couple more hours at most."

"Then, we oughta be on our way at daybreak."

"How'd you make out findin' us some drovers?"

"Better'n I expected. Couple of 'em greener'n meadow grass, but otherwise it's a pretty good crew. Old Charley Green is probably as good a pot walloper as you'll find on the trail -- or anywhere else. And that's half the battle.

"Ain't nothin' keeps hands riled up more'n somebody makin' a mess of the cookin'. And nothin' makes 'em happier than good grub on the trail.

"Young Cliff, the horse wrangler, ain't quite ready for a drover's job -- but he knows what he's doin' with the horses, and he's willin'. Booger Jim, Cisco Red, Pedro, Short Stuff, and Fred Smith are all good boys. I've worked with 'em before. They'll do to ride the river with. Then, there's you'n me and your nigger, Mike -- and your friend George Gibson. Don't know much about the rest of the boys, but they seem to be all right. With the MacDuff remuda, we'll sure enough have good horseflesh."

Lance stood in his stirrups as another bunch of cattle moved in over the ridge, followed by a lone rider on a blaze-faced chestnut.

"Here comes George now. Hell, Guy, if we was a mind to, we could leave this afternoon."

Guy chuckled. "Don't cut yourself much slack, do you, boy? I think we'd all better get one more good night's sleep. Likely it's the last bit of comfort we'll have for a while."

The herd strung out – a mile-and-a-half of bobbing horns and swishing tails. Lance noticed that, after a couple of days, the same cattle took the lead every morning, and another group could be depended on to be at the drag. Each animal had his own position on the trail and took it, unerringly, every day.

Each drover had his own position as well. The point men were the most able and experienced of the group. They held back the leaders and spread the herd to afford, as much as possible, fresh grazing to every animal. Greener drovers were given positions at the drag where they attended to stragglers and ate the dust of fifteen hundred Longhorn cattle from dawn to dusk. The swing and flank men were responsible for seeing the cattle didn't spill out the sides of the herd.

Lance spent the first few days watching the drovers at work. In spite of himself, he felt a twinge of envy at the seemingly effortless way they handled even the most arduous chores on the trail. The men themselves were a source of fascination and puzzlement to him. They seemed completely self-contradictory. Whippet lean and rock hard, they were virtually tireless in the saddle through a fourteen-hour day. Yet, when not actually working, they gave the impression of uncaring indolence. But again, even in repose, their rest was that of a cocked hammer, ready to explode into action at the touch of a trigger.

In age, they tended toward youth, yet their grizzled, deeply creased faces marked them as veterans of the fiery sun and drying winds of the *brasada*. At the end of a hard day, they were outwardly playful as a pen of puppies. But as the evening progressed, most of them showed a distinct bent toward reflective thought. Lance never tired of listening to their stories of past experiences – both in and out of the cow camp – and their often fanciful theories of why things were as they are.

Guy Madden was the acknowledged master of "cow psychology." When it came to methods and techniques of handling cattle, even the most experienced listened carefully when Guy chose to enlighten them. Lance was impressed by the respect accorded his trail boss by the drovers.

As they moved up the trail, they swung a little east of north to afford better grazing, more frequent watering holes, and to avoid the dangerous Comanchero country which lay to the northwest.

They soon hit up against the Colorado River. Upriver rains had water running bank to bank – lipping full. As the herd eased against the surging waters late in the afternoon, Guy decided they should drink and bed down for an early morning crossing when the sun would be at their backs.

The lead steers hit the water on the run – straight into the stream -- and lit out for the other side. Booger Jim, who'd ridden in just ahead of them, slipped out of the saddle, and holding to his horse's tail, was towed quickly to the far bank. The other riders whooped and chased the cattle – crowding them right in behind the leaders.

Everything went smoothly until the lead steer hit the opposite side. As he tried to scramble up the steep bank, the ground caved in under his hooves, and he was thrown back into the faces of those behind him. Panic seized the animal, and he pulled for shore – but in the wrong direction.

With the suddenness of a thunderclap, the water filled with cattle, some headed in one direction and some the other. As they collided in mid-stream, the herd went into a deadly mill, a line of cattle turning in on itself in an ever-tightening coil. Cattle on the inside were quickly pushed under the water by those crowding in from the outside.

Without a word, Lance nudged Captain Jess into the current. Lunging the powerful horse against the outside of the mill, Lance tried to force his way into the herd to break the swirling motion. However, the harder he pushed the tighter became the death spiral of the rapidly tiring animals. Lance could see Mike and Pedro trying to force their way in from the other side and were having no better luck than he.

Then, he heard the voice of Guy Madden from the near bank. "Cisco! Straighten them damn cows out."

He saw Cisco Red pull past him, roll off his horse right on top of a steer on the outer edge of the spiral. As Lance watched in amazement, the young drover jumped, scrambled, crawled, and rolled from the back of one steer to another until he reached the very center of the tightly wound coil of cattle. He crawled onto the back of one of the largest steers and let out a loud whoop. As the steer floundered toward the bank, Cisco flogged his hat into the faces of the other cattle, turning them toward the far shore. Within seconds, the mill was broken, and the cattle formed an orderly line moving across the torrent.

As the big steer neared the shoreline, Cisco dropped off

91

and staggered out of the water on foot. Lance caught Cisco's big brown horse and brought him over to where the drover stood ankle deep in water and mud.

The freckled face broke into a big grin as he rubbed his hand over a shock of bright red hair. "Mr. Morgan, reckon you owe me a new hat."

Lance was learning. "Maybe, Cisco. Be more careful with the next one."

After the entire herd had crossed, Guy called out, "Looks like we lost a couple of head. One of the calves took off downstream and his mammy took off after him. Think it was one of Mr. Gibson's cows."

George laughed. "That figgers. Easy come – easy go."

The herd turned northward toward Waco, Dallas, and the Red River Crossing. By then, the herd was trail-broken and rose each morning facing north ready to move out in proper formation. Several days passed without incident.

Then, the benevolent weather they'd enjoyed all through the drive turned on them. The day started hot, muggy, and still. The oppressive heat built steadily through the day, and by late afternoon, a solid band of puffy clouds could be seen on the western horizon. The sky darkened early.

Guy Madden watched the boiling clouds nervously as he prepared to bed down the cattle. He turned back at a gallop to where George and Lance were riding on the swing. "It's festerin' up for a booger tonight. Tell Charley to get everything under cover and tied down for tonight."

Lance could see lightning blinking through the darkness of the gathering clouds. He trotted Captain Jess back to the wagon. "Hey, Charley, Guy says you better get your stuff ready for a storm tonight."

Charley paused as he took an armload of firewood from Cliff, the wrangler. "Oh, he said that, did he?" Charley shuffled toward the fire and threw on a couple of sticks. "Well, you can tell that peckerwood he don't need to waste no breath tellin' Charley Green a storm's comin'. I was ridin' out storms while he was still in knee pants. Don't worry 'bout ol' Charley, young feller; I'll take care of my stuff right enough."

As riders began to drift in for supper, they could hear the rumble of thunder approaching. The drovers were edgy as a compressed spring but covered it with their usual banter.

Fred Smith rode up, dismounted, and in his rolling pigeon-toed gait, made his way up to the group. Without a word, he sat, unbuckled his spurs, and tossed them into the wagon. His pistol was next, then a long-bladed knife.

One of the drag riders, a young Georgia boy, stared wide-eyed. "What the hell you doin', Fred?"

Booger Jim laughed scornfully. "Aw, Fred thinks anything made of metal attracts lightning."

Pedro looked up from across the fire. "Fred's right, Booger. I ain't wearin' no spurs tonight -- knife neither."

Cisco Red joined in the argument. "That's not right. Heat's what draws lightning. Ever'body knows that. I'm leavin' my slicker behind tonight. Better to be wet'n cold than dry'n dead. Ain't I right, Guy?"

Guy shrugged. "Damned if I know, Cisco. I've heard both ways. And then, I've heard don't neither one make no difference. Some says it depends on how you been livin'. As for me, I figger lightning hits where it wants to and don't make no never mind what's there."

Short Stuff dragged himself up and took a long look at the sky. "Gonna be darker'n the inside of a nigger's pocket tonight. And me with first guard. Who's with me?"

Mike raised a hand. "Afraid it's me, Short Stuff."

"Oh, cripes. How'n hell am I gonna be able to see you out there tonight, Mike? Maybe if you'd smile a lot, I could see you."

"Don't reckon I'll be smilin' much tonight. But if you listens close, you might hear me prayin'."

Short Stuff picked up his saddle. "Just as well. Some of them idiots prob'ly think your smile would draw the lightning."

Mike drained the last dregs from his cup. "Guess we better get at it."

Guy stirred himself. "Don't want no stompedes tonight, boys. Best you sing to 'em."

Mike and Short Stuff mounted and turned toward the resting cattle. As they moved away, Short Stuff's voice rose high in a wordless, quavering tune known as "The Texas Lullaby," the eery, but cattle-soothing "song of the brush."

Guy spoke dryly. "You boys best sleep while you can. May be little enough chance for sleep tonight."

In spite of Guy's admonition, there was no way Lance could force himself to sleep. He sat by the fire, watching the oncoming storm in awe. Flash lightning soon turned into forked lightning accompanied by ear-splitting claps of thunder. Then came the peculiar blue lightning carrying with it the acrid smell of brimstone.

As he watched in silence, the sky poured down balls of fire that rolled across the ground like tumbleweeds. He got to his feet to look for the herd -- and felt a clammy chill run down his back. A ghostly ball of fire encircled the tip of every horn in the herd. Streaks of fire ran up and down the backs of the cattle, and each swish of the tail was accompanied by fiery sparks. He could hear the riders circling the herd with Short Stuff's haunting "Texas Lullaby" rising in volume as he came to the near side, only to be shortly replaced by Mike's deep bass intoning "Jesus, Lover of My Soul."

Lance could sit idly no longer. He crawled over to where Guy had bedded down. "Hey, Guy."

"Yeah, boss. What is it?"

"I was thinkin' I oughta mount up and help the boys on guard tonight. All right?"

Guy sat up and rubbed his eyes. "Yeah. Couldn't hurt. But be careful out there, Lance. If they start to run, it's like the boys say, 'one jump to their feet – next jump into hell.'"

"Yeah, I'll be careful, Guy. I just gotta do somethin'."

Guy watched him catch Captain Jess and step into the saddle. "That boy's gonna be a cowman someday -- if he lives long enough." He pulled the covers over his head.

Captain Jess had enjoyed plenty of rest that day and was eager to work. Lance held him up and spoke softly. Take it easy, fellow. We don't wanta make any sudden moves."

Lance glanced toward the wagon and gasped in surprise. Rings of fire encircled the iron bands around the wagon wheels. Captain Jess nickered softly and pointed his ears straight ahead. Like two demon eyes, little fireballs appeared on each ear as sparklers raced up and down his mane. Lance's hands went clammy as he realized the only thing he could see in the direction of the herd was the foxfire playing on the horns of the cattle.

He sat quietly and listened. He could tell Captain Jess was moving on instinct alone. The little fireballs shot back and forth as the horse's ears were never still. He let out his held breath in one short gasp as he heard the rising melody of Short Stuff's singing. When the sound seemed to be as close as it was going to get, he whispered into the darkness.

"Short Stuff."

The singing stopped instantly. "Damn, boss. You damn near scared me to death. What're you doin' here?"

"Thought I'd come out and try to help. Couldn't sleep anyhow."

He could make out Short Stuff's horse by the fire playing off the bridle bit and the animal's ears.

"Couldn't hurt none. Glad to have you. Try to keep spaced between me'n Mike. And, boss, sing your heart out. Them cows is gettin' mighty nervous."

Lance waited until Short Stuff's voice began to fade, then started Captain Jess at a slow pace hoping to work in a circle around the fire-lit herd. Not a sound came from the cattle, and Lance took this as an ominous sign. Normally, there was a certain amount of noise from a bedded herd. Cattle changing positions, a calf bawling for its dinner, a disagreement over sleeping arrangements. But nothing!

He could barely hear Mike on the other side of the herd switching songs to "Nearer My God to Thee." He could even hear the little click-clack of Mike's spurs against the fenders of his saddle. Then he heard what seemed to be a collective sigh – as if fifteen hundred head of cattle all let out their breath at the same time. As a flash of lightning lit up the area, he saw a big dun steer shaking its head.

It was as though the world had come to an end. A tremendous flash of zigzag lightning forked down over the seething mass of cattle accompanied by a crash of thunder he could feel throughout his body. At that exact time, as though the lightning had knocked the bottom out of a huge barrel in the sky, the rain poured down in sheets.

With a mighty roar, the herd was up and running. The prairie lit up in yellow and blue as sheet lightning descended as a great blanket encompassing the running cattle and the riders trying to stay with them. He'd heard drovers talk about "stompedes," but nothing could have prepared him for the madness of the real thing. He knew that to stay with the herd, he would have to ride with the same wild and reckless abandon as the herd itself.

At the first signal from Lance's legs, his big bay horse was at full speed. Plowing a furrow in the wind, he went to his knees as a forefoot stuck in a prairie dog hole. His nose slid across the muddy ground, but the agile animal caught himself and regained his feet without missing a step. The lightning let up just a bit and came in intermittent flashes. By the light of one of these flashes, Lance saw Guy riding hard off to his left. Slicker flapping and hat brim blown up against the crown, he was bent low over his mount's neck and gaining rapidly on the fear-crazed herd.

Above the din of six thousand pounding hooves, he could hear Guy shouting, "Turn 'em right, boys. Get 'em millin'."

Lance signaled Captain Jess, and the bay responded with a burst of speed that took him up beside the flying Guy Madden. Guy looked across, obviously surprised to see Lance coming up on him. "Push against 'em from this side, Lance. I'll cut in front of 'em."

Across the herd, lit by an occasional flash, they could see Mike keeping pace with the cattle. He looked across and seemed to sense Guy's purpose. With a wave of his hand, he pulled up to allow the herd to wheel in that direction. Short

Stuff was nowhere in sight.

Guy spurred his horse to the front of the lead steers, and Lance could hear his voice raised in "The Texas Lullaby" -- except this time, he put words to it. "Whoa up! Whoa up, you slab-sided sonsabitches."

There was more, but Lance couldn't make it out. Now the trail boss rode back and forth across the front of the herd, gradually taking charge of the run. The cattle began to slow their headlong rush to nowhere and Guy, turning in his saddle, shouted. "Now! Turn 'em off. Turn 'em right."

Lance pulled his mount against the side of the run, chanting slowly and rhythmically. Suddenly, as though a string had broken, the leaders cut quickly to the right. Guy slowed his pace, turning them back on the others. Soon the entire herd was circling in the same type coil they'd been in at the river crossing. The herd was milling.

The rain had stopped except for an occasional sprinkle, and thunder could be heard only as a distant rumble as it moved off to the east. One by one the drovers drifted in, some bringing a few cattle with them that had dropped out during the stampede. Each was crooning his favorite cattle soothing melody.

Daylight seemed an eternity in coming. In the light of predawn, Lance searched the faces of each drover as he circled by.

"Mike!" he called out as the black face came into view. "You seen Short Stuff this morning?"

"Nossah. I ain't seen him since them cows started runnin'. I thought he was over on your side."

A hastily convened council decided that Lance, George, Mike, and Pedro would backtrack toward the wagon to search for the missing man while the others maintained control over the quiet but still nervous cattle.

About halfway to the wagon, they located Short Stuff's horse. He was standing still, right foreleg dangling from the knee. Mike dismounted and ran his hand gently over the leg. "It's broke, Mistah Lance."

Lance shook his head. "You know what to do, Mike."

"Yassuh." He slipped the revolver from his holster and shot the animal between the eyes.

Pedro stepped off his horse, leading him as he ran along the back trail plainly marked on the muddy ground. Within a quarter of a mile, they could see a spot of yellow on the prairie ahead. It was Short Stuff's slicker and as they approached, they could see the drover was still in it, sprawled on the prairie mud.

The sight of the wagon, flanked by four riders, was a welcome sight to the drovers who had been in the saddle most of the night and all of the morning with nothing to eat or drink. Guy rode up to where Lance sat shifting in his saddle.

"Did you find Short Stuff, boss?"

"Yeah, we found him, Guy. Horse stepped in a hole and busted a leg."

"Is he — did he make it?"

As the question was asked, a roar came from inside the wagon. "Damn it, Charley. Are you through bouncin' me around back here for a while? If I hadn't already had a busted leg when we started, I'd sure have one by now."

Lance grinned. "Charley and Mike rigged up a splint for his leg, but he won't be doin' any ridin' for a while."

Charley winked at Lance and Guy. "Whatta you expect me to do, you dad blamed whippersnapper? Carry the damned wagon on my back? I gotta go where the trail goes. Now stop your whinin' and get some rest."

"You old beanburner! I hope you done a better job on my leg than you did on your own. I'd hate to think I was gonna hafta hop around like you do for the rest of my life."

"Why, you dumb little bastard. We shoulda shot you and fixed up the horse. You think I did the work on my laig. If I hadda, it'd be good as new. But no. I had to depend on some young sprout like you."

Guy turned back toward the herd and pushed back his hat. "Well, Mr. Morgan, best I make out, we ain't short a head."

"Thanks to you, Guy. But how come it was Lance last night, now it's Mr. Morgan?"

Guy raised his eyebrows. "Hell, last night you was a cowboy. Now, you're just the owner's rep again."

He put spurs to his horse and galloped back to the herd.

CHAPTER 14

Bain MacDuff paused in the saloon doorway. Ordinarily, he didn't care much for the barroom scene, and he knew it distressed his mother to even think of him going in one. But Mr. Simpson was still getting the supplies together for loading on the wagon, and he still had a few minutes to kill. Better than waiting around in the hot sun, he rationalized.

One look at the crowd inside didn't do much to justify that decision. The usual scattering of drunks and drifters -- plus the ubiquitous group of carpetbaggers who seemed to have acquired a rather well-developed herd instinct since moving south.

He made his way to the bar and asked for a beer. As he sipped the lukewarm brew, he became aware that three of the carpetbaggers to his left were getting rather loud. They had obviously been at the bottle a bit longer than their respective capacities could tolerate.

Then, the name, "MacDuff" caught his ear. He turned to look at the men. One, a florid faced, pudgy man was waxing enthusiastically over some exploit of his. ". . . and they tried to say he was the wrong man -- not even a Reb. I say 'Nonsense'! We got the right man all right,"

One of his companions, a thinner man with drooping mustache, interjected, "You say he tried to make a fight of it? Drew a gun?"

"That's right," the first man muttered. "While we was tryin' to talk. Pulled a pistol outa his coat. That's when I drilled him -- dead center -- and he dropped like a sandbag."

Bain took one step toward the man and hurled the mug of beer into his face. "You're a damyankee liar!"

The man sputtered and tried to wipe off the beer with the sleeve of his checkered coat. "Now see here, young man."

Bain's face was rigid with fury. "The name's MacDuff."

The man with the droopy mustache stepped between them. "You mean you're a — ah — relative of . . ."

"His son. And if you want to live to see the sun go down,

98

you'll stay outa this."

The man stepped back quickly. "No business of mine. Just happened to be here."

The pudgy man tried to bluster his way through. "You can't bluff me, kid. I'll have the law on . . ."

"You'll be stone dead in two minutes, you cheap bastard. You been talkin' about handlin' a gun. Now's your chance to prove what you can do. I see it stuck there in your waistband. Draw it. I mean right now. Draw it."

Sweat poured from the man's pores. He started to whimper. "I won't. You can't kill me if I don't draw!"

Bain brought the back of his hand smashing across the puffy face. "What makes you think that? Fair play?"

He came back with the open side of his hand across the other side of the man's face. "I'll show you the same fairness you did my father if you don't draw."

The man struck out weakly with both hands. Bain brushed the hands aside and smashed his fist into the bridge of the carpetbagger's nose. The man crashed heavily to the floor, rolled over to his hands and knees, and crawled quickly toward the door. Just before he reached it, Bain stepped up and landed a hard kick to the man's posterior. It drove him headlong through the swinging doors and out onto the street.

When Bain stuck his head out the door, the man was well down the street chugging along at a fair clip considering his build and condition.

Bain turned back to the bartender who stood grinning behind the bar.

"Any damages I can pay for?"

The man shook his head. "Nope. And if there were, it would be my pleasure to pay them myself, Mr. MacDuff. And by the way, the beer's on the house."

Bain touched a hand to his hat brim and sauntered into the hot streets of Terwilliger.

Nearly five hundred miles to the north, the MacDuff trail herd spread out over the fine grazing lands of the tallgrass prairie. Expertly spaced and guided by Guy Madden, every animal in the herd had ample untrampled grass to graze during the slow trek to Red River Crossing -- and Indian Territory just on the other side.

Short Stuff was dropped off at Red River Crossing to recuperate in relative comfort after the jarring ride in Charlie's wagon.

Once in Indian Territory, they were confronted by a small band of Crow Indians who turned out to be more hungry than hostile. Lance watched closely as Guy moved out to negotiate with their leader.

During the conference, Lance saw the Indian hold up four fingers. But very shortly afterward, Guy rode back to the group. "Cut out a couple of those worn-out steers," he shouted."

Cisco Red moved expertly into the drag and chased out two leg-weary animals.

Lance moved up beside Guy. "Looked like he wanted four head."

"That's what he wanted. Asked for four, hoped to get three, and settled for two."

"Reckon that'll keep 'em off our backs?" Lance asked.

Guy frowned. "Once they accept them -- that'll be it. Indians pretty well keep their word. Be a different story if it was meskins or comancheros – or white men for that matter. But Indians — they won't bother us again."

As they drew near the shipping point, the grass grew shorter. Earlier herds converging on the area kept it perpetually overgrazed. However, under Guy's watchful eye, the cattle neared the railhead in sleek and fat condition with a hard layer of tallow under their hides.

Camped about thirty miles from their destination, they received a visitor as they prepared to bed down the cattle. The man was stocky with a square jaw, clear brown eyes, and a head of dark brown hair greying at the temples. He had the well-fed look of prosperity and was dressed to match in a dark broadcloth suit under his linen duster.

He introduced himself as Col. Mel Rankins, a cattle buyer for Mayes Company in New York City. After looking over the herd, he complimented Lance and Guy on the condition of the cattle.

"Looks like just what my company wants," he said. "Mr. Morgan, I'm prepared to offer you $20 a head for the entire herd – and I'll take delivery right here. Send my own men out to bring 'em in."

Lance considered the offer. "What do you think, Guy?"

Guy tilted back his hat. "Hell, I don't know. Somethin' could happen between here and town – maybe lose a bunch of cattle. Guess it's up to you, boss."

Lance reflected another minute, then spoke. "We'll have to pass on your offer, Colonel – but with thanks. I guess we'll just test the market."

"You'd best think it over again, young man. You'll have a nice profit in hand. No guarantee you'll get near that much even if you get 'em all to town."

Lance felt unaccountably irritated at being addressed as

"young man."

"Colonel Rankin, we've stuck with these cows through a thousand miles of bad weather, stampedes, hungry Indians, and river crossings. I don't reckon we're gonna get overly excited about thirty more miles of prairie. We're just gonna play this hand out. If we lose — we'll just lose."

Rankin flushed, and his voice took on an edge. "Have it your own way, young man. Let's hope you don't lose the whole damn herd."

The town of Wilson's Gap, Kansas, was new. Its sole excuse for being was a pair of shining rails that slithered through the prairie, connecting the area with the population centers of the Northeast. As the rails snaked their way westward, little towns sprang up at their terminal points like the regrowth of heads on a mythical serpent.

As the railhead moved on, most of the towns withered and died to be supplanted by those springing up ahead of them. But for now, Wilson's Gap was in full flower.

Railroad workers, buffalo hunters, hide shippers, freighters, sod busters, cowmen, and their drovers flocked into the jumble of hastily erected buildings both for pleasure and business. That group, in turn, attracted the gamblers, merchants, whores, thieves, and outlaws. The latter two groups made it necessary for citizens to recruit men to enforce their rules -- many of whom, from time to time, had worked both sides of the law with even-handed equality.

This was the immediate destination of the MacDuff trail herd. And shabby as it was, it was a welcome sight to Lance and Guy as they trotted down the single street. The herd was being held two miles east until a deal could be struck with a buyer.

"Reckon the boys might be a little miffed at having to stay with the herd while we came to town?" Lance wondered aloud.

"Probably," Guy surmised. "But they know how it is. Herd sells first -- then comes the play. Wouldn't do 'em no good to come to town nohow. Ain't none of 'em got two nickels to rub together 'til we get this herd sold."

After hitching their horses to the rail in the middle of town, the pair separated. Lance to see if he could find a buyer and Guy to wash the trail dust out of his throat.

Guy decided he would try one more saloon. Everywhere he'd been so far, the prices were high and the beer warm. He pushed through the doors of the Red Rooster and made his way to the bar. Glancing around, it seemed pretty well a

101

duplicate of the three he'd already seen.

The patrons consisted of the usual mixture of gamblers, sod busters, and buffalo hunters. A half dozen saloon girls solicited business by word and close contact. However, at a back table sat two men who stood out from the rest.

The most striking was a young man dressed completely in black except for a fancy pattern of gold embroidery on his vest and a white linen shirt. A flat-crowned, broad-brimmed hat was pushed back above cold, pale blue eyes set close together. Curly, golden hair tumbled from under his hat down to his shoulders. Long, nervous fingers were constantly in motion – lifting and sifting through a stack of silver dollars – or toying with his half-filled glass of whiskey. His face was thin and sallow in contrast to the sun-darkened complexions of the men around the room.

The other was larger and older. His face showed more effects of outdoor living in the sun and wind. He wore a tan pullover shirt laced at the throat with leather string and faded, Union blue trousers.

Both wore shiny tin badges of City Marshal.

Guy nodded at the pair as a salute to the law and turned back to his beer. Then, he froze as a voice raised above the saloon noise.

"Now, we're all gonna drink a toast to the greatest army general of all time – General U. S. Grant." The younger of the city marshals was on his feet, glass hoisted in air.

Guy smiled and raised his own glass. "And to be sure we're drinkin' to the greatest -- one to General Robert E. Lee." He drained his glass at a gulp.

The patrons, mostly Yankees with a few Rebel sympathizers, laughed and shouted good naturedly and downed their drinks. However, the young marshal tossed his drink on the sawdust covered floor. "Hey, Reb, ain't them grey britches you got on? They so dirty I can't hardly tell."

"Yeah. They're grey, Marshal."

Guy turned slowly, hands plainly visible. The young marshal was still standing. His pant legs disappeared into the tops of shiny black boots. A bone-handled revolver hung on each hip.

"I ain't so sure. Maybe we should take a better look. Take 'em off, Reb."

The room turned suddenly silent. No movement -- no sound.

Guy nodded again. "You've had your little joke, Marshal. He turned back to the bar.

The young man's voice rose higher. "Don't you turn your back on me, Reb. I said to drop them pants."

Guy turned back to face the marshal. His hand started toward his gun but stopped as he looked down the barrels of the marshal's twin revolvers.

"I said to drop them britches! Now!" The man's voice was almost hysterical and the flicker of a sardonic smile played across his lips.

"Back off, Marshal." The voice came flat and deadly from the third step leading to the upstairs area. "Or, I'll blow a hole right through your blue belly."

Lance Morgan held the shotgun rock steady, pointing right into the marshal's eyes.

The marshal looked around frantically. "Clint!"

The older man spread his hands flat against the table. "Not me, Frank. It's your play -- not mine. I don't argue with no loaded shotgun."

"Drop 'em, Marshal." Lance's voice was calm but firm.

The two revolvers clattered to the floor. The marshal backed up and knocked over a chair. "I'll have your badge for this, Clint Murdock. You're through in this town."

The other man looked at him in disgust. "As for this badge — you can have it, Kennedy. It's time I was movin' on anyhow."

Lance motioned with the shotgun. "You want 'im, Guy?"

The big trail boss shook his head. "Not now, thanks, Lance. If I change my mind, I'll come back for him."

The two men backed out the door into the street.

Frank Kennedy dropped to his knees scrambling for his revolvers. As his hand closed on one, a booted foot came down on hand and pistol alike. He looked up into his deputy's face.

"Don't be a bigger fool than you already are, Kennedy."

"Damn it, Murdock. I'm gonna kill them Reb bastards."

"No you won't. One, I ain't gonna let you and two, I ain't sure you could. You oughta thank that kid for puttin' that shotgun in your face. Likely saved your life."

"What you talking 'bout?" The young man's face turned livid with anger. "I had the drop on him. I woulda killed him for sure."

"Even so, your troubles would have just started."

"How come? I'm the law here."

"I ain't talkin' no law, stupid. That wasn't just some drifter you would rawhide anyway you want. That was a Texas trail boss. Don't you know there woulda been a dozen Texas drovers who'd just as soon tack your hide to your office door as to look at you?"

"Whatta I care? I could take any of 'em."

Clint Murdock looked at his superior in a mockingly quizzical manner. "You think they're gonna come in here one at a time and call you out in the street?" Murdock snorted scornfully. "They ain't gonna play your silly gunfighter games. They'd just come in here and swarm all over you. Take 'em no time to kill you – and two days later they wouldn't even remember doin' it."

The marshal's voice turned whiny. "Now, Clint, what you takin' up for the Rebs for. You was a Union man."

Murdock's voice filled with disgust. "I wear blue britches -- I fought for 'em -- and that trail boss wears grey. But I figger I got more in common with him than with a fool like you who, so far as I can tell, never wore no britches of either color. Now I'm goin' over to the hotel and pack my gear for California. And I'd advise you to do the same before that trail boss decides to come back and cram them fancy guns down your scrawny throat."

Following Guy's lead, Lance didn't mention the encounter with the marshal when they got to camp. After all, their first concern was the well being of the herd. This was no time for distractions.

However, early next morning, the matter was taken out of their hands. They received a visit from a gentleman of ample proportions and attired in the fashionable garb of a prosperous merchant which he almost certainly was.

He addressed himself to Lance. "I, sir, am Dick Marlowe, chairman of the Wilson's Gap Merchant's Association. We – that is the entire association – wants to express its regrets for the incident in town last night.

"Our Town Marshal, who has outlived his usefulness to this town, has departed on the early morning stage. I believe we had a committee present to see him off. We hope -- we all hope – that you'll not hold it against the town."

In spite of his attempt to remain grave, Lance couldn't help smiling at the tone of the man's delivery. "Mr. Marlowe, I'm responsible for this herd of fifteen hundred cattle. Getting them sold is all that's on my mind right now. I assume you've made arrangements for new law enforcement."

"Ah yes, of course. I believe we've prevailed on Deputy Clinton Murdock to accept a promotion and to remain as Town Marshal."

"That's good," Lance said. "We certainly want to conduct our business in a law-abiding town."

The man smiled with relief. "Well, we certainly have the buyers, Mr. Morgan. And when they're sold, we want you to know that any business you or your men might care to transact will be mighty welcome in Wilson's Gap."

Lance grinned. "I'm sure the boys will give your merchants all the business they can handle as soon as we get the herd sold."

The buyers came and when all offers were made and considered, Lance accepted a bid of $35 a head made by none other than Colonel Mel Rankin, the man who had offered just $20 a head a few days before.

"You got the makin's of a good cowman, Morgan," the Colonel said, "and a good business head. I wonder if you would consider an offer to work with our firm. We could use a young man like you."

"I appreciate that, Colonel," Lance answered. "But no thanks. I like fine just what I'm doing."

"Well, think it over. It's a standing offer." The man reached inside his coat and pulled out a handful of cigars. "Keep these for yourself -- or spread 'em out among your boys. Pleasure doin' business with you, Mr. Morgan."

The man swung lightly into the saddle and followed his herd of Texas Longhorns on their way to the shipping pens.

The Penrose was the only hotel in town. Lance, George, Mike, and Guy sat in early morning conversation while the desk clerk dozed in his chair.

"Guy, you're more than welcome to come with us," Lance said. "We're gonna take a look at the Staked Plains on the way back."

"Guess not, Lance. Me'n Cisco gonna catch the stage -- go back in style."

"How about the other boys?"

"Well, Guy said, "Booger Jim hired on to push a herd up through the North Platte country. Pedro's gonna backtrack and check in on Short Stuff at the Crossing. Fred and the others ain't quite decided. Likely blow all their money and have to work their way home."

Lance stood up awkwardly. "Damn, Guy, it just don't seem right with everybody splittin' up and gone. I was kinda gettin' used to 'em."

"Yeah — well — that's the way it goes. George, Mike, take care now, y'hear?"

CHAPTER 15

As the three riders picked their way toward the rising escarpment, the big and little bluestem, Indiangrass and sideoats grama of the tallgrass prairie gave way to the buffalo grass, blue grama, and curly mesquite grass of the High Plains. The landscape became dotted with bear grass thrusting its dagger-like leaves out in all directions while the flower stalk grew straight up out of the middle much like a long stake jabbed right through its heart giving the area its common name *llano estacado* – the Staked Plains.

As they reached the top, they could see that what had appeared to be flat land was actually quite rolling. It contained numerous "wet weather lakes" that filled during rainy season and -- lacking an outlet for the water -- often retained it during dry spells of up to two years. These lakes were complemented by smaller replicas created by the wallowing of generations of buffalo.

Here on the plains, they got their first look at the small but swift pronghorn. Flashing alarm signals from a white patch on their rumps, the dainty antelope-like creatures leaped and dashed across the riders' path in a dazzling display of animal ballet.

George, in particular, was entranced by the region. Pausing at a running water draw to refresh themselves with cold, clear water, he jabbed the toe of his boot into the turf. "Look at that grass, Lance. Thick as fur on a cat – and cured on the stalk good as the leafiest hay. This is cattle country. That soil would grow anything – just look at it, boys."

Lance stroked his chin. "That may be true, George. But I don't think the Comanches would take kindly to your moving in right across their hunting grounds."

"Guess you're right. But, some day – I don't know."

A couple of days after they topped the escarpment, the land suddenly fell out from under their feet in a vast gorge with precipitous banks that blazed with reds and purples in the afternoon sun. The walls dropped hundreds of feet to a relatively flat, broad bottom. Grass, boot-top high, showing amber out toward the tips but tinged with green on the lower leaves, waved like the waters of a vast lake.

The canyon was so wide, the far side was barely visible on the distant horizon. The bottom was laced with a network of channels through which the running water snaked its way south and east toward Red River.

The floor was alive with game. Large herds of pronghorns stepped daintily toward the creek until, at a signal from one of their lookouts, they broke away in a scrambling dash to make way for a solitary lobo wolf to stroll leisurely to the water. The men sat for the better part of an hour as a huge herd of buffalo made its way ponderously across their path.

After most of the herd had passed, a flock of prairie chickens exploded out of the grass just ahead of the herd. Startled by the sudden action, the leaders snorted, shied to one side, and started a lumbering run. Within seconds the entire herd was running full speed, tails upraised, down the canyon then lunging up the other side. The riders sat in awe at the tremendous power generated by the thundering mass of animals as their hooves pounded the shaking ground.

So far, the men had seen no sign of Indians, yet they rode carefully, keeping themselves off the skyline. At night, fires were kept small and relatively smokeless. Noise was held to a minimum.

About a week into the crossing, they came upon a fresh trail made by a fairly large body of men on horseback. George dismounted to examine the trail more closely.

Lance rode up beside him. "Indians?"

George didn't look up from the tracks. "Don't think so, Lance. Had several two-wheeled carts with them. Must be comancheros."

Mike looked puzzled. "I've heard about them comancheros. I thought they was some kinda Indian."

George shook his head. "Naw. They're renegades -- mostly meskins and half-breeds. They trade whiskey, guns, and trinkets to the Indians for stolen cattle and horses."

Lance said, "Not above a little thievery on their own."

George nodded. "Especially if they find an isolated homestead or a shorthanded drove of cattle. Anyhow, gives the Comanche a ready market for whatever he can steal."

After another week in the saddle, the men neared the edge of the plateau where the Staked Plains break off into canyons and draws running down toward the Gulf of Mexico. The men were extra cautious now for this was the "trading ground" where Comanche and comanchero meet -- usually just after the "raiding moon."

Skirting the edge of one of the sizable breaks leading into a maze of canyons and flat-topped hills, they heard the unmistakable sound of gunfire coming from the other side of the ridge. Dismounting and walking the last fifty yards, they finally positioned themselves just under the protective ledge of the ridgeline.

"Wait here," Lance whispered. "I'll crawl up there and see what we've stumbled into."

He unbooted his large caliber rifle, and pushing it ahead of him, crawled to an uplifting of rock at the crest. Raising himself slightly to get a better look down the slope, he beckoned the others to join him.

"Comancheros," he muttered. "Got a settler's cabin surrounded down there."

Below, on a gradual downslope, three men could be seen overlooking a dugout "soddy" below. Utilizing buffalo wallows, the raiders had virtually a solid earthen barricade between themselves and the defenders. Searching the terrain carefully, Lance made out five others forming a roughly circular pattern around the besieged.

Occasionally, one would fire into the cabin walls, but the effect was negligible, and Lance was convinced the firing was simply to keep those forted up in the house nervous. The comancheros seemed to be in no hurry. After all, time was on their side.

Answering fire came from two distinct weapons. One was the thunderous roar of a heavy buffalo rifle, the other the sharp bark of a lighter caliber. Although the firing from the cabin seemed to be quite accurate, there was little chance of actually scoring a hit because of the position of the raiders in their carefully chosen shelters.

Lance looked at the others questioningly.

"Hell yes," George grunted. "Let's cut ourselves in on this action."

Mike nodded in agreement. "Let's fair this fight up some."

The closest man to them was about fifty yards directly down the slope. Lance pointed to him. "Think you can take him out, Mike?"

Mike grinned. "Yassuh. Easy."

Lance nodded. "Get him."

Lance and George watched as Mike slipped over the ridge and down the slope. Moving quickly, he stalked the man with amazing stealth for someone of his bulk. The two nodded at one another in satisfaction as Mike leaped the last few feet into the raider's position.

A strong hand around the throat throttled off any outcry

108

as the comanchero was dragged to the bottom of the wallow. Shaking him as a terrier shakes a rat, Mike squeezed until he stopped struggling.

Lance indicated a man to their left. "Take the one on the left, George. I'll get the one on the right."

George nodded.

The comancheros were not prepared for an attack from the rear. While well protected against fire from the cabin below, they were alarmingly exposed from any other angle.

This was no confusing gunfight in dark streets – no short range "draw-and-fire" affair. This was an out and out shooting match, and Lance was in his element. His .44-.70 spit leaden death as quickly as he could load and fire.

In less than ten minutes it was over. As the withering fire raked their ranks from behind, the confused attackers tried to shift positions to get some protection only to expose themselves to the deadly fire of the sharpshooters below. Five of the attackers died quickly on the slopes while the other three fled in a flurry of whip and spur. Two carts, laden with trade goods, were left behind.

Lance and the others mounted and rode down the slope to where the nester leaned on the doorsill of his cabin, the octagonal barrel of a heavy Sharps buffalo rifle tucked under his arm. Gaunt and pale, eyes set well back in their sockets, he looked out of place in this rugged country. His features, while delicate, were sensitive and alert. He appeared to be in his late thirties.

He stepped forward to greet his visitors. With laughing eyes, he paraphrased, "I looked to the hills from whence my deliverance came."

His voice was surprisingly deep.

He offered a hand that was thin but strong. The long, slender fingers were heavily callused.

"Gentlemen, I am deeply in your debt." He nodded his head. "My name is Henry Porter."

He glanced toward the doorway where a small boy of about four was being ushered out by a slender woman of medium height.

"This is my wife, Helen, and my son, Phillip."

The woman had obviously been at one time very attractive with bright and shining grey eyes, but a windy and arid climate, coupled with a blazing sun, had robbed her skin of its youthful glow. Little creases showed around the eyes and crisscrossed her upper neck. The lips, still full and generous, seemed to be a perpetually chapped condition. Yet, a warm smile and easy manner gave evidence that this was a woman at peace with herself and her way of life.

The small boy was casting a wary eye in Mike's direction and sliding away to conceal himself behind his mother's long, full skirt.

The woman flashed a smile at Mike. "Forgive my son, please. He's never seen a colored man before."

The sod-covered hut was somewhat larger than George's, and a small lean-to on the east side of the house sheltered a rock and mud cooking pit for hot weather use.

The floor was clay, hard packed and swept clean. A small counter in one corner was built around a hand pump for the family water supply. Under the pump spout was a hand-painted enamel basin snug up against a bucket of similar design which held a gourd dipper also painted and lacquered to a high shine.

In the opposite corner stood a bed made of rawhide stretched over a sapling frame. A small fireplace built into the back wall provided for cooking and heat. A hand-hewn table, flanked by six chairs, stood in the middle of the room.

Near the right-hand wall, in near perfect condition in spite of the rough journey it must have had, was a spinet piano gleaming with the well-cared-for look of an object much prized by its owner.

A shaggy buffalo robe in front of the fireplace and a large combination chest and chifforobe completed the room's furnishings. A short loft overhanging the room was proudly identified by Phillip as "my room."

The evening meal consisted of dutch oven bread, a large bowl of baked beans and meat strips of alternating fat and lean.

George was enthusiastic. "Mrs., Porter, I do believe that's the best meat I've ever eaten. What kind is it?"

"Why, thank you, Mr. Gibson," she responded. "Would you like some more?"

"Yes, please." George held out his plate as she heaped it full again.

Lance said, "I do believe George is going to wipe these people out of their winter rations as quickly as the comancheros would have."

George spread his hand helplessly. "I truly am ashamed, Lance. I just can't help myself."

After supper, as the men went outside to enjoy the cool breath of the high country's evening breeze, the visitors stared curiously at the wall of a small shed which was covered with the pelts of small animals turned flesh side out over boat-shaped boards to keep them smooth as they dried.

"That's where I dry my pelts," Henry said, noticing their curiosity. One of the few cash crops I've been able to come up with so far. Doesn't bring in much, but it pays for my staples and a few seeds for the garden."

Lance asked, "What kind of pelts are they, Mr. Porter?"

Henry lifted one off the wall and turned back the skin to reveal the distinctive black and white markings of the common skunk.

Lance looked quizzically at the settler who merely chuckled and nodded. "Yes, Mr. Morgan. We can afford to waste very little here."

Lance cut a quick glance toward George who was beginning to turn pale; his Adam's apple bobbed up and down as he swallowed hard. Gradually, he took control of himself and squatted on his heels. "I don't care, fellers. I still say that's about the best meat I ever ate."

They spent two more nights, sleeping outside in their bedrolls. They learned that the Porters were from Philadelphia where Henry had been a portrait painter of considerable reputation until an unfortunate lung condition required his removal to a higher and drier climate. Helen was an accomplished pianist, and the men spent their evenings in pleasant attendance at her improvised concerts.

In spite of his protestations, George was obviously relieved that the remaining meals featured more conventional fare than the first.

He also plied his host with questions about the region and its potential for ranching. He learned that the comanchero attack was the first of its kind experienced by the Porters. So far, the Comanches had been no problem although there were signs that they frequently passed near the Porter's soddy.

It was with a lingering tinge of regret that the men made their farewells and departed.

Single file, the men made their way down the brush-covered slope off the plateau of the Staked Plains. As they rode, the air became noticeably heavier and the heat more oppressive. Trees reappeared as a feature of the landscape, at first as scattered mottes of giant live oaks with thick trunks and wide ranging branches that offered welcome shade for a mid-day rest stop. Later, there were thick groves of post oak, hickory, bois d'arc and pecan trees -- growing sparse and spindly on the uplands but tall and sturdy in the bottoms.

George had been riding with furrowed brow for most of an hour when Lance pulled up beside him. "What's on your mind, George?"

George shifted his cud of tobacco. "Aw, nothin' much."

"You been studyin' about somethin' – or you're comin'

111

down with somethin'. Got anything to do with the Porters?"

"Not exactly. It's that country they live in, Lance. Did you ever see such country? It'll be the best ranch country in Texas one day."

Lance grinned. "And . . ?"

George pursed his lips and squirted a stream of tobacco juice. "And nothin'. I just think, that's all."

"Thinkin' you'd like to be part of it?"

"I reckon so."

"Can't blame you for that." Lance pushed back his hat. "You'll need money, George."

George's chin jutted stubbornly. "I got about five thousand now."

"It ain't enough, George."

"No, but it's all I got."

Lance leaned forward and caught George's arm. "Don't be a fool, George. We both need more money, and we know where we can get it."

"You're thinkin' Confederate gold."

"It's not Confederate gold," Lance snapped. "The Confederacy doesn't exist. At five dollars a head, that gold would buy twenty-four thousand cows in Texas – worth some $840,000 in Kansas.

George shook his head firmly. "It may not be Confederate gold, Lance, but it sure as hell ain't ours."

"That's crazy, George. If it ain't ours, just tell me whose it is. Who owns that gold, George?"

George shook Lance's hand off his arm. "I don't know whose gold it is, Lance. I just know whose it ain't."

CHAPTER 16

The country took on a more familiar look as the men neared the MacDuff Ranch. Since their sharp words over the gold, Lance and George had spoken little more than necessary. Lance finally eased his horse over next to George's.

"George, I been thinkin' about that gold. You're right about it not bein' ours. Lookin' back on it, I think I musta sounded like Roy O'Neil."

George laughed. "Not quite, Lance."

"I don't know what I was thinkin' – let's forget the gold. We'll find some other way, okay?"

George took the younger man's hand. "I don't think you woulda gone through with it nohow."

Colleen wore her depressed feelings like a banner. Her usually animated face was quiet and grave. Her movements were listless as she pulled a handful of blackeye peas from a burlap bag close by her feet. Placing the peas in her lap, she took one, ran a thumbnail down the center, and stripped the peas out of the hull into a small bucket between her feet.

She didn't see her mother in front of her until the woman spoke. "Good heavens, Colleen. With all that concentration I'd think you'd be doing a better job. You've put some snaps in that bucket big as my finger."

At the sound of Erin's voice, the girl looked up, her expression unchanged. "I'm sorry, mother, I didn't notice." She picked out a few of the larger ones and placed them back in her lap.

"I know, dear, but try to pay a little more attention. You know how your brother hates stringy hulls in his peas."

"I don't think he's going to be worried about our blackeyed peas for a while, mother -- if ever." The young woman's eyes filled with tears.

Erin put her arm around her daughter's shoulders. "Of course, he will. Just as soon as we get this incident straightened

113

out. We have friends who are trying to make the authorities see reason."

"I'm afraid, mother, that our friends have very little influence with the damyankee authorities."

Erin looked surprised. "Colleen! Our problems do not excuse that kind of language. Kindly remember that a lady is a lady under any circumstances."

"I'm sorry to offend, mother, but being a lady won't get Bain out of jail."

"Neither will conducting ourselves as trash. Please use some restraint."

"Yes, ma'am."

Erin started to speak, stopped, and shaded her eyes to peer down the road.

"What is it, mother?"

"I don't know for sure. Something's moving out there. Yes, it is. Riders! I think it's Lance and the others. Thank God. They're home."

"In jail?" Lance blurted out. "Just for slappin' that scalawag around a little. He's lucky Bain didn't kill him."

Erin sat at ease in the porch swing while Mike and George hunkered on their heels near the steps. Colleen sat next to Lance clutching his right hand with both of hers.

George stirred himself enough to move to the top step. "Just what could they do to Bain, ma'am?"

Erin hesitated then spoke stiffly. "The man is asking for the maximum penalty for assaulting an officer under martial law — death by hanging."

Lance's face convulsed with shock. "They go too far. Those bast — I'm sorry ma'am — but this is too much. The peace is over."

Colleen clutched his arm. "Please, Lance, you're beginning to sound just like Bain."

Erin nodded. "Nothing will be gained by losing our temper. There have been several young men in this part of the country who have been goaded into what appears to be permanent outlawry by our present officials."

Colleen spoke. "My father, my brother, I just couldn't stand it if . . ."

She fled into the house with her hands over her face.

Erin's face was grim. "What Colleen was trying to say is that to lose any of you right now would be unbearable."

George climbed slowly to his feet. "You're just as right as can be, ma'am. But when's the trial set for?"

"Colonel Whitaker will be in town first of next week. That's when Bain will be tried."

"And the procedure?"

"It will be a military trial under martial law. No jury. Yankee officer for a lawyer appointed by the court. I'm afraid it's strictly a formality."

George sauntered down the steps. "I hate to leave your hospitality so soon, but I feel like that carpetbagger can be reasoned with, don't you, Lance?"

"I have no doubt," Lance replied. "Set an extra plate for supper, ma'am. I think Bain will be home by then."

"Yes siree," the bartender said. "I saw the whole fracus right here in this saloon. Young MacDuff tried ever' way in the world to make that carpetbagger draw his gun – but that javelina showed his yellow streak plain. So MacDuff kicked him right through the door."

Lance leaned across the bar. "You know this carpetbagger's name?"

"Yeah. Smedley, Clarence Smedley."

Lance turned toward the door. "Much obliged."

The sign over the door proclaimed, "Land Sales, Clarence Smedley, Prop."

George and Lance walked through the door into a tiny outer office with a rickety table, a cane-bottomed chair and a set of files against the wall. A thin-faced man with a long nose, a fringe of hair just above his ears, and virtually no chin sat in the chair.

"What can I do for you, gents?"

Lance paused in front of the table. "You Smedley?"

"No, I'm not. Did you have an appointment to see Mr. Smedley?"

George pushed against the table. "Where's Smedley at?"

The clerk put on an air of indignation. "I'm afraid if you don't have an appointment, Mr. Smedley is not available."

George put a little more weight on the table which began to creak and lean. "Is Smedley in that back office?"

"Well, yes, but you can't . . ."

Lance started for the back office. As the clerk raised himself from the chair, George pushed hard down on the table which collapsed on the floor. As George followed Lance into the office, he glanced back. "Ain't much of a table."

The inner office was larger but had the same look of being temporary and shabby. Behind a desk, sat the rotund Clarence Smedley.

"What's the meaning of this intrusion?" he blustered. "Jenson!"

The little clerk scurried into the office just behind Lance

and George. "I'm sorry, Mr. Smedley. I told them they had to have an appointment."

Smedley scowled from behind the desk. "Jenson, fetch the marshal."

The man hurried for the door, opened it, and ran headlong into an unexpected barrier. He rebounded flat on his back on the dusty floor and looked up at the huge black man filling the door. Mike's smile lit the whole room.

"Oh, I'm sorry, sah. Now I done got you all dirty." He picked up the clerk and shook him vigorously, the little man's head popping back and forth like a popper on a bull whip. Then, he placed him gently back on his feet.

"Better you sit down — Jenson, is it?" Lance said.

The man collapsed into the only empty chair in the room. Smedley had slid open a drawer and was stealthily reaching a pudgy hand inside. Lance leaned across the desk and slammed the drawer shut.

Smedley shrieked in pain, cradling his right hand in his left. Lance leaned across the top of the desk, his face just inches from Smedley's.

"You must be Clarence Smedley." Lance's smile was without humor.

"That's right, and since you men have forced your way in here, what can I do for you — before you go to jail?"

George hoisted a leg up and half sat on the desk. "Well, you see, we're friends of Bain MacDuff, and we thought it'd be nice if you went down to the marshal's office and dropped them charges against him." George shifted his wad and spat a stream of juice at the spittoon. He missed.

Smedley tried to laugh. "You're wastin' my time. Them charges gonna stick – as well as them I'm filin' on you for criminal trespass."

Lance shook his head sadly. "Damn. That's too bad, Smedley. I was hopin' you'd be reasonable so you could stay alive just a while longer."

George looked at Lance. "Guess there ain't no use talkin' no more, Lance. Let's just do what we came to do and get the hell outa here."

Smedley's face turned frantic. "You wouldn't dare shoot me down right here in front of a witness."

"He's got a point," Lance muttered. "Guess we can't leave any witnesses."

Jenson jumped straight up from his chair, voice piping shrilly. "I ain't no witness, men. I don't see nothin' – don't hear nothin' – don't tell nothin'."

"So much for your witness, Smedley," Lance snarled. He grabbed the carpetbagger by the coat front. "Now, what's it

116

gonna be?"

George stepped closer, drawing his revolver. "We're in a kinda hurry."

"All right." Smedley slumped against the wall. "I'll drop the charges."

He straightened himself and tugged at his waistcoat. "We can go down to the marshal's office right now. After all, there was no real harm done. I can afford to be generous."

He stepped toward the doorway while George and Lance exchanged amused glances. Mike stayed in the passageway.

Smedley looked back. "Let's go. Tell your nigger to get outa the way."

George thumbed back the hammer. "Smedley. I oughta shoot you just for thinkin' we're that dumb."

Smedley turned to Lance. "What's he talkin' about. I'm willin' to do what you asked. What are we waitin' for?"

Lance stepped up to the man and brushed imaginary dust off his lapels. "I think he means we ain't goin' down to the marshal's office where you can have us tossed into jail. You're gonna hafta go down there all by yourself.

"Then you're gonna find yourself real sick of our Texas climate. You're leavin' on tomorrow's stage – clean outa this country."

"But I have property here. I can't just go off and leave it."

George grinned at him. "It's better'n bein' dead. And you'll be dead if you don't do exactly as we say."

Smedley staggered out of the building and down the street. Lance jerked his head after him. "Go along with him, Mike. George and I better make ourselves lost."

As Bain and Mike rode out of town together, Bain touched heels to his horse's flank and put him into a brisk foxtrot. It was time to go home.

It was three days later before George and Lance showed up at the MacDuff Ranch. They had seen Smedley board the northbound stage with four full carpetbags. From the look on his face, they didn't think he'd be seen again in Texas.

With Bain's enforced absence, ranch work had gone neglected. Lance, George, and Mike pitched in with willing hands to take up the slack.

After a hard day's work, Lance had washed up for supper and paused for a moment near the corral to enjoy the sheer sensual pleasure of early evening on the *brasada*.

The sunset streaked the sky a heavy rose broken by streaks of yellow and slate grey across the rimrock of the western horizon. A breeze, laden with fragrance from the herb patch, stirred the tree leaves along the stream bank. At that moment, a meadowlark struck up its evening lullaby.

Lance hooked his heel into the bottom rail of the corral and leaned back against the fence to savor the moment. Touching the light layer of perspiration on his face, the evening air cooled the fever left over from the blazing heat of the afternoon sun. He took a deep breath and tilted his head back awash in a general feeling of well-being.

He started at a light touch on his arm and looked down into the smiling face of Colleen MacDuff. Her eyes sparkled as the last rays of sun glinted off her auburn hair, tinting it with gold. The starched prettiness of white cotton draped her body with the purity of carved ivory.

"Beautiful, isn't it?" she said. "I've seen father put into a trance by such an evening. He loved this place so much."

Lance pushed his hat back to expose more of his head to the soothing air. "I can see why. It's beautiful — not just the sight — but the sounds, the smell, the feeling. It's like the whole world is there just for you to enjoy."

He let his eyes drift over this girl — turned goddess — turned woman. She smiled softly, and he flushed as he became aware of the boldness of his stare.

"I'm sorry, Colleen. I don't mean to be rude. It's just that you're so beautiful tonight. I've never seen you like . . ."

"I'm not so bad — once you get used to me. Is that what you're trying to say, Lance Morgan?" she teased.

"No — not at all. It's just . . ."

She stepped forward into his surprised arms, put both arms around his neck, and kissed him lightly on the mouth, shutting off the words.

He reached up and pushed his hat all the way back, letting it fall unnoticed to the ground. He put a hand on each side of her face holding it firmly. This time, he initiated the kiss -- again lightly. The next was longer -- more urgent. Their bodies pressed closely together in mutual hunger.

"I want you, Colleen. I want you now – and forever."

She whispered in his ear. "I knew it all the time -- but I thought you'd never figure it out."

CHAPTER 17

Erin's happiness radiated from her shining face. "Lance, I am so pleased. I've long thought of you as a member of this family – and now you really will be.

"I'm happy for you -- and for Colleen. You'll be good for one another. I can only wish you a portion of the joy that Scotty and I had for nearly twenty-five years."

She paused to dab at her eyes with her apron, but the smile never left her face. "Have you decided on a date?"

"Right away," Colleen exclaimed, "the sooner the better."

Lance smiled indulgently. "I think right away – after a proper mourning period."

Colleen placed both hands on her hips. "That's nonsense, Lance Morgan. This is the Texas frontier – not Charleston or Atlanta."

Lance scratched his head. "I'm from Alba, Tennessee, Colleen. That's a long way from either place – and not just in distance. But it seems, out of respect for your father, we ought to wait a while. Don't you agree, Mrs. MacDuff?"

Erin rose from her chair and faced her future son-in-law. "Lance, I'm afraid I'm going to have to agree with my daughter. Maybe I shouldn't say so, but I know that Scotty wanted this to happen, and he'd not want to be the cause of its delay. I say that if you're both sure of your love, there's no reason to put it off – not for Scotty MacDuff."

"Well," Lance scuffed his boot against the floor. "I kinda wanted to get another herd up the trail before winter hits. I got Guy Madden getting the drovers together now. I've already got enough cattle committed for a trail herd. Won't be much time."

Colleen sensed victory. She flew across the room into his waiting arms. "Better than no time at all. I'll get right to work on my dress."

Erin moved quietly out the door, only to reappear a moment later almost hidden behind an armload of white

119

organdy and lace. "Colleen," she said softly, "it would make me very happy if you'd wear this one."

Tears streaked the young girl's face. "Mother, your wedding dress. I didn't even know you still had it. I'd love to wear it."

Bain had gone to town and returned with broadcloth suits for himself and the groom. His usually tousled hair was slicked back with the help of rose oil and water. Mike and George had gone to infinite pains to make themselves appear presentable. All passed even the bride's critical inspection.

The wedding day brought out neighbors, many of whom they hadn't seen since Scotty's funeral. Dressed in their finest, they came, the men stiff and slightly uncomfortable in unaccustomed starched collars and string ties, the women fluttery and sentimental, the youth-robbing drudgery of day-to-day living brushed aside by surging memories of brief, tender interludes of the past.

The women overflowed the house and spilled over onto the spacious veranda, while the men sought the cooling seclusion of the big shade trees. Erin, with the capable assistance of Mike, had prepared great quantities of food including a giant pound cake, laden with butter, to top off the feast.

Outside, where the men had gathered to swap news and their respective views on events of the day, one of them had buttonholed Lance under the shade of a huge pecan tree. "Mr. Morgan, I understand that you intend to take a herd north before winter."

"Yes, sir. That's correct. I leave within the month."

The man rubbed his chin. "May run into some weather leavin' this late."

"Well sir, that's possible. But if I can push 'em through before mid-December, they ought to make it all right."

"Well, if you're gonna try it, I got 'bout two hundred head I'd like to send along."

"Gather 'em. I'll pick 'em up at your place."

"They'll be ready, sir."

Nothing detracted from the most festive day in recent memory for most of the guests and participants alike. This was Colleen's day, and she dominated it totally.

Soft and radiant, she floated through the ceremony and the remaining amenities. Her beauty and manner captivated everyone -- including her new husband, who was immediately transformed from calm and confident cowman to a callow, awe-stricken youth in the presence of his bride. He hardly noticed when the last of the guests had pulled away from the ranch gate. Witty remarks of Bain and George passed without response. Even Mike's sincere best wishes were acknowledged perfunctorily.

The entire family smiled with relief when Colleen led her bewitched groom off to their room.

While Lance immediately began the task of assembling the cattle for the drive, his new bride was not to be left behind. The honeymoon was as hectic as the wedding was festive. On the road every day, often the nuptial bed was a bedroll on the ground or in the back of a wagon.

In spite of his determination to not let anything distract him from getting the herd headed north, Lance found the magic spell cast by his diminutive mate so strong and compelling it was difficult to think of anything else. The sight of her firm and trim young body, athletically eager to join with his, the fresh, clean scent of her skin, and the soft, warm taste of her mouth on his, fueled a fiery passion that drained the strength from his body, leaving it languid and sensitive to the slightest stimulation. Her nearness during the day brought an overwhelming flow of tenderness washing over his spirit. The touch of her fingers on his arm sparked a long-lasting tingle throughout his body.

Erin wiped her hands on her apron and paused from cleaning off the breakfast dishes. "Lance, you've seemed a little preoccupied the last couple of days. You and Colleen haven't had a spat have you?"

He dropped his head shyly. "No ma'am. Nothing like that."

"Is everything going well with gathering the herd?"

"Why, yes. It's coming just fine."

"Then, what is it?"

"It's nothin' – just an impossible thought I've had."

"What's that, Lance?"

"Aw, that big Circle-T Ranch over to the west. Mr. Thompson didn't want to send any cattle on the drive, but he said he'd like to sell about a thousand head right here."

Erin smiled. "Well, we can't expect everyone to go along with you on this drive. Some are just going to be skeptical."

"It's not that so much; it's just that I'd sure like to be able to buy that herd."

"What's he asking for them, Lance?"

"Five dollars a head – range delivered."

"That sounds like a fair price. You could make a good profit if you get them to Kansas."

Lance shook his head. "What little I had is already tied

121

up in this drive, and Mr. Thompson wants cash money."

"Well, maybe something will turn up. Don't give up on it completely."

Erin swept away the remaining dishes as Lance and Bain headed for the door.

George sat quietly in the saddle, but he shook his head vigorously. "We've been over this before, Lance. It's just plain wrong. That ain't our gold."

Lance pressed closer. "Look, George, we wouldn't need to take it all – just a little bit. And, we could replace it after the drive. We'd be richer, the gold would be the same. What would it hurt?"

"I ain't worried about the gold, Lance. I'm worried about us. What would it do to us if we used that gold for ourselves?"

"What would it do to us? It would make us rich – that's what it'd do to us. So rich we could spit in a carpetbagger's eye. And that's what I aim to be -- no matter how long it takes. This would just shorten the time, that's all."

George continued to shake his head. "I understand how you feel, Lance. And if you wanta take that gold and use it, I'm not gonna shoot you over it. I just don't want any part of it. So, don't ask me about it again."

Lance's shoulders slumped in defeat. "You know I can't take that gold unless you go along with it, George."

George pulled his mount around. "I wish I could see it your way, Lance, but I just can't."

When Lance and Bain returned in the evening from a long day in the saddle, Erin met them at the door. "Lance, you can pick up your steers at the Circle-T day after tomorrow."

Lance stared at his mother-in-law, mouth agape. "What? I don't understand."

"I mean you have your steers for the drive. Mr. Thompson said he'd have them gathered by tomorrow."

"Erin, what have you done?"

"I drove over there today and spoke to Mr. Thompson. He agreed to accept payment after you sell the steers in Kansas. So, they're all yours, Lance, hoof, hide, and horn."

Lance let out a whoop of joy and lifted Erin off her feet in an exuberant hug.

The cattle were gathered in a large, low-lying flat near the Circle-T ranchhouse. Lance and Guy Madden sat their horses looking down at the herd.

Guy scrutinized them with a practiced eye. "Looks like a good herd, Lance. Oughta bring top dollar in Kansas."

"Sure hope so, Guy. These are really mine."

The two loped down the slope to where the Circle-T owner sat in the shade of a scrub mesquite.

Lance was smiling broadly. "Mr. Thompson, I appreciate your sellin' me these cattle on tick."

"Just good business, son."

"Still, I appreciate your confidence that I can get you your money after the drive."

Thompson peered up at the young man quizzically. "Don't know as I can take much credit for that, son. The MacDuff Ranch will more than cover any risk I'm takin'."

"The MacDuff Ranch? What's this got to do . . ." His voice trailed off as he knew what he was going to hear.

"Why sure. Erin MacDuff pledged the ranch against these cattle. Didn't you know?"

"I knew. It's just that the pledge won't be needed."

The rangy cattleman swung into his saddle. "Hope not, boy. I just wouldn't feel right takin' a widow's ranch away. Well, they're all yours now. Good luck to you."

He set spurs to his sorrel and turned him toward home.

Bain's raised his voice in indignation. "I stayed at home on the last drive – but I aim to go on this one."

Lance, George, Mike, and Erin all looked at each other as though waiting for someone else to speak. Finally Erin broke the silence. "I know you want to go, son. And I remember we talked about you going on the second drive. But someone has to stay. Colleen and I can't run this ranch all by ourselves."

Mike rose slowly to his feet. "S'cuse me, Miz MacDuff, but if Bain wanta go on this drive, I be proud to help out 'round here while he's gone."

Bain brightened instantly. "That's great, Mike. That'd be all right wouldn't it, mother?"

Erin looked thoughtful. "But Mike might also have an interest in going on the drive."

"No, that's all right, Miz MacDuff. If I can help you and Miz Colleen, I'd shore be proud to do it. If you think I could do it all right."

"I have no doubts about that, Mike."

Bain leaped to his feet. "Then it's settled. Mike can take care of things as well as I could."

Erin failed to suppress a note of sarcasm. "He'll probably even manage to stay out of jail."

Along with the herds sent by neighboring ranchers on speculation, the thousand head from the Circle-T made up a

123

large herd on the gathering grounds. Lance and Bain rode to the chuck wagon where Guy was instructing several drovers.

Lance saw a familiar face. "Hey, Booger Jim."

The rider touched his hat. "How you been, Mr. Morgan?"

"Fair to middlin'. How about the drive to North Platte?"

The man sidestepped his horse nearer to Lance. "Mighty wooly, Mr. Morgan."

"Bad weather?"

"Worst I've ever seen. We had a storm that'd tear the hinges off the gates of hell. The lightnin' was crackin' and poppin' like a panful of bacon grease. I was on night watch after midnight, and you couldn't told the difference than if'n it'd been noon. The whole herd turned into a giant fireball. I could feel my hair stand straight up inside my hat.

"My pore ol' horse jest squatted down and wouldn't move – no matter what. And I didn't much keer one way or 'nother nohow. I jest knowed them cows was gonna stompede and run over me any minute, but I couldn't move no more'n my horse could.

"Them cows was moanin' and a'bellerin' like some critter caught up in hell. I was prayin' for all I was worth, makin' all kinds of promises if the Lord would jest get me through the night.

"But you know, them damn cows was too scared to run. Guess they was 'bout like me and my horse. Jest froze stiff. When it let up, jest before daylight, they got calm and bedded down right away."

Lance grinned at him. "Well, did you keep all the promises you made?"

"Aw hell, Mr. Morgan, the Lord knowed them promises was too much for a man to keep."

George approached the wagon at a trot, swung down, and headed for the coffee pot. "Well, that's the last of my cows. What's left to gather?"

Lance took a swig from his cup. "Got a few more down south about ten miles. We should have the whole herd here and ready to go by tomorrow afternoon."

Guy looked up from where he squatted on his heels near the fire. "Everything else is ready to go. Just as soon as we get that last herd. How many in that bunch, Lance?"

"A couple hundred. Amos Carter's herd. I'm ready to go get 'em right now. Carter said they'd be ready this morning. Who you wanta send along, Guy?"

The trail boss tossed the dregs of coffee into the fire. "Won't take many hands to hold the herd here. I figger if

Bain, Pedro, Fred, and a couple of the new hands would hold the main herd here, the rest of us could chase the new ones in pretty quick. Sound all right to you?"

Lance nodded. Bain eased back up into the saddle. "We'll take care of 'em, Guy."

There had been some delay in gathering the Carter cattle, and they weren't quite ready when the men arrived at the Carter Ranch. Amos Carter met them at the holding grounds and explained that it'd be just a short time before the cattle were all gathered.

He turned to Lance. "Looks like married life agrees with you, son. You're gettin' fat as a town dog."

"Can't complain none," Lance said.

"Wal, they say that kissin' don't last – cookin' do."

Lance grinned. "Nice when a feller can have both."

Carter laughed and slapped his leg. "Shore right. You sound like a Texican already."

"I'm gettin' there, Mr. Carter. Sometimes it seems like I never lived anywhere else."

With Guy and the trail drovers lending a hand, the missing steers were quickly found and thrown in with the others. Slowly and calmly, they pushed the herd out of the gathering grounds and started on the trek to the jumping-off point near the MacDuff Ranch. By late afternoon, the drovers brought the cattle over the rim to where the main herd had been left.

Not a cow – not a rider in sight.

Lance and Guy rode hard down to the deserted flats. The ground had been churned up all across the valley floor and out through one end. Lance looked about frantically, then rode up beside Guy. "Stampede?"

Guy was looking at the ground. "I guess you could say that. But not by their selves. Look at all the horse tracks. Musta been twenty maybe twenty-five riders."

Leaving two riders in charge of the small Carter herd, the others spurred hard in pursuit of the missing cattle. The trail was broad, deep, and easy to follow.

As the sun plummeted behind the hills, they could hear the unmistakable lowing of cattle just over the ridge. Suddenly, a rider appeared, skylighted between them and the setting sun. Flourishing a rifle over his head he shouted, "Ayee, Gringo! Santiago say he will take the cattle now -- for the gold he doesn't yet have!"

Guy threw his rifle to his shoulder and got off a snap shot at the rider, but in the uncertain light, the bullet flew well off its mark. The rider let out a derisive laugh, whirled his horse, and disappeared into the brush across the ridge.

125

Guy looked puzzled. "What the hell was that all about?"

Lance shrugged his shoulder. "Who knows?"

He felt uneasy at the idea that his old foe knew exactly where he was and what he was doing.

Further questioning by Guy was averted by the arrival of a flushed, wet, and dusty Bain MacDuff on a horse lathered with sweat.

"Big bunch," he panted. "Hit us about noon. Swarmed on us like a hive of bees. Fred Smith cut 'em off. Held 'em maybe fifteen — twenty minutes. Dropped a couple of 'em. But, Lance, they got him. By the time I got there, they'd put three holes in his chest.

"I didn't even get to know him good. Now I never will. Anyhow, thanks to Fred, we got back maybe half the herd.

"Pedro is stayin' after 'em. Says he thinks he knows where they aim to cross the Rio."

Lance's face was grim and set. "You did right, Bain. Stay with the cattle you got; the rest of us will go after 'em. Maybe we can beat 'em to the crossing. And Bain, I'm really sorry about Fred Smith – really sorry."

Heading straight for the Rio Grande, the men raced into the darkness after the stolen cattle. At the river, the roiled water and churned-up mud told the story. They were too late. They heard the shouts of the Mexicans as they drove their booty on into the interior.

With a snarl of rage, Lance plunged his mount into the water. Guy Madden, following closely, cut in front of him. "Hold it, Lance."

With a sweeping arm, Lance motioned the man out of his way. "I'm goin' after 'em, Guy."

"Get ahold of yourself, boss. You can't do that."

"Why not?" Lance tried to push past the trail boss.

"Dammit! Because you'll get yourself and the rest of us killed. That's why not." Guy took a firm grasp of Lance's bridle. "That's Mexican country. They know ever' rock – ever' box canyon – ever' brush patch

"Not only that, but the Mexican troops would shoot us on sight if we go tearing through their country after those cattle. If we managed to get 'em away from the bandits, we'd never get 'em back across the river."

Lance grabbed off his hat and slapped it hard against his leg. "Where'n hell are the Mexican troops right now? Why ain't they here to help us get our cows back?"

"I'm afraid," Guy said, "they're a might selective about when they go into action. But believe me, it would be suicide to go into Mexico after them cows right now."

Reluctantly, Lance turned his horse back to the Texas side.

"All right, Guy. I sure don't want any more boys killed over them cows. But this just about wipes me out."

Lance felt a wrenching in his gut when he thought about the MacDuff Ranch pledged as security for the missing herd.

As they reached the bank, they came instantly alert at a sound from the edge of a large thicket near the upper bank. A rider emerged with two men on foot. It was Pedro with a rifle across the pommel of his saddle. The two men had hands tied behind them, and Pedro had a loop from his *reata* over their heads. At any hesitation of the men, he gave a sharp jerk on the rope which brought them reeling after his horse.

"*Señor* Madden!" Pedro shouted. "These two seem to have lost their horses in the brush."

Guy turned toward Lance. "Your call, boss, what do we do with 'em?"

Lance rode in close to the men. Dressed in loose fitting, once white pants of the peon, they also had the crossed bandoleers of bullets favored by Mexican fighting men on both sides of the law. Black hair hung down in ragged bangs on their foreheads and strung unevenly down their backs. Empty holsters swung from their belts.

Lance pivoted his mount to face Guy. "Would they have any information we might want?"

Guy considered the question for a moment. "Naw, I don't think so, Lance. Even if they knew where the cattle were going, it wouldn't help us much."

Lance rode slowly to the clearing, turned, and faced the other drovers. He burned with the idea that his ambition was to be the cause of Erin MacDuff losing the ranch she and Scotty had worked so hard for, and these men helped cause the problem

"Hang the bastards," he said.

CHAPTER 18

On the edge of the holding grounds, in a grove of live oak trees, they dug a rectangular hole in the prairie. In a rough, board box, the body of Fred Smith awaited burial. Erin MacDuff and Colleen drove out in the wagon and stood in the shade of the trees. Lance, George, Bain and Guy stayed nearest the grave while, just behind them, the other drovers waited beside their mounts.

Guy spoke. "Somebody oughta say somethin', boss."

"Not me. I never done anything like this."

Guy persisted. "You talk better'n any of us. You gotta do it, boss."

Reluctantly, Lance stepped up beside the box. Sweeping off his hat, he motioned everyone closer. "Now, folks, I don't really know what to say, but I reckon that don't matter much to Fred anymore. I didn't know ol' Fred very long. Likely some of you knew him a lot better'n I did. But I reckon I knew him well enough to like him – which I done.

"Now, we're fixin' to put Fred Smith in the ground. At least we all knew him as Fred Smith. Maybe that was his name, and maybe it wasn't. Don't make no difference to me. I knew him as a good man -- a hard worker -- a man that'd never let somebody else do his job for him.

"He was a purely good companion and would stand by his own crowd. The way he hung up his saddle would tell you that. Maybe some would think we shoulda took him into town to get buried, but I reckon not. The *brasada* was home to Fred. Maybe it was a little rough at times, but it gave him the kinda livin' he loved. I don't think Fred woulda wanted it any other way.

"I don't know nothin' about his religion, but I reckon he had one. And if God has any work to be done in the next world, I reckon He couldn't ask for no better hand than Fred Smith. I guess that's all I got to say."

Lance and Bain caught each end of a rope slipped under the crude coffin and lowered it into the hole. Erin and

128

Colleen stepped up, and each lay a small bunch of flowers from the MacDuff garden at the head of the grave.

Then, there was a rustling at the edge of the clearing as the drovers mounted their horses. Bareheaded, they approached the open grave, hats held on the saddle horns. One at a time, each rider rode to the edge of the grave, tossed in a single wild flower, whirled his horse, and rode at a gallop back to the waiting herd.

In a narrow swale at the end of the MacDuff holding grounds, the remnants of the trail herd were funneled through in a narrow stream. Booger Jim, stationed on one side of the herd, kept a running tally as the cattle were fed through. Cisco Red, sitting his horse on the other side, kept his own count.

After the cattle spilled back out onto the holding grounds, Booger rode over to where Guy and Lance watched the operation.

"I counted seven hundred forty-two head – Cisco caught seven hundred forty even. I think maybe he missed a couple that sneaked by over on my side."

Guy waved him off. "Close enough. Thanks Booger." He turned to Lance. "Got about half of 'em, the sunsabitches!"

"Dammit!" Lance exploded. "Hold 'em here a while, Guy. I gotta talk to George and Bain."

The men squatted on their heels to talk in the shade of the chuck wagon. Lance started the conversation. "Half the herd's gone, boys. Most were the ones I bought from Circle-T. George, most of yours are still here – and all of Mike's. Bain, a couple of hundred head stolen were MacDuff steers."

Bain wiped sweat from his face. "It was my fault. I was responsible for the herd when it happened."

"Not so!" George contradicted him. "You did the best anyone coulda expected. Musta been thirty or forty meskins against you and a handful of men."

Mike nodded in agreement.

Lance said, "No one blames you, Bain. Besides, it don't matter now. The cows are gone, and we ain't gonna get 'em back. What worries me is the note Erin signed pledgin' the MacDuff Ranch against the ones I bought."

George scratched his chin. "Hell, Lance, dig out that damn gold. I'll go along with it. I sure don't want Erin to lose her ranch."

Lance pursed his lips. "Don't think I haven't thought about it. But hell George, if it wasn't right to use it before, it

129

ain't right now. Just to get my butt outa a jam."

George laughed. "You thought it was all right before. You gave me hell."

"Yeah, but I was wrong."

They were interrupted by the arrival of Guy Madden at a lope.

"Hey, boss, I got a idea."

Lance walked over closer to where Guy had pulled up his horse. "What's on your mind, Guy?"

"Well, I know you bought a bunch of them cows on tick, and it's got you in a tight. But I know where we can get another buncha cows, and it won't cost you nothin'."

"What you got in mind, we turn rustlers?"

"Hell no. But over in the breaks of the Nueces, they's big bunches of cows -- wild ones -- don't belong to nobody. I think we could catch enough of 'em to fill out the herd in a couple of weeks with luck."

Bain sauntered up. "Wild cows? Yeah, they're there; I've seen 'em, but catchin' 'em is somethin' else again."

Guy nodded. "Never said it was easy. But it can be done. I've seen it done, and I've done it myself."

Lance frowned. "Reckon we could do it in two weeks, Guy? We'll be cuttin' it mighty thin with winter comin' on."

"Ain't no guarantees, boss, but it's a chance. Trouble is, we gotta risk some of the herd."

Lance glanced toward the others. "Most of them that's left don't belong to me, Guy. They're George's, Mike's, and Bain's."

"You wanta do it, Lance, you got mine," Bain said with a wave of his hand.

George chuckled. "Didn't have no cows when I came here. Reckon the world wouldn't end if I lost 'em now."

Mike said. "You don't even gotta ask, Mistah Lance."

The first days were spent building a sturdy log and brush corral. From the single opening left in the structure, two wings were extended out in a "V" shape with mounds of brush piled against it to disguise the man-made look. Once this was completed, the men were ready for the cow hunt.

Led by Guy Madden, the drovers rode single file into the brush, driving a number of cattle from the herd before them. About a mile from the corral, he led the cattle into a thick motte of brush and eased out the other side.

Dropping off a couple of new hands to stay with the cattle, the others strung out along the edge of the brush and continued the slow fox trotting pace. Lance was last in line.

There was a sudden crashing of the brush ahead, and every

130

rider leaned low over his horse's neck and thundered ahead at full speed. As a Southerner, Lance had always been at home in the saddle, an excellent horseman. But this wasn't riding -- it was a fight for survival. Captain Jess plowed straight ahead, crashing through whitebrush and guajillo, dodging the thicker limbs of mesquite.

Lance found himself all over the horse's back, and often as not, down on the mount's side. Spiny limbs slashed at his face and body as the animal plunged ahead on the heels of what Lance could only suppose to be the wild cattle. He quickly lost visual contact with the others and could trail the group only by the crashing sounds of brush and limbs.

He smashed through into a small clearing and saw Pedro up ahead, his mount standing perfectly still. Pedro motioned for him to stop. As Lance pulled up, he caught a glimpse of cattle moving through the thicker part of the brush.

He looked questioningly at Pedro who shook his head and held a finger to his lips. Then, he heard, once again, the familiar sound rising softly from all around – the quavering melody of the "Texas Lullaby" – the song of the brush.

He heard Pedro take up the tune, blending his voice with those of the other riders as he turned and walked his mount slowly through the brush. Some cattle came crashing into the clearing right at him. His mouth felt dry and his nose itched, but he sat still. The cattle stopped quickly, turned with a snort, and disappeared back into the thickness of the motte. As he turned to follow Pedro, he realized that he was crooning the same haunting tune as the others.

The riders continued their slow circling of the cattle for more than an hour. Then Lance saw Guy ride slowly out of the circle and off to one side. He dismounted and pulled the cinch of his saddle tighter, remounted, and returned to the circle. One by one, the other riders did the same.

Guy's voice rose louder as he moved out toward the corral. The other riders closed in on the cattle, pushing them toward the sound of Guy's voice. Lance could make out some decoy cattle among the skittish wild ones.

As Guy led the cattle into the wings of the corral, some of the wild cattle sniffed the air suspiciously. They darted in a group to one side, and seeing the barrier facing them, whirled in confusion.

The riders' voices grew louder, almost pleading, but the cattle bolted back in the direction from which they had come. Now, the riders gave a piercing yell and spurred their horses in a near solid front facing the oncoming herd. Confronted by this host of their most feared enemy, the cattle swerved back toward the wing, then straight into the corral entrance.

131

Quickly the men leaped from their horses and lashed strong poles across the opening. The herd was trapped.

There was no chuck wagon on this trip to serve as a welcome source of hot, strong coffee, sourdough biscuits and boiled beans. The men made a small fire to boil coffee beans, crushed and tied in a clean sock, which washed down dried jerky carried in wallets across their saddles.

Guy stood by the fire noisily slurping from a tin cup of boiling hot coffee. "Pretty good day, boys. Got seventy-five head – and got all our decoys back."

Lance sidled up beside Guy and spoke so no one else could hear. "Is it always that rough, Guy?"

"Rough?" The trail boss looked at Lance questioningly. "They won't get no easier than today. Usually it's a helluva lot tougher."

Lance sighed and went back to picking cactus thorns out of Captain Jess.

Guy Madden was right. None of the runs they made in the next few days were easier -- and some flirted with total disaster.

Once, as the cattle turned toward the corral, a herd of javelinas jumped out of the brush. All at once, the riders were caught in a melee of snorting javelinas, bellowing cattle, and plunging horses. All the wild cattle escaped and only with great effort were the decoys recovered.

But Lance was learning quickly the ways of the *brasada*. He learned there is never an opening – a soft spot – to enter a brush motte. As Guy put it, "No more'n you can find a warm spot to dive in an icy stream." He learned to hit the brush dead center at a hard run and "tear a hole through it."

He learned to ride all over, under, and alongside his horse and to fend off threatening branches with his arms, shoulders, and the top of his head. He learned to dodge one way, and in a split second, back the other. He found he had to keep his eyes open or risk having them gouged out.

Experienced hands "born to the brush" could follow a cow wherever that cow could go. Once he expressed disgust at himself to Booger Jim for falling behind in a chase. The cowboy hooted. "You're doin' fine, bossman. Ain't many of them prairie hands could stay with you now.

"Hell, we had one of them fellers out here a while back. He thought he was a real ripsnorter. We came outa the chase and found him sittin' in a clearing. He said he'd headed into the brush with the rest of us. Then, as the brush got thicker, he seen a rattlesnake start into it then have to stop and back out. Said if a damn rattlesnake can't get through that brush

132

he didn't figger he had no business tryin' it."

Lance cocked his head to one side. "Is that a true story, Booger? Or, just one of your windy tales?"

"True as can be, bossman. I kilt that rattler and kept the rattles to prove it."

He pulled up a string of rattles tied to his saddle strings.

Lance chuckled. "Don't see how anybody could doubt you now, Booger."

Booger pulled his horse away humming a tune. Then he broke into song about "*Little Bill and the Mean Black Steer.*"

"The steer he hit for nearby brush
A'snortin' fire and smoke.
And Bill he dabbed a brand new loop
Around ol' Blackie's throat.
The horse he squatted like a rabbit,
The cinch it broke like straw.
Both Bill's new saddle and his new catch rope
went driftin' down the draw."

Once on the drive, the mossy-horned wild cattle were edgy as a coyote in a dog kennel. Lance had thought that regular Longhorns off the range were wild and free creatures -- but these *cimmerones* were completely feral. Lean but muscular, they had the innate athletic ability of the wild beasts they were.

Guy Madden said they could "kick a tick off their nose with either hind foot, and with their horns could jab through a gnat in full flight."

Lance took his place near the wagon while Guy scouted out the area ahead. The nervous cattle were much harder to break to the trail than the ones Lance had taken earlier. The one advantage was that they covered more miles in a day -- and winter was coming fast.

Early in the drive, the cattle developed the habit of a nightly stampede. Not the bone rattling wild run of panic-stricken beasts, but just a brisk gallop to keep the drovers alert and away from sleep. This continued for five nights until Guy rode into the herd, spotted the brindle steer that was leading the runs, and shot him dead. After that there were no more routine stampedes.

Unlike the earlier drive, there was no lush tall grass to meet them at the edge of the prairie. Thousands of cattle preceding them up the trail had grazed and trampled the grass down to harsh nubs sparsely scattered on the brown prairie soil. The riders worked to keep the herd spread in a loose formation to give them maximum grazing from what little grass was available.

Crossing into Kansas, the drove passed through a dense thicket growing alongside a series of draws. The lead cattle had hardly passed out of sight into the brush when, with an unearthly bellow, the herd was scattered and running.

It was five miles of wind-splitting ride before the run was under control. It was obvious, even without a tally, that a large number of cattle were missing from the herd. With a flourish of his hat, Guy shouted, "Booger, Cisco, Pedro -- come on. Let's go get them cows."

Lance watched them ride into the brushy draw.

Lance trotted Captain Jess up to where Bain and George sat at the flank of the herd. He tugged his watch out of his pocket and frowned. "Boys, it's been two hours since they left. Think I'll drift back and see if they need any help."

"Good idea," George said. "Fire two shots if you need any help."

Lance turned back at a lope toward the distant brush. Entering the thicket, he backtracked the herd to the point where they'd entered. Still no sign of cattle or horsemen. He dropped down the draw about four hundred yards and reentered the thicket. After about ten minutes he heard the faint bawling of cattle from farther ahead in the bottom. He pointed Captain Jess toward the sound and let him pick his own way through the stunted timber.

Suddenly, the animal's ears started working back and forth. His front feet started a nervous prancing, and he nickered softly. Lance leaned up along his neck to peer into the glade just ahead. An object appeared to be hovering in the trees at the edge of the clearing. Lance could feel the hair prickle at the base of his skull and work upward over his ears. He could now see that the object was tied with a rope and was swaying in the breeze. A little closer and it was no longer an object but a man wrapped in a buffalo robe and hanging by his neck.

He gave Captain Jess his head and tore out toward the bawling cattle in a clattering run. As he broke out of the heaviest brush, he saw the missing cattle, now gathered into a small herd, and being moved into the open by Guy and the others. He slid the big bay to a stop beside Guy.

"Hey Guy, there's a feller back there hangin' in a tree."

Guy canted his head. "Sonuvagun."

Lance frowned "What's goin' on, Guy?"

The trail boss hooked a leg over his saddle horn. "Well, we found these cows in a little corral hid out back there a ways. There was a feller had a buffalo robe that coulda been used to flap to set off a stompede. So, we opened the corral and got our cattle back."

"And the man?"

Guy sat up straight. "I reckon he musta felt real bad about what he done. Guess he hung hisself so he wouldn't be tempted to steal any more cows."

Lance asked no more questions, but he felt a chill run up his back that had nothing to do with the approach of winter. He was committed to building an empire in the *brasada*, and this was going to be part of the price.

The wind was blowing cold out of the north by the time the drive reached the holding grounds outside Wilson's Gap. Big flakes of snow shifted with the wind before settling on the tops of brush or stubs of the grass. None seemed to be sticking on the ground.

Guy pulled the collar of his sheepskin jacket up around his ears. "Dammit, boss. Looks like a stomp lot around here. Ain't a blade of grass in sight."

Lance stared at the bawling herd. "Cows lookin' awful snaky too."

Guy nodded. "Like a bunch of gutted snowbirds."

This time there was no delegation to meet them -- no buyers driving out from town. They hunched their shoulders against the chilling wind and rode slowly into town. They found most of the buyers' offices closed and padlocked.

They lurched into the Longhorn Saloon to escape the cold. As they opened the door, a cold blast of air swept into the room with them. George struggled to close the door behind him. As they turned toward the bar, they could see that virtually every patron in the bar was staring in irritation at the source of the icy blast.

Lance looked around the room until he saw a familiar face, Dick Marlowe of the Merchant's Association. "Mr. Marlowe. May I buy you a drink?"

The pudgy merchant indicated the glass in front of him. "No thank you Mr. — ah — Morgan, isn't it? This one is enough for me then I've gotta get home."

"Suit yourself," Lance said amiably. "Where are the cattle buyers today?"

The man glanced up briefly then back down at his glass. "Most of 'em have been gone several weeks. Maybe they'll come back in the spring -- maybe not."

Lance's eyes clouded. "Man, I've got fifteen hundred head of cattle up here. What in hell am I gonna do with 'em?"

The man shrugged and averted his eyes. "Couldn't say. Might try Omaha. I've heard they was buyin' there."

Lance whirled back to the bar. "George, what the hell is goin' on here?"

George dragged out a chunk of tobacco and fitted it into his cheek. "Looks like we done brought somethin' up here, Lance, that nobody wants."

Bain looked bewildered. "Afraid he's right, Lance."

Lance started to speak but was interrupted by another cold blast from the door. The newcomer looked familiar to Lance, but he was unable to place him. The man stomped his feet vigorously to stimulate the circulation, then unbuttoned his Mackinaw and stepped to the bar. His eyes moved over the room as though he were taking inventory and assigning each person a place in his mind. He hesitated when he came to Lance, then lit up with recognition.

"Say, I know you. You're the young feller that faced down Frank Kennedy this last summer."

Lance faced the newcomer warily. George took a couple of steps to one side, and Bain put one hand on the butt of his revolver. Lance peered into the man's face.

"I'm Clint Murdock, town marshal. Hell, I owe you a drink. Hadn't been for you I'da been driftin' around out in California somewhere."

He stepped forward and extended his hand.

"I was deputy the night you tangled with Frank. You shoulda gone ahead and bought the little fool a one-way ticket to hell."

Lance smiled with relief. "Yeah, I remember. A lot's happened since then."

The marshal turned to the bartender. "Set 'em up here for my friends."

As the bartender poured the drinks, Murdock asked, "What are you doin' up here in the north country? Figgered you to be baskin' down in Texas this time of year."

Lance snorted. "I kinda wish we were. We got a herd outside of town. Now they tell us the buyers are gone."

"You got a herd out on that bald spot. Good Lord, they'll starve to death if you don't move 'em pretty soon."

George responded. "Move 'em where? With no buyers here — we got no place to go."

Lance jumped in. "Guess we could start 'em back toward Texas – but there ain't no grass left on that trail neither."

"Wait a minute," Murdock said. "All the buyers ain't gone yet. They's still a couple around gettin' their stuff together to leave. Prob'ly over to the hotel right now."

"Thanks a lot, Murdock." Lance was calling over his shoulder as he and the other two were almost out the door.

136

The hotel hadn't changed a bit. The room clerk, snoozing in his chair, didn't even glance up as they clomped straight through the lobby and into the dining room.

"Well, well, well. Looks like the Texians are back," one of the diners boomed as he pushed back his chair and dabbed at his mouth with a napkin. It was Colonel Mel Rankin who'd bought their earlier herd.

Lance moved quickly to his table. "Colonel Rankin, am I glad to see you."

"My pleasure, I assure you," he responded. "What are you gentlemen doing here? Riding the railroad north?"

Lance impatiently introduced George and Bain then launched straight to the point. "We brought up another herd, Colonel. We hoped you might make us an offer on it."

"A herd? You got cattle here?"

"Yessir. About fifteen hundred head."

"Son, I guess you haven't heard. We got us a full scale depression up north. No market for cattle right now."

"No market?" The words came up from Lance's gut.

The cattle buyer got to his feet and dropped a handful of coins on the table. "When you got no job -- you don't eat beef. It's about as simple as that. Jobs are scarce up north."

Lance gritted his teeth. "Gotta be a market somewhere."

Rankin pulled a coon's pecker toothpick out of his vest pocket. "Tell you what. I might be able to help you out a little. My company's got a government contract to get some beef out to the Indian Reservation in Nebraska. You ain't gonna like the price though."

"How much?" George asked.

"What kinda condition your cattle in. They in as good a shape as those you brought in this summer?"

Lance paused. "No sir, they're not. Tell you the truth, they're pretty damn skinny. Not much grass on the trail this time of year."

The cattle buyer laughed. "You're an honest man, Lance Morgan. I knew those cattle wouldn't be fat. I've seen that grass. Well, my company authorized me to pay $7.00 a head for those Indian cattle."

Bain and Lance exchanged distressed looks.

George muttered, "Won't more'n pay expenses."

Lance tugged at his hat. "If even that," he agreed.

"Wait a minute," the colonel continued. "I'm not through. I'm taking it on myself to bump that price a couple of dollars because you didn't try to pull a fast one on me."

George blurted, "Doggone Colonel, we appreciate that."

Lance made some quick mental calculations. That price would cover expenses and almost redeem Erin's pledge on the ranch. He held up his hand. "George is right, we do appreciate the offer, but where were you going to get your cattle if we hadn't come along?"

Rankin looked puzzled. "From our pens in Saint Louis, why?"

"Could you deliver them for $9.00 a head?"

The man threw back his head and laughed uproariously. "Lance Morgan, you're a pistol for sure. I like you, boy, but you're barkin' up the wrong tree. I can deliver out of Saint Louis for less than $9.00 a head. Now, do you want $9.00 for your starvin' cattle or not?"

Lance stuck out his hand. "You gotta deal, Colonel."

With a pale face, Lance counted out money to pay the drovers and watched the stack of bills shrink to almost nothing. He turned and walked away with the feeling that he was dead broke and was still about two thousand short of redeeming Erin's note. So much for dreams of quick riches on the cattle trail.

No one was in the mood to celebrate the end of this drive. Even the reckless drovers left town with most of their pay still in their pockets. In small groups, they turned their backs to the cold north wind and started drifting toward the *brasada* hundreds of miles to the south.

CHAPTER 19

Lance, George, and Bain drifted into the *brasada* just ahead of the coldest part of winter. They paused where the trail forked and George would split off toward his own spread. He eased up beside Lance.

"How much you short, Lance?"

Lance pursed his lips. "Need about two thousand to pay off Mr. Thompson. And I ain't likely to get it this winter."

George unfastened his saddlebag and removed a small packet. He thrust it into a startled Lance's hands.

"My share is $840, Lance. It won't cover it, but it might help."

Lance's face flushed. "I'll take it, George, because of Erin and the ranch. But it makes me feel mighty low."

"Since you're already feelin' that way, I might as well throw in my $935 right now," Bain said.

Lance smiled wryly. "That leaves me only about $325 short."

Bain shook his head. "You're not short at all, Lance. Mike told me if it was needed to make good that note, to use his share. His cattle brought a little over $500."

Lance trotted his horse a little to the side of the trail so no one could see the wetness on his cheeks.

Lance and Bain reached the comfort of the MacDuff ranchstead a week before Christmas. After paying his obligations at the end of the drive, Lance had allowed himself one small extravagance. Tucked down in his saddlebags, carefully wrapped in tissue paper, was a beautiful new blue dress for Colleen and a pair of tortoise framed reading glasses for Erin.

His blood raced with excitement as he swung off his horse by the gate. He had taken two steps toward the house when the door burst open and Colleen dashed across the porch to throw herself into his arms. Until he actually saw her, smelled the freshness of her silky hair and held her warm body close

139

to his, he didn't realize how much he had ached for her presence.

Over her shoulder, he could see that Bain had engulfed his mother in an embrace, and right by the porch, face split in a huge grin, stood Mike.

The fire crackled and popped, noisily ingesting a green stick of cedar that had been thrown on top. The snug warmth of the ranch house was a welcome luxury to Lance and Bain who had been weeks on the chilled prairie with nothin but a slicker for a ground cloth and the vastness of space for a ceiling. Just about every detail of the trip had been pumped out of them by Erin when she asked about George.

Lance frowned and stared into the fire. "Looks like George is gonna give up his place here. Wants to strike out to the plains up on the caprock."

"What?" Erin seemed startled by the news.

"Bain and I both tried to talk him out of it. Told him he ought to wait a year or so anyhow – get better prepared. But he just can't seem to wait."

"But that country's completely unsettled," Erin protested.

"Right, but he said somebody had to be first."

"When does he plan to leave?" Erin asked.

"Don't think he said exactly, did he, Bain?"

Bain crossed a booted foot over his knee. "I gathered he was gonna go early in the spring. Take his little bunch of cows and head out."

Erin frowned. "I hope that boy knows what he's doing. I sort of liked the idea of having him as a neighbor."

Christmas morning dawned clear and mild. After the usual early morning breakfast, at which Erin asked a special blessing "on this first Christmas day with our new family member," the MacDuff/Morgan clan tumbled happily into their seats around the tall and bushy juniper which, after being decorated with glass ornaments brought from the British Isles and strings of berries, served as an excellent Christmas tree. Colleen was radiant. Her sparkling eyes darted about the room, taking in every detail of the scene, but never for long before they rested again on the clean shaven face of her husband.

The room fell quiet as they heard a deep bass voice raised in the strains of "Silent Night." Mike had come up from the bunkhouse. Somehow he had managed to accumulate a small burlap bag of gifts. A little something for everyone.

There was a Spanish shawl for Erin, a new leather-bound tallybook for Lance, a pair of hand-tooled spur straps for

Bain, and a pair of silver earrings for Colleen.

Then, more gifts began appearing. Dug from the bottoms of trunks and drawers – dumped out of the depths of satchels and saddlebags — out of hiding places where they'd been secluded for months.

Lance proudly slipped on a new vest made of calfskin with the hair still on it – a gift from Colleen. It was from a lineback dun animal and had a dark brown stripe down the middle fading to lighter shades of tan toward the edges.

Colleen tucked her feet under her on the settee and snuggled close to Lance, hugging his arm close to her breast. "Darling, I love my new blue dress. But I'm afraid I won't be able to get into it for a while."

A look of consternation crossed his face. "Oh no," he groaned. "I thought I got it right. Did I make a mistake?"

She smiled at him. "Depends on how you feel about being a father. How do you feel?"

His eyes widened at the realization of what she had said. "Are you sure?" Knowing how inane the question was.

She nodded, her eyes never leaving his face, her question not yet answered.

She had to wait but an instant. With a whoop that turned all eyes his direction, he shouted, "I'm going to be a father!" He looked around. "I'm going to have a son," he said.

"Your first statement is almost certainly correct," said Erin. "I've suspected it for some time. It remains to be seen about the second."

Lance turned red, looking both confused and happy at the same time.

Erin continued. "Babies have been known to be girls, you know."

"Yes, I know," Lance responded. "Hey, Mike, did you hear about my boy?"

Mike grinned and bobbed his head toward the giggling Colleen. "I surely did, and I figger most of the county heard about it just now."

Bain, down on one knee putting on his new spur straps, raised his head. "What about me? I'm gonna be an uncle. But — when?"

Lance blinked rapidly. "When?" he asked Colleen.

"About the first week in May."

Lance was beginning to feel light-headed. "I've got a lot to do before then. I've got a son coming."

He suddenly discovered his mouth was dry. He stumbled toward the water bucket, took a long drink, and looked about in wonder. "My boy'll be a native Texian."

By midmorning, George Gibson arrived. With a loud

shout of "Merry Christmas," he swung down carrying a string of prairie chickens he'd shot for Christmas dinner.

Even before his foot hit the ground, Lance bolted out the door announcing the expected arrival of "his boy." Erin dug into her bottomless trunk and fetched out a wrapped and waxed package of chewing tobacco "shipped in straight from Virginia." George, knowing his habit was somewhat at odds with the woman's fastidious nature, was flabbergasted.

"If you're going to use the stuff," she sniffed, "you might as well chew the good kind."

Spring came early, as it often does to the *brasada*. Well before the Ides of March, the mesquite thickets were showing tiny pale green buds, which almost all the inhabitants took to promise no more freezing weather. Tallow weed, buttercup, and, when moisture conditions were favorable, wild vetch gave the cattle and horses an advance taste of spring greenery. Cattle sales of the year before had reduced grazing pressure and pasturage was plentiful.

Lance was anxious to avoid the disaster which had come so close in the fall of trailing cattle a thousand miles only to find no market for them. But trail cattle he intended to do. Texas was full of cattle -- both branded and unbranded -- and they had proven themselves capable of walking to market -- wherever that market happened to be.

The saloon in Terwilliger was about empty. Guy Madden and Lance sat alone at a small table near the back. Each had a mug of beer in front of him.

Guy furrowed his brow and gazed thoughtfully at the bottom of his glass. "Dunno, Lance. So far as I know, it ain't never been done. But — what the hell — don't mean it can't be done."

Lance leaned forward intently. He had just outlined a plan to start three herds of cattle to market at the same time. The total of six thousand head would be unmanageable in a single herd, but broken into three herds of equal size, could be handled very well. Through Indian country, and during other particularly dangerous circumstances, the herds could be combined at night for extra protection.

"And this time," Lance said, "I'll go into Wilson's Gap ahead of the herd to check out the market. If it's still down, we'll swing west into Colorado or up into Wyoming. Those gold miners will give us a market for beef."

"Who'd you have in mind to ramrod all those herds?" Guy inquired.

"That's something I wanted to ask you about. You'll be in charge of the first herd and overall. I figger Booger Jim

142

and Cisco Red ought to be able to handle the other two -- or Pedro maybe."

Guy drummed the tabletop with his fingers. "Yeah. Booger can do it. So can Cisco -- if he really wants to. He's not quite as settled as Booger. Still a lot of kid in him -- but he knows cows about as well as anybody I know. As for Pedro -- it'd never work. You won't find no cowboys that'll work for a meskin no matter how good he is. Reckon we're a little too close to 'remember the Alamo' for that. Never mind that Pedro's uncle died at the Alamo fightin' for Texas right alongside Col. Travis. But that don't matter to some folks. They still just see a meskin. May not be right -- but that's the way it is."

Lance settled back in his chair. "That's about what I figgered to hear. So, let's get at it."

Lance was in an expansive mood at the supper table. With enthusiasm running high, he failed to notice the warning frown on Erin's face as he rattled on about the upcoming cattle drive.

"George will be trailing with us as far as the turn off to Fort Griffin, then he'll cut over toward the plains country. We'll spread the three herds so they can get good graze and take 'em on to market. I'll be going ahead to check markets and prices."

Colleen didn't feel well at all. Even she had noticed extended periods of irritability. Her expanding body made her feel clumsy, awkward, and vulnerable.

Lance chuckled. "We expect to take the three . . ."

Colleen slammed her knife and fork to the table. "I don't want to hear any more about your dumb cattle drive! That's all I've heard from you for weeks -- and I'm sick of it!"

She pushed back her chair, and leaving a shocked and dismayed Lance in her wake, she bolted to her room.

Lance looked hastily around the table. "I'm sorry, Erin. This is my fault. I'll go talk to her."

"Just a minute, Lance." Erin lay a hand on his arm. "Things are just going fast for her right now. Maybe a little scared with the baby coming -- and you going to be gone."

"But I'm doing this for her -- the baby -- for all of us."

"Are you, Lance?" the older woman smile patiently. "We have a fine ranch here. Enough for almost any family."

"But, I didn't do anything to build it. Scotty did it — you and Bain — it's not really mine. I have to . . ." He stammered to a stop. His excessive use of first person singular was obvious even to him. He continued weakly, "build something myself."

"I understand how you feel, son. But I can assure you that no one thinks there's anything wrong with it but you. If you could only be content with what we have . . ."

"I'm sorry, Erin, I don't think I can do that."

Erin sighed deeply. "I was afraid that was the case. I'll try to help Colleen understand – but she's not exactly in her most reasonable state of mind."

Erin gazed fondly at the miserable young woman who sat defiantly vulnerable in the wooden rocker in her bedroom. She knew something of the feelings that dominated her daughter's emotions. The unreasoning shame for her misshapen body and failing complexion. The resentment that she alone carried physical evidence of the upcoming event. The paranoid sensitivity to the slightest sign of neglect from her partner – real or imagined.

She knelt at her daughter's side and placed an arm across her shoulders in a protective gesture. "He doesn't mean to be uncaring, my dear. He loves you very much, and he's very excited about the baby."

Colleen's lips were a thin line. "He has a strange way of showing it."

"He doesn't understand, Colleen, what it means to carry a baby in your body twenty-four hours every day, seven days a week. He doesn't know how your changing body can seem like that of a stranger – the feeling that you're swollen and unattractive – that your feet hurt – that you want someone to hold you and tell you everything's all right."

"All he really cares about is that stupid cattle drive."

"No, dear. He really believes that he's making these cattle drives, expanding our operations, mostly for you and the baby. He wants you to have everything success can bring. Most of all, he wants you to be proud of him."

"But that's not what I want. I could be very proud of him if he'd just stay home -- if he'd be by my side when the baby's born -- be in my bed at night. We already have a ranch good enough for anyone."

"Not good enough for your husband, my dear. You're married to a very proud and stubborn young man. The war, and now Reconstruction, has been very hard on him. He intends to operate on a scale so large that nothing – no one can take it from him again. Try to understand."

"I do understand. I just want him to understand me sometimes."

The leave taking at the MacDuff Ranch was one of the low points of Lance Morgan's young life. Colleen said her goodbye sitting despondently on the edge of her bed. No

144

amount of tender persuasion nor ambitious promises of what the drive would mean to their future could coax a smile to her lips. Only after Lance had mounted and was riding away did she rush to the window and press her face against it in the agony of futility. Lance rode straight toward the dawn-streaked sky without looking back.

This time, Lance welcomed the mind-numbing stress of driving six thousand fidgety Longhorns over the trail. The activity soon dulled the guilt and afforded him at least some respite from the painful memories of the parting with Colleen. As Guy put it to one of the trail hands. "The boss is in a real horn-tossin' mood – got his dauber 'way down."

He drove himself with little regard for fatigue or pain. He spread himself between the three herds, overseeing every detail of the operation in spite of the unquestioned competence of his drovers. His self-imposed responsibilities denied him even the satisfaction of staying with the herd until George turned off toward Fort Griffin. Instead, he had to move well out from the herd so that if a market failed to materialize at Wilson's Gap, they could turn toward another destination with a minimum of delay.

CHAPTER 20

A week remained in June as Lance rode down the familiar single street of Wilson's Gap – still early for Texas trail herds. He found buyers, many with fat government contracts for beef to feed the reservation Indians. Among the buyers, their old associate, Colonel Mel Rankins.

He seemed genuinely pleased to see the young cowman. "Got three herds comin' at once? I swear you Texians would walk those cattle into hell if the devil would furnish a market. Let's get somethin' to eat. Here — have a cigar."

An hour later, the colonel pushed back his plate, putting a match to his big cigar. Squinting his eyes against the ensuing cloud of smoke, he got down to business. "I'm gonna put it to you straight. I want those cattle of yours – and I want 'em bad. I got contracts in my pocket for more cattle than these other buyers around here ever hope to see.

"I can give you a price that'll make your eyes bug out and still make a nice profit for myself. But you gotta deliver. How you figger to get around the quarantine?"

Lance just stared blankly.

"You don't know about the quarantine?"

"Not until now. What quarantine?"

"Aah, those grangers down around the state line have been claimin' that Texas cattle been spreadin' a fever among their farm cows down there. Pushed through a law that says you got to winter your cows above the fever zone, or you can't take 'em through."

"Never heard of such a thing!" Lance's face mirrored his disbelief. "I can't hold three herds through the winter up here. Where does the quarantine line run?"

Rankin's face creased in a frown. "The legal line runs just about straight south of here to the border. You could swing a few miles to the west and miss it. But there's a bunch of jayhawkers and redlegs left over from the war who've taken it on themselves to enforce their own quarantine wherever they find a herd of Texas cattle."

A slight smile crept over Lance's face. "Just why is that bunch worried about the fever?"

Rankin puffed furiously on his cigar. "They don't give a damn about the fever. It's just an excuse to take over the cattle. Now, I don't like to deal with those people, but if they come in here next week with your cattle, well — I'd rather buy from you – but I gotta buy from somebody."

Lance stood and tugged his hat down firmly on his head. "You just sit tight, Colonel Rankin. You'll get your cattle -- and you'll get 'em from me. And thanks for the information."

Rankin chuckled and shook the young man's hand. "I believe you aim to do it. Good luck to you."

Lance traveled light and fast. He put Captain Jess into a ground-eating lope that soon left Wilson's Gap far behind.

Well along the road toward Fort Griffin, George Gibson stood in his stirrups and twisted to watch the line of cattle file past him. Heads bobbing up and down as they walked, the procession moved through a shallow swale. Edging through the narrow gap, the popping of horn against horn was almost continuous. As the last of George's one hundred fifty head passed through, a young rider with bandana pulled up over his nose and mouth pulled his mustang up beside George.

"They travelin' good, Mr. Gibson."

George shifted his cud from one cheek to the other. "Yeah. Don't reckon they'll give me any trouble, Cliff. Fact is, I feel kinda guilty takin' you away from the big herd. I could handle 'em now, if you wanted to get on back."

"Don't know about that, Mr. Gibson. You'll have to be drivin' a wagon after we pass Fort Griffin. Besides, Mr. Madden told me to see that you got these cows up to the plains country, and I reckon that's what I better do."

The rider tugged down the bandana to reveal the beardless but freckled face of a boy looking to be about sixteen years of age. Hair so blond it was almost white showed from under a shapeless hat pulled low on his head. His grin exposed a row of even white teeth.

"Besides, this is the first chance I've had to work with cattle on the trail. Been wranglin' the remuda for several drives now. It'll feel good to get away from ol' Charlie. That ol' belly-cheater always kept me hoppin' to fetch firewood and prairie coal for him."

"Before we get where we're goin', Cliff, you just might like the idea of gatherin' cow chips for ol' Charlie."

Far to the east, Lance drew near the main herd. He could

hear it well before he could see it. The creaking and clanking of Charlie's wagon was a staccato counterpoint to the low bawling of cows and the rumbling of the herd bulls, all coming from over a low rise covered with tall prairie grass and bordered by a ragged line of bois d'arc trees. Lance paused at the crest of the ridge almost stunned by the spectacle before him.

From his vantage point, he could see two thousand Longhorn cattle loosely spread over two miles of verdant prairie. Back another mile, came a second herd of equal size. And on the far horizon, was a third herd just barely visible. Each herd was offset from the others so none of them had to trail directly behind another. For the first time, the true magnitude of what he was trying to do came through with the clarity of the cloudless sky over his head.

His nostrils dilated as he drew in the first warm, clean bovine smells of the advancing herd. With a touch of his spurs, he trotted down to where Guy Madden rode in the lead of the first of the herds.

Lance nudged Captain Jess into step with the trail boss's big dun. "How's it been, Guy? Any problems?"

"Pretty smooth, boss. Smallish bunch of Comanches tried to make off with some of the remuda, but we managed to hold 'em off. Had to fire a few shots. Thought we might have a real stompede — but the cows never turned a hair. Got real lucky there. How about yourself? We gonna have a market in Wilson's Gap?

"Yeah. Good market. But we gotta loop around a little west of town. They got some kind of quarantine set up on our old trail."

"Quarantine? What the hell for?"

"They claim our cattle carry a fever that kills their stock."

Guy turned to Lance, "That's crazy, boss. Our cows ain't sick."

"Just some Yankee trick to get our cows cheap. Anyhow, better not mess with 'em if we don't have to."

That night, Guy pointed the wagon tongue a little west of north to give the herd a new direction, and the next morning the combined herds swung well west avoiding the settlements of seething grangers.

Three days later, the drove crossed the line out of Indian Territory and into the state of Kansas. Late in the afternoon, they approached a timbered creek to the right of their path. Guy swung his horse around to meet Lance coming in from the swing position.

"Lance, I think we'd best give the cows a drink here and

bed 'em down on the other side of the creek. I'll ride up and check out the best waterin' spot."

Guy rode toward the brushy bottom at a gallop. Just before he reached the first timber, the big dun squatted and slid to a stop. Out of the brush rode a large band of mounted men loosely grouped around one Lance took to be their leader, big and burly with a bushy, red beard. As Lance touched spurs to his mount, he saw the man ride out from the group to face Guy Madden.

Lance pulled up beside Guy. "Any problem, Guy?"

Lance's short shotgun rested lightly on the pommel of his saddle.

"These fellers say they're gonna take the herd."

Lance made a quick count – about thirty-five hardcases.

"The hell they are!" Lance said calmly. He stared, unblinking, at the red-bearded man.

The man frowned and fidgeted. "We're the Grangers' Protective Association. And we ain't lettin' them Texas cattle spread poison to our herds."

"Like hell!" Lance exploded. "You're a thief and liar. You're no more a farmer than that lead steer back there."

Lance heard the horses coming up behind him. Without looking, he could sense the other drovers spreading out in a single line behind him. Guy sidestepped his horse to open up a space between himself and Lance.

The redbeard grimaced. "I'll tell you what I'll do. Them cows look purty healthy. I'm willin' to pay you two dollars a head for 'em — so you won't have a total loss."

Lance smiled grimly. "And I'll tell you what I'm gonna do for you. If you and your men just turn around and ride away, I'm gonna let you live.

"I got twenty-three Texas cowboys here that cut their teeth on rattlesnakes and mesquite limbs. If you're huntin' trouble you can call in the dogs and put out the fire — your hunt's all over."

Lance heard the soft-stepping ponies of his drovers moving up beside him. The redbeard tried to stare back at the young man, but his gaze dropped. He jerked his head in a signal to his men, whirled his mount, and the entire band galloped back down into the creek bottom. Lance watched them until they were out of sight.

Colonel Melvin Rankin was true to his word. The price was $50 a head in Yankee greenbacks – more than Lance had imagined possible for cattle valued in Texas at no more than five dollars a head.

Lance stretched out, fully clothed, in his hotel room. But

149

in spite of his fatigue, excitement banished any possibility of sleep. He paid the men a bonus equal to their pay for the drive, calculated all the expenses, and found he had a profit in excess of $100 thousand dollars. Even with a split to the other owners back in Texas, his share would come to more than $50 thousand.

He rolled onto his back, hands clasped behind his head. Judging by the noise outside his window, the boys were getting full use of their extra money. He rose from the bed, walked to the open window, and drank deeply of the night air. He would have a son by now -- a son with a wealthy father. Life was good.

After a hearty breakfast in the hotel, Lance sauntered out onto the shaded porch taking a look up and down the street. A drummer's wagon moved slowly down the street toward the hotel. A whirl of wind kicked up dust and paper off the boarded walk. Nothing else seemed to be stirring.

Lance idly watched the wagon pull off to the side of the street and the driver lock the brakes. The man was tall and heavyset. Dark hair showed around the edges of a black derby hat. He wore a black suit, white shirt and black string tie. He gazed at the vacant street and consulted a gold, flip-top watch attached to a slim gold chain strung across his vest.

He snapped the watch shut and nodded toward Lance in a friendly way. "Appears early for the folks hereabouts."

Lance returned the nod. "If you'd tried to sleep in this town last night, you'd understand why."

The man chuckled appreciatively. "No matter. I've got the time to wait. In the meantime, sir, if you have a few moments, I'll show you a marvel that'll change the lives of every person in the West."

Lance strolled toward the wagon. "I could hardly turn down a chance like that."

"You won't regret it, sir." The drummer beamed. "Name is Hartley — William F. Hartley of the Winchester Repeating Arms Company." He reached into the wagon pulling out a sleek rifle with gleaming brass frame and butt plate. It had a lever just over the trigger through which Hartley put his fingers.

"I have here a brand new weapon – the Winchester Model 1866. Holds fifteen .44 caliber cartridges which it can fire as fast as you can work the lever and pull the trigger. You have my personal guarantee, sir, that a resolute man, well-mounted and armed with this weapon cannot be captured under any circumstances."

Hartley handed the rifle into Lance's willing hands. He

put the weapon to his shoulder and sighted down the barrel. "How many shots did you say it would hold?"

"Fifteen shots, Mr. . . . ."

"Morgan — Lance Morgan."

"Yes sir, Mr. Morgan. This is a repeating rifle. Gives you the effective firepower of a whole platoon."

"How much?"

"Sir?"

"How much? What do they cost?"

"Well sir," the drummer started, "I've been selling these fine arms for $50 all the way from Kansas City to here – but I'll make you a special price bein' you're the only one here right now – just $35."

Lance took another look down the barrel and worked the lever a couple of times. "Give you $250 for ten."

Hartley paused as though making mental calculations "You gotta deal, Mr. Morgan. Where do you want 'em?"

"Just hold them here for me, Mr. Hartley. I'll bring your money within the hour."

Lance moved on down the street to the livery stable. The door to the little office was open, so he walked straight in. A smallish old man, made smaller yet by a slight hunch in his shoulders, scurried from behind the table which served as his desk.

"Mr. Morgan it's all ready for you just like I promised."

"And the grey trotter?"

"Yes sir. Got him at a good price – $45 cash."

Lance smiled. "You did a good job, Otto."

Lance unbuttoned his shirt, opened a leather pouch buckled around his waist and extracted a handful of bills. "That's $350 for the buggy – $45 for the horse – and here's an extra $10 for doin' such a good job for me. Now, let's get hitched up, and I'll be ready to go."

They stepped through a side door into the large barn adjacent to the office. Down both sides were box stalls for horses and mules with a wide aisle down the middle. In that aisle sat the object of their immediate attention, a two-wheeled buggy with a gleaming lacquered finish decorated with gold leaf designs. The wheel spokes and shafts were deep wine red.

"She's a beauty, Mr. Morgan. Brought in from St. Louis. Ain't never seen nothin' like that around here."

Lance laughed. "Nor anywhere else I allow. What was a cattle buyer doin' with a rig like that?"

The old man scratched the end of his nose. "Beats me. Reckon he liked that false bottom for carryin' money. His company didn't want it -- told me to sell it."

"How'd he die anyway?"

"Lead poisonin' – bad case. Him and a tinhorn tangled over a game of faro down to the Texas House. Reckon his temper was a little faster'n his gun."

The little man opened one of the box stalls and led out a sleek dappled grey gelding. Within minutes the animal was hitched to the rig, and Lance drove it down the street to the hotel. Guy Madden was sitting out front.

"Whooee, boss! Some kinda rig. Where'd you get that?"

Lance grinned sheepishly. "Got it off a dead cattle buyer you might say. Fair takes your breath away, don't it?"

Guy stepped down from the porch to take a closer look. "Damn, that thing is built."

"Yep. She's made for the rough roads all right. Say Guy, you seen Booger or Cisco this morning?"

"Naw. I figger they're still poundin' their ears this morning. They were really puttin' on the rollers last night."

Lance looped the reins around the brake handle and swung to the ground. "Yeah, I heard 'em most nearly to daybreak. Guess they aimed to hang and rattle 'til sunup."

Guy chuckled. "I saw Cisco 'bout midnight. Had on some new duds -- purple silk bandana around his neck, a brown checked cottonade suit with the legs tucked into a pair of red top boots. Had a snootful of Kansas sheep dip and a rimfire cigar in his mouth."

Lance said, "I'd appreciate it if you could round 'em up. When I pull out, I'll have a boodle of cash in this buggy. I'd purely welcome some company on the road home."

Guy rubbed his chin with his thumb. "Yeah, I'll bet. I 'spect me'n the boys'll be pleased to ride shotgun for you."

Shortly after noon, the little caravan pulled out of town heading south. Lance drove his shiny new buggy with the high-stepping dappled grey between the shafts. Captain Jess, secured to the back with a brand new plaited horsehair halter, trotted serenely alongside. Flanking the buggy was the trio of Guy, Booger Jim, and Cisco Red. Proudly displayed by each of the riders was a gleaming, brass clad Winchester booted on the saddle.

Lance's voice boomed over the clatter. "How you boys feelin' today?"

Booger Jim rode close to the buggy so he wouldn't have to raise his voice. "Boss, my head feels so big it'd throw a rat into a sweat just to run around it. And just between us," he whispered, "that Cisco's gonna be useless as a knot in a stake rope for a couple of days."

CHAPTER 21

The breaks leading from the prairie up the escarpment to the High Plains, so easily crossed on horseback, was a much more formidable obstacle to George Gibson in his heavily loaded Murphy Wagon pulled by a team of four mules. Leaving his small herd in the care of Cliff, the young wrangler, he spent half a day riding the edge of the plateau in search of an easy way up. Cliff had coffee and beans boiling in the coals by the time he rode back in.

His smile flashed up at George. "How's it look, Mr. Gibson?"

George swung heavily off his horse. "Ain't no easy way up. They's a little draw 'bout a mile south we can follow part of the way – but we'll have to figger a way to get to the top. May have to backpack it up."

George's words were accurate. After going as far as they could go up the draw, they unloaded the cargo, dismantled the wagon and using the mules and themselves as pack animals, they carried the outfit up the rugged slope.

"Let me tell you a thing, Mr. Gibson," Cliff panted as he leaned against a jutting rock. "My feet jest ain't made right for this ground work. My butt's made to fit a saddle. Don't nothin' function right scufflin' around here in the dirt. I make a better hand from the hurricane deck of my pony than I do afoot."

George moved up and looked down from the top. "Rather be hustlin' cow chips for ol' Charlie, would you?"

Cliff took a deep breath and straightened under his load. "If that's a feller's choice in life – it's a mean one."

Henry and Helen Porter heard the faint but unmistakable lowing, bawling, and clattering sounds of an approaching herd. Picking up his Sharps .50 caliber, Henry eased into the doorway and gazed across the swale. "Looks as though we're about to have company, my dear."

Helen sent the youngster scooting up to his loft, picked up

a leather bag of ammunition, and stood behind her husband. The first cattle just nosed over the ridge when a rider swung past them coming toward the cabin at a lope.

Henry stepped outside, making sure to stay in the shadows of the portico. The rider rode straight to the house stopping his lathered mount at the hitching rail in front. He pushed back his hat and squirted a stream of tobacco juice. "Howdy, Henry."

Henry leaned his rifle against the house and stepped off the porch. "Howdy, George." He turned and spoke to Helen. "It's just George Gibson."

The woman rushed outside. "You men, I declare. 'Just George Gibson' indeed! Get off that horse, George Gibson, and come in this house."

Grinning broadly, the two followed through the door.

Glancing furtively over his shoulder, Lance spoke softly to the horseman riding nearest to the buggy. "They're still there, Guy. Been doggin' us for a half an hour now. What do you think they're gonna do?"

Guy didn't need to look. "Hard to tell, boss. But they're Comanches right enough. And whatever they're gonna do, they've already decided."

Just then, the warriors let out a series of high-pitched yelps and galloped past the men about a hundred yards to their left. Circling back, the Indians formed a line, eighteen abreast, directly across the buggy's line of travel.

Then followed a spectacle such as Lance had never seen before. The Indians' faces, as though split down the middle, were painted half black and half bright carmine red. Most had headdresses of buffalo horns and carried red-painted lances with feathers attached. Shields were painted in gaudy colors and enclosed in a circle of feathers that fluttered with every movement.

As he watched, two of the warriors broke to the front of the group and put on a dazzling display of horsemanship, riding at breakneck speed, vaulting on and over their ponies.

Lance pulled the grey to a halt. The three horsemen took positions a few steps in front of the buggy. One of the Comanches, with a shrill yell, galloped straight toward Lance and the drovers. About thirty yards away, he slid his pony to a stop and plunged his lance into the ground.

Guy muttered out of the side of his mouth. "Stay here, boys. I think they wanta talk."

Guy moved forward at a slow dogtrot, hand held palm out in the sign of peace.

The Indian sat with his arms folded until Guy approached

within about ten yards. Then, he pointed a finger at Guy's face and grunted, *"Tejano!"*

Guy replied quickly, "No." He pointed toward the north. "Kansas."

The Indian frowned and made motions with his hands.

Guy nodded. "Kansas."

The warrior scowled uncertainly, pulled his spear out of the ground, and made a move to turn away. Then, suddenly he whirled and jabbed a finger toward Guy's saddle rig.

"Tejano!" He screamed and lunged his pony forward, drawing his spear back alongside his ear.

Guy's hand flashed toward his belt and the bark of his .44 revolver echoed across the prairie. The Indian toppled backward over his pony's hips and hit the ground hard. He rolled and struggled to his feet, but Guy fired again, and he pitched forward on his face.

The other warriors, with shrill yipes and shrieks, dashed toward the trail boss, nocking their arrows to their strings as they rode. But by then Booger and Cisco had pulled their Winchesters and spurred forward. Lance, siting in his motionless buggy, pulled up his rifle and fired quickly. The lead warrior, hit in the middle of the chest, slowly slipped off his galloping mount.

The three drovers opened up on the advancing warriors with devastating effect. Three more Indians fell dead under the withering fire and another was unhorsed. One of the others pulled him up behind him as they all turned to flee from the unexpected firepower of the repeating rifles.

The three drovers, exulting in the effectiveness of their new weaponry, spurred in hot pursuit of the confused enemy. Lance set the brakes on the buggy, untied Captain Jess, and leaped into the saddle. Although the Indians' flight had taken them out of sight over the ridge, he followed quickly after the sounds of battle.

Topping the ridge, he could see the drovers close on the heels of the war party. Even with the superior firepower of the new rifles, they could not be fired accurately at a gallop, and he could see little effect from the shooting.

He saw Guy give the signal to pull up, and the three stopped and turned back toward Lance. He trotted out to meet them. He could no longer see any signs of the savages. Then, with the suddenness of a panther attack, a figure hurtled out of the scrub brush in front of his horse and leaped high to drag Lance from the saddle.

He lashed out with the shotgun he carried across his pommel and felt it jar heavily against something solid. Instinctively, he hit the ground rolling, but the brown

155

apparition was with him all the way. A strong feral scent assaulted his nostrils, and he swung his gun barrel at it.

As it fell back from the blow, Lance could see it was one of the Comanches who had apparently lost his mount and was hiding in the brush. Blood ran from a gash on the Indian's forehead. But, with a snarl, the savage launched himself forward, a flashing knife held low and forward.

Lance stepped backward, but his heel caught in tall tangled grass, and he fell on his back. With a yell of triumph, the Indian leaped at him, knife extended. Desperately, Lance thumbed back the hammer of his short shotgun and jerked the trigger. He felt smothered by the weight of the Comanche who collapsed across his face. With a shudder of revulsion, he pushed the body to one side.

He struggled to his feet and stood panting over the body of his fallen adversary. Only then did he begin to feel a dull pain in his side. He put his hand to it and felt the warm wetness of his own blood oozing through his fingers. He sank slowly to his knees, then everything went black.

"Say, boss. You had a close one for sure."

Lance could hear the voice he recognized as Guy Madden's, but the blackness remained. Panic engulfed him, and both hands went to his eyes. They were tightly closed. Gradually, he eased open the lids and was rewarded with a blurry view of three faces peering down at him. He rubbed his eyes, and the blurriness disappeared.

"What happened?"

Guy said, "That injun tried to put his knife in your gizzard. Damn near done it too. But I reckon it missed the vitals. Gonna have a sore side for a while though."

"Everybody else all right?"

Guy replied laconically, "Ever'body on our side."

"What about the other side?"

"I reckon we furnished 'em plenty of stories to tell their grandchildren. Reckon we stretched out seven or eight of 'em. I don't s'pose they'd ever seen repeater rifles before."

Lance pulled himself to a sitting position and found he'd been carried to the shade of the buggy and stretched out on his bedroll.

Cisco squatted beside him. "You makin' it, boss?"

"Yeah, thanks, Cisco. Just a little light-headed. What do you think set those Comanches off anyhow?"

Guy scratched his chin. "Maybe they wanted to show what great warriors they was. But I think mostly was 'cause they just don't like Texians. I almost had 'em persuaded we was from Kansas, then they took a good look at our saddle

156

riggin'. Toe fenders on the stirrups, brush-rigged all the way. Soon as he seen that saddle that Comanche wasn't buyin' no story 'bout Kansas. But I bet next time, they look for them Winchesters a'fore they light into somebody."

Cisco looked over his shoulder as he sauntered out toward his grazing horse. "Hell, I may just change my nationality 'fore I run into any more of them redskins."

"Hoo boy!" Booger called out. "What you gonna do — pass yourself off as some fodder forker? Brush popper stands out all over you – jest like you'd done fell in a big bucket of Texas. It won't wipe off — it won't wash off. You gonna be Texian 'til you turn toes down – that's a fact."

Lance got to his feet and gingerly climbed into the buggy seat. He looked over at his trail boss. "Erin's liable to give you what-for for usin' the material for her new dress to wrap my rib cage."

Guy stepped into his saddle. "I think she'll figger it was well used."

Brent MacDuff Morgan lay flat on his back in a pile of clothing in the middle of the floor checking out his toes. His mother mentally inventoried the large cupboard, now lined with canned food prepared for the coming winter. Nearby was a handsomely crafted cradle of oak, temporarily deserted for the coolness near the floor. Wet cheesecloth covered the open windows on the south to cool the hot August wind as it entered. Erin sat comfortably on the couch stitching up a tear in one of Bain's shirts.

The women looked up as Bain walked quickly through the room to take a rifle from the rack. "Riders comin'."

Colleen looked out the window, and saw Mike easing up to the corner of the yard with one of Scotty's old shotguns. She could see a wisp of dust from beyond the horizon. "Not enough riders to be bandits," she whispered.

Bain nodded. "Not if that's all of them."

He slipped quickly out the door and stationed himself at the opposite end of the house from Mike. Erin rose, quietly took another rifle off the rack, and stood just inside the half-opened door.

The riders came straight over the ridge, making no attempt at concealment – a good sign. Two – then three – riders and a buggy pulled by a grey trotter. Erin glanced back into the room where Colleen had picked up the baby and moved to a rocker in the corner. "Better make yourself pretty, girl. Your husband is home."

The harsh bitterness that had raged inside Colleen at

Lance's departure had been dispelled by long months of empty loneliness and the pain-washed ecstasy at the birth of their son. Lance returned home to a woman much like the one he'd married, loving and passionate. Plus, she had an additional measure of warmth and tenderness that childbirth instills in many women. Her childlike playfulness, her open and vulnerable wonderment remained, but tempered by a new sense of maturity and calm assurance that made her even more wonderfully enchanting than before. By mid-afternoon, oblivious to appearances, she and Lance deftly maneuvered themselves into the privacy of their own room.

Their hunger for one another was an electric current that set off tingling sparks of passion at each touch. His mouth hungrily searched out hers. Her lips yielded, not passively but as active participants inviting his invasion. His hands explored every contour of her body which flexed against his in response. Hastily, they moved to the bed where, with both fully clothed, he took her with her dress pulled up around her waist. Then, with the fierce intensity of their hunger sated for the moment, they began the leisurely rediscovery of one another – body and soul.

Days passed quickly at the MacDuff Ranch. Lance bought the twelve thousand acre Hayden Ranch, which had blocked MacDuff expansion to the south, for $9 thousand. Guy Madden, Booger Jim, and Cisco Red hired on as full-time ranch hands. As northern money began to trickle into Texas, there was renewed interest in the excellent horses turned out by the MacDuff *manada*.

All winter, creaking wagons rolled into ranch headquarters discharging loads of cypress and pine lumber and other building materials hauled in from Louisiana and East Texas to go into a major expansion and renovation of the ranch house. Under the critical eye of a contractor brought in from San Antonio, a crew of local laborers painstakingly transformed the former home of Scotty MacDuff into a splendid mansion of English Tudor design.

While she uttered no word of protest, Erin's eyes sometimes misted as she watched the secure haven of many memories submerged beneath the huge and impressive but alien structure taking shape over her head.

Brent MacDuff Morgan, unconcerned with any happening outside his immediate vicinity, grew fat and sturdy – gurgling happily over the lavish attention of a doting father and mother, a grandmother, a proud uncle, four affection-hungry cowboys, and a former slave who delighted in remembrances of a one-time master.

158

It was soon December, and the first chilling norther of the winter whistled down the dusty streets of Terwilliger. Lance stepped out of the courthouse in the middle of the square and turned up his collar against the bite of cold air. The faint odor of wood smoke teased his nostrils an instant before being snatched away by the swirling wind. He thrust hands into his pockets and half-ran across the street to the Terwilliger Bank. Shoulders hunched, he burst through the door and pushed it shut against the pressure of the norther.

The potbellied stove in the small lobby shimmered with heat waves. The room felt uncomfortably hot after the chill of the outside air. Lance strode across the lobby, unbuttoning his jacket as he went. He stuck his head in the largest of several offices in back. "Hey, Robert, you in?"

Robert Decker peered up from his desk, looking over rimless half-glasses perched on the end of his nose. His face was round and had a well-scrubbed look, blue eyes set well apart. The top of his head protruded from a fringe that encircled his dome.

He pushed back his chair and came around the desk to greet his visitor. Slightly shorter than Lance, he was heavier in build and broad in the shoulders. He stretched out a strong, square-shaped hand. "Lance Morgan, you comin' in with another big deposit for me?"

"This time of year? Hell, Robert, you know better'n that." Lance flopped into a straight-backed, cane chair.

"Then, what can I do for you? I know you didn't come out in this norther just to chin with your friendly banker."

Lance leaned forward placing both hands on the desk.

"I just came from the courthouse. There's about eighty thousand acres just west of Big Frog Spring in one big Spanish land grant that'd be an ideal addition to the MacDuff Ranch."

Robert Decker frowned and leaned back in his chair. "So? It's open range. You're using it now."

Lance spoke quickly, drumming his index finger on the desktop to emphasize his point. "And so is everyone else in the county. Then, they push over around Big Frog Springs for water. Keeps our grass grubbed down around there."

"Tell me what you have in mind, Lance."

"I want to own that country -- buy it from the owners. There's not but three meskin families involved."

The banker leaned toward Lance, eyes popping with surprise. "What for?"

"I've got plans for that land -- and they don't include lettin' ever' ragtag outfit in the country run their cattle on it."

159

"I wouldn't exactly call Zeb Marlin's outfit 'ragtag.' And just how you aim to keep those ranchers off that graze? Some of 'em been pasturin' it for ten years or more."

"I'll fence it if I have to."

Robert Decker laughed without humor. "Now I know you're crazy. Nobody can fence that much land."

Lance jumped to his feet and paced to the far corner of the office. "Nobody has until now. Dammit, Robert, you gonna let me have the money to buy that land or not?"

Decker's eyes narrowed shrewdly. "Hold your horses, Lance. You haven't told me how much you need – when you'll pay it back – nor what you gonna put up for security."

"Security? Hell, that land's its own security. I'll pay you back when I can. And I'll need about $100 thousand."

The banker whistled through his teeth. "The depositors would hang me from the nearest tree if I made that loan – and rightly so."

Lance slapped the top of the desk. "What's it gonna take to get me that money, Robert?"

Decker rubbed his hand over his bald head. "First, more security. A definite time for repayment. When could you pay it back, Lance?"

"By end of summer – nine months – how'd that be?" He paused and Becker nodded.

"How much security you need, Robert?"

The banker grinned. "Everything you've got, Lance!"

CHAPTER 22

The raging norther, which had probed an icy finger even deep into the *brasada*, lashed across the High Plains virtually unopposed by any natural obstructions. The wind hurled the icy sleet with stinging force and piled the meager snowfall higher than a man's head on the lee side of any protrusion.

At the head of one of these long, narrow drifts, a skinny black stovepipe emerged from the flat prairie. Wisps of grey smoke appeared briefly only to be whisked away by the howling wind. About twelve feet from the stovepipe was a slanted rectangular hole in the ground about three feet wide. A green-tanned buffalo hide hung at the base, effectively blocking further encroachment of wind or snow.

George Gibson pushed aside that makeshift door and stuck his head up into the raging gale. He flinched at the sting of the wind-driven sleet and glanced over to a similar structure close by, where two horses in their long winter coats stood stamping their feet and snorting at the flakes of snow which occasionally drifted down on their noses. He hastily grabbed up a gunny sack filled with cow chips and ducked back inside the shelter.

He stamped his feet on the dirt floor and swung his arms against his sides. "Cliff, it ain't let up one damn bit."

His companion knelt beside a cast iron stove carefully feeding it the last of a small pile of cow chips. "Hope we don't run out of prairie coal. Is that the last sack?"

"Naw, there's one more."

Cliff tossed on a couple of chips from the sack, replaced the lid, and put a blue enameled coffee pot on it. "Sure hope it lasts. I'd hate to go lookin' for more in this weather. It'd be a lot worse that rustling' 'em for ol' Charlie. At least the weather was warm."

George dragged his plug tobacco out of his jacket pocket and bit off a chew. "Just don't let that fire go out. This damn stuff is hard enough to start when it's dry."

"Reckon the cows'll be all right?"

161

"Yeah. I ain't worried about them. They'll drift down into the breaks to the south. They'll be just fine."

That night, the wind stopped as suddenly as it had started. The whistling, moaning, and creaking sounds that had been the men's constant companions for thirty-six hours stopped abruptly. George rolled over, stuck his head out from under his blanket, and raised himself on one elbow. Young Cliff was sitting straight up in his bedroll.

"Well, reckon that's it," George said before he slithered back into his bedroll and was soon fast asleep.

George's homestead was about ten miles to the west of Henry and Helen Porter's place. Henry had helped him pick it out, giving George a running description as they rode. The land fully matched Henry's enthusiastic assessment. Spread out in the swale before them was a vast meadow of knee-high grass, waving and rippling in the wind.

The meadow was split down the middle by a slow moving stream that emerged from a series of short, rocky cliffs that broke the landscape to the north. At the southern end of the meadow, with its path blocked by rocky breaks leading down the escarpment, the stream spread into a wide bog of cattail, reeds, and water grasses, then disappeared into the sandy subsurface. Even in late summer, when most grass was brown and dry, this grass was still lush, green, and thick.

George had been impressed. His mind translated the scene into terms of the map shown him at the homestead office. The meadow was about a mile long and a half mile wide. His ranching homestead allowance allowed him six hundred forty acres – one square mile. He could claim the meadow plus some of the upland and the rocky breaks below.

Henry said, "The next closest water is ten miles to the east, fifteen miles south, twenty-five miles to the west and Lord knows where to the north. Homestead here and you control more than a hundred thousand acres of good grassland."

George shook his head in wonder. "How does it stay so green, Henry? That stream couldn't account for any of it except right near the edge."

"Sub-irrigated," Henry replied. "Those grass roots reach down to the permanent water level. This country has quite a few of these meadows scattered around. The breaks will give your stock winter shelter. Perfect cattle country."

George remembered he had turned to the young drover holding back his herd. "Turn 'em loose, Cliff. I think we done found our new home."

The early morning came crisp and cold but dead calm.

George led the way up out of the dugout, tugging the collar of his heavy coat over his neck. His breath hung like smoke in the still air. Across the meadow, a thin ribbon of steam hovered over the stream that ran through it. Narrow bands of faint color on the eastern horizon signaled the predawn.

Cliff was stepping on his heels. "Lemme outa here, willya, George? I gotta have some fresh air."

George stepped aside. "I know what you mean, kid. It was gettin' some close in that dugout."

Cliff sucked in a deep breath of the frigid air, and the sudden drying of his throat brought on a fit of coughing.

George chuckled. "Take it easy on that fresh air, Cliff."

Cliff recovered enough to lurch to the horse shelter. "Want me to hobble 'em and turn 'em loose, George?"

George rubbed a three-day stubble on his chin. "Naw, we may need 'em. Just stake 'em out so they can graze."

The faint hoof beats carried far in the stillness of the morning. Looking to the east, there was a speck moving toward them. George moved quickly back into the dugout to emerge with his breech-loading musket. Cliff had dropped over the rim of the breaks and was now out of sight.

By the time the dot could be distinguished as horse and rider, he recognized the dappled roan of Henry Porter's. He waited as the man pulled up nearby the dugout.

"Good mornin', Henry."

The horseman threw back his head and laughed. "Good morning? My goodness, George, has four months on the edge of the Great Escarpment gotten you completely out of touch with the world?"

"What the hell you talkin' about, Henry?"

"You don't know what day this is? Merry Christmas."

"Oh, cripes! Hey Cliff, we done forgot about Christmas."

The youngster came climbing up the edge of the rocks grinning. "Dang, I didn't hang up my socks."

George winked at Henry. "With them socks of yours, Cliff, we coulda just kinda leaned 'em up against the wall.

"Well, we ain't got much Christmas cheer, Henry, but get down. At least we got coffee."

"No thanks, fellows. Can't stay. Just came to deliver an invitation. My good wife and I would be pleased to have you gentlemen spend Christmas with us if you can fit it in to your social calendar."

"I don't reckon a whole tribe of drunken Comanches could make us miss that."

"Good. We'll be looking forward to it." Henry turned his horse and started away.

George shouted after him. "Henry, I hate to ask this, but

163

what're we havin' for Christmas dinner?"

Henry laughed. "Don't worry, George. I haven't trapped a skunk in weeks."

"You want what?" Bain's face turned dark with anger.

"Now simmer down, Bain," Lance said. "It's just a technicality. There's no danger of losing the ranch or anything like that."

"Then, what's a mortgage for, Lance? Anytime you have a mortgage, you've got a chance of losing it."

Lance shook his head. "No, Bain, you don't understand. Robert Decker just needs it to satisfy his depositors. We'll clear the mortgage with the first couple of herds we send up the trail, and we'll have twice the land that we have now."

"Dammit, Lance. We got all the land we need. There's more open range than we can use now."

"We can't use it the way I wanta use it." Lance's chin was beginning to jut stubbornly. "I'm gonna make this the biggest and best ranch in Texas."

"Sure you will," Bain bit off the words, "at the risk of everything we already have. Mother could wind up with nothing – and everyone else." Bain jumped to the ground. "I seem to remember that almost happening once before."

Lance flushed angrily. "No way that could happen now. We're too big an operation. At the worst – there's still that gold hid up there."

Mike, who'd been standing by quietly, spoke for the first time. "'Scuze me, Mistah Lance, but wouldn't you hafta ask Mistuh George about that?"

Lance looked from one to another as though confused at the seemingly unanimous and unreasonable opposition.

"It's bad enough that I hafta argue with a kid that's just barely dry behind the ears," the words snapped out seemingly of their own volition, "but now I gotta explain to an ignorant field nigger who knows nothing about it."

Even as the words rattled from his mouth, Lance wanted desperately to choke them back – even before he saw the pain cloud the big brown eyes of one of his best friends.

Mike stooped and picked up a saddle which lay on the ground. With sagging shoulders, he walked to the bunkhouse.

Bain's face, which had been dark with anger, suddenly drained and turned pale with shock. "Lance, I don't mind for me – but Mike didn't deserve that."

"I know — I didn't really mean it," Lance mumbled. A wave of regret washed over his mind. "I just wish he wouldn't get into things he doesn't understand."

"You might as well of shot him with a bullet." Bain's

eyes narrowed at his brother-in-law. "Lance, if you want your damn land that bad, I'll sign the papers for you. But you'll still have to convince mother and Colleen."

Erin MacDuff strolled to the window in her upstairs suite and stared out over the familiar landscape. "I've always loved this place very much, Lance. To me it's always been everything a ranch should be."

"I know how you feel about it, Erin." Lance stood, holding his hat across his chest.

"When Scotty and I moved here right after the Texas War For Independence, I had dreams of us building a secure little kingdom that would continue for generations."

Lance shuffled his feet. "You've done everything right so far. And I want to continue that work."

Erin chuckled. "I think your plans are well beyond anything Scotty and I ever had in mind."

"There's nothing wrong with planning big, Erin. I want to contribute to what you and Scotty have already done."

"Don't get me wrong, Lance. I'm not opposed to your plan in general. I just want you to consider whether you're trying to do it too quickly. Scotty and I took years building this place to where it is right now."

"Times are different now, ma'am. Things are changing faster. If we don't take advantage of opportunities as they come up, they may not be there later on."

She turned to face him. "You may be right about that. But do you think it necessary to risk losing everything just to make this latest quick expansion?"

"Yes, ma'am. I think it's worth the small risk."

The woman frowned. "I've always thought you were a good man, Lance. From the very first, I hoped that you and Colleen would hit it off. Does that seem scheming to you? Never mind, maybe it was.

"At any rate, I thought you were just what she needed, brave and resourceful -- but more than that, there was a kindness about you that I could feel. I sensed that you'd never hurt anyone unless you had to. And that, Lance Morgan, is what makes you strong.

"Now, you ask us to risk everything on your dream of building an empire here in the *brasada*. A huge empire . . ."

Lance fidgeted with his hat. "It's more than a dream, Erin. I got it all figgered . . ."

She lifted a hand. "Don't interrupt me, please. Nothing wrong with dreams. They can make you strong too. Scotty had a dream, and I shared it with him. He wanted to be a master breeder -- to work with living things and make them

165

better. He lived that dream until . . ."

She dabbed at her eyes with her handkerchief.

Instinctively, Lance went to her and put his arm around her shoulders. She smiled through her tears.

"Forgive me, Lance. I'm not ungrateful for what Scotty and I had together. We lived our dream for years – and that's much more than many people ever have."

"And now, you think I'm asking you to risk all that?"

"Oh no, not at all," she said. "My dream is done. Actually, from a business standpoint, I think your plan is sound – if all goes according to plan. You *could* fail – but you'd only start again. I could easily forgive your failure."

"Then why . . ."

"Why do I hesitate? Because if you fail – if we lose the ranch – I'm afraid you'll never forgive yourself. That would destroy the Lance Morgan I know and love.

"You must be sure you never trade your soul for more and bigger. But if you feel that your need is greater than the risk, I'll cooperate fully in what you plan to do, and the resources of MacDuff Ranch will be at your disposal."

Bain leaned against the doorway leading into the bunkhouse. Mike sat on a bunk piecing together the broken straps of a harness.

"Mike, Lance didn't really mean what he said. He's so worked up over this expansion thing, and he was upset with me, he just hit out and you happened to be there."

Mike looked up with a slight smile. "I think I had that all figgered out. It's just that my heart don't understand. Sometimes I jus' don't recognize that boy no more."

Letter, Feb. 16, 1869
From: MacDuff Ranch, Terwilliger, Texas
To: Mr. Guy Madden, Brazos Crossing, Texas
Dear Friend,
I have been advised that there have been heavy rains in your area. I trust you have not been overly hindered in your passage and that the drive is going well. As stated in the note you carry, you have full authority to sell and deliver any or all stock as you deem desirable. You are aware of my need for money, so do not fail to expedite the disposal of the herd as quickly as you can obtain a satisfactory price.

We have had some good rains and the grass is coming on good at present. If you anticipate any kind of trouble, make your own study and do what you think is necessary to protect our mutual interests. Do not fail to keep me informed. Use the telegraph freely when you have opportunity.

Yours truly,
Lance Morgan

Letter, March 2, 1869
From: Camp at Ft. Worth, Texas
To: Lance Morgan, Esq., Terwilliger, Texas
Deere Lance,
    Have rec'd yrs of 16 inst. The herd is doing well except we lost eight head at Brazos Crossing. We had ever thing across the river when some tomfool dog run out barking. and we had a turruble stomPead. We was lucky to only lose 8 head.
    However, the Boys are all good ones and are awful good hands with the cows. We had some truble with the waggin and had to get the wheel fixed here in Ft. Worth. It cost $3.50. I have spent 50 cents on a sack of onions because the Boys favors them with their beenes and $2.50 for a sack of spuds.
    I scouted ahead of the trail yesterday. It looks like ever cow in Texas is headed north. I saw three droves strung out up ahead and when I got back they was two more moving up on us from behind. Looks like about 1500 in each herd.
    We are resolved to head strate for Wilsons Gap. If we kaint get thru there, we will turn west around the quarantine line like we done before. My regards to the Boys at the ranch.
Yrs truly
Guy Madden

    Pedro Ramos Alvarado stood uneasily on the big veranda of the MacDuff ranch house. With his dark brown hat he slapped at the dust on his pant legs. Never before had the *patrón* summoned him to the main house. He made a quick attempt to brush the hair back off his forehead.
    The iron-studded door swung open and Lance stood inside in the passageway. "Ah, Pedro, come in please."
    The young *vaquero* stepped uncertainly into the house. His eyes darted quickly back and forth in an effort to orient himself in the unfamiliar surroundings. Lance took no notice of the man's trepidation and motioned him into a leather chair. Pedro took the precaution of dusting off the seat of his trousers before he sat.
    "Would you like a glass of lemonade? I believe there's a pitcher already made."
    "*Como no?* Yes, thank you, *señor.*"
    As the *vaquero* took the first tentative sip from his glass, Lance pulled his chair up to face Pedro. "How much money do you make now, Pedro?"

Pedro frowned slightly, as though he were not sure he liked the direction the interview had taken. "Twenty-five American dollars every month, *señor*."

"You know that I ... that is, we have bought more land."

"*Si, señor*, I know the country. My people call it *Rincón de Laguna*."

Lance leaned forward. "Pedro, I want that land cleaned out – a big cowhunt. Round up every hoof on the place. Can you do it?"

Pedro's face looked stricken. "By myself?"

Lance laughed. "No. Not by yourself. Can you get a crowd of men together to do it?"

The confidence returned. "Of course, *señor*. But they must be Mexican you understand."

"I understand. Your pay will now be $50 a month. You will be in charge. Hire as many men as you need – but no more. Agreed?"

The jaunty air characteristic of Pedro returned – plus a little extra. "Agreed, *patrón*. I will hire the men cheaply, and they will work very hard – for me."

Letter, April 20, 1869
From: Red River Crossing
To: Lance Morgan, Esq., Terwilliger, Texas
Good Friend Lance,

We been stuck here at the crossing more than a week now. She is a roaring and foaming like nothin I ever seen before. Theres a half a dozen herds strung out as fur as I can see up and down the near bank. Hole dam valley is full of cows waiting to get across. One herd tried to cross yesterday and we berryed two of his Boys today. Haff his herd must be halfway to the Gulf of Mexico by now.

So far we have lost no more cows since the StomPead on the Brazos. The Boys are eager to cross Old Red and get the jump on these other herds a waiting. But I figger to be prudent and wait at least one more day. I had the Boys find some big logs and drag into camp. I figger we can flote the waggin across on them.

I am sending this letter by mr. Jake Swain who has turned back to Ft. Worth. He will try to come through later. I have had to get some more supplies spending $4.75 for same as we needed more flour and beenes. I hope all is well at the Ranch and give my best to the Boys. I remain
Yrs truly
Guy Madden

Letter, May 28, 1869

From: Territory - Kansas line
To: Lance Morgan, Esq., Terwilliger, Texas
Dear friend Lance,

If you rec'd my last inst. you will be advised we got across Old Red. Although we lost 18 head in the crossing all the Boys made it and we are ahead of them other herds who maybe are still waiting to cross. The Boys worked like Heroes and took much risk of there lives to get the herd across. I am very proud of the hole bunch.

We have seen several bunches of Indians but they was Mostly Cherokees none of them Comanche and have had no truble with them. But we run into a hornets nest here at the Kansas line. They was a bunch of grangers standing there with shotguns in hand and a saying they did not want Texas cows passing thru theyre land. I was minded to go on across smoking, but then I seen a little snot nose kid a holding a gun biggern he was with teers rolling down his cheeks he was so scared and I pulled back my horns.

We drifted a ways west and a feller came out to say that Abilene was clear and clean. We are now resolved to point toward that town. They have swear papers ready there that say we wintered north of the fever line. Then we can ship into Illinois where the feller says the price is right dandy just now. I will check the post in Newton to see if you have any new orders for me.

Yrs truly
Guy Madden

Letter, June 21, 1869
From, MacDuff Ranch, Terwilliger, Texas
To: Guy Madden, Newton, Kansas
Esteemed friend Guy,

Rec'd yours of 28 last. I am grateful that none of your men were lost on Red River and that the herd got through all right. No doubt you were right and prudent to turn away from the granger quarantine. Knowing you to be sober and reliable always, please be sure to remember you have full authority to take any action you see fit to protect our interests.

Please be advised to do all in your power to remit proceeds from the sale of the herd to my account at the Terwilliger Bank no later than Aug. 1. You know the importance of this matter. As we will have no time to send another herd this year, we must hold for the best sale we can get. If the market in Abilene is down, you might consider heading for Omaha direct. Don't fail to sell promptly if the price is right. Keep me informed always.

Yrs. truly
Lance Morgan
P.S.
Bandits are still very active and have stolen 300 dry cows last week. We caught one and found that he was one of Santiago's men, he talked before he "died." Our friend Santiago has declared himself a "Juarista" and has assumed the title of "General."

The parlor of the MacDuff ranchhouse was bedecked with tinsel and crepe. Bain was there, prosperous looking in a new grey, fine-checked wool suit tucked into shiny black stovepipe boots. Booger Jim had his hair slicked back with pomade and his skin rosy from a brisk scrubbing. Mike was decked out in new boots and light tan shirt with orange cuffs and collar. Pedro sat stiffly in a high-backed chair. His new city-bred white shirt featured a boiled, stand-up collar. Colleen MacDuff served cups of punch and glanced uneasily from time to time toward the door.

"I'm sure Lance will be here in a few minutes," she said. He must have been delayed getting away from Terwilliger."

There was a pounding of hooves and the clatter of a rig. Colleen brightened. "That must be Lance now."

The door to the hallway opened just a bit and Lance's head stuck through. "Give me just a minute to clean up, and I'll be with you. Bain, could you give me a hand here?"

"Sure, Lance." Bain stepped into the hall and closed the door behind him.

Within ten minutes, the men reappeared, Lance wore clean trousers and shirt, and his smooth face was fresh from recent scrubbing. Bain walked behind carrying Lance's coat which he hadn't bothered to put on.

"I'm sorry to be so late; I was delayed in town. Where's the birthday boy?"

Colleen frowned in mild rebuke to her husband. "He's been in his room waiting for his father to show up. I'll go fetch him now."

Young Brent struggled out of his mother's arms at the sight of his father and set sail across the room in a tiptoe run into Lance's arms. Lance hoisted him high in the air, bringing a gurgling laugh from the youngster.

At that instant the door to the kitchen opened, and Erin MacDuff marched in bearing a large angel food cake with sugar frosting and a single lighted candle in the middle.

All eyes turned toward the cake, and only Bain, standing slightly behind Lance, saw the small dark red spot on the underside of his sleeve start to grow and widen.

170

He stepped forward. "If we're gonna have a party, Lance, you really oughta wear your coat." Lance put Brent down and slipped his arms into the coat Bain held for him.

Letter, July 2, 1869
From: MacDuff Ranch, Terwilliger, Texas
To: Guy Madden, Omaha, Nebraska
Friend Guy,
I must presume you are now in Omaha or will be by the time this reaches you. The draft for $75,000 for 1,500 hd sold in Abilene has cleared the bank in Terwilliger. I sincerely hope the remaining 1,200 odd head sell quickly. As you know of my need for cash, I will say only that a small profit quickly will be more suitable than holding for more at a later date. My future and that of my family is in your capable hands. But I know you are doing your considerable best. The bank note is due the last of Sept. so do not fail to expedite any additional funds rec'd for cows.
Thieves and bandits from across the border are still very active here. Pedro and his cow bunch on the new range ran afoul of a mob of about 20 in April and put them to flight leaving 2 of their number behind very dead. I was ambushed early in May on my son Brent's birthday. My rig was fired on as I drove home from town. They put several holes in my fancy buggy and I sustained a slight wound in my upper arm. My scattergun blew out one of them's lamp and the rest lit a shuck for the border. I have no proof but I am sure most of our troubles are with Santiago's band. Luckily, so far, we have beaten off every attack with no losses on our end.
Do your best to get the cows sold soon!
Yrs. truly
Lance Morgan

Letter, August 4, 1969
From: Omaha, Nebraska
To: Lance Morgan, Esq., Terwilliger, Texas
Friend Lance,
As you know from the draft you rec'd the price was good in Abilene, but the buyers were very picky and refused to buy without a deep cut in the herd. Cows were beginning to spread all over the prairie for a dozen miles around Abilene with more coming ever day. I determine to head for Omaha with the rest of the herd. I told the Boys they would have to wate til the rest of the herd is sold to be drawing there pay. As they don't know about your pressing need for money they got a little huffy about it but have settled down to work again. The herd is coming in today and will try to sell if possible.

171

A local constable tried to impound the herd for crop damage to some grangers farm, but I told him he would have to put up a $50,000 bond to take the herd and he backed off. Had to pay the granger $50 cash to settle. I am considerably short of funds right now and if you could send a letter of credit or tell me someone to see in Omaha to put up some cash or credit. Grub is very low. Knowing you will help as you can, I remain.

> *truly yrs*
> *Guy Madden*

Robert Decker leaned back in his chair with both hands behind his head and fastened his eyes on a small spider trying to get a web started in a corner of the ceiling.

"Lance, tell your man to contact Wilford Grub of Merchants' & Cattlemen's Bank in Omaha. He'll let him have whatever cash he'll need while he's there – which you and I both hope won't be long. Right, Lance?"

Lance smiled weakly. "Right. However, Robert, I've already got $75,000 for just a little over half the herd. If we have trouble selling the rest, I may have to ask for a short extension on that note. All right?"

The banker leaned over the desk. "Doggone, I'd like to be able to just say 'yes' and that'd be it. Most times I could do that, but right now is a tough time for the bank. That money you got was from a foreign investment firm. Now, they're gettin' cold feet and want their money back."

"You tellin' me you'd sell me out for $25,000 if I don't have it by the end of September?" Lance's eyes narrowed.

Decker looked away and sat back in his chair. "Naw, Lance, that's not exactly what I'm sayin'. You know I'll do everything I can – but it won't be easy. I might have to call your note. Let's just hope you get your cows sold and make it a lot easier on both of us.

Lance stood by the corral fence watching Bain put the finishing touches on gentling a two-year-old lineback dun. As many times as he'd seen him work with horses, he still enjoyed the sight. Those lean, strong hands that handled a Colt with such swift sureness were equally effective in communicating a calm confidence to a nervous young horse. Pedro Alvarado came in at a lope and pulled to a sliding stop by the corral flashing a shiny smile. "*Señor*, the cattle have been gathered in the *Rincón de Laguna*."

"Very good, Pedro. How many?"

"I think about twenty-two hundred, *mas or menos*."

"What brands they carryin', Pedro?"

172

"Many carry the Box-A, some have the Bar-Dot and Circle-T, most are the Long-Z, and some no brand at all."

Lance pulled a couple of cigars from his vest pocket, handed one to Pedro and fired up the other himself. "Send a rider to the other owners and tell 'em we cut the herd day after tomorrow. Tell 'em to have someone there to take charge of their cattle."

"And those without a brand, *señor?*"

"Put the M-Bar on 'em, Pedro. Those are our cows. You need any help?"

"*No, señor.* It will be done." Pedro whirled his horse and moved off in an easy lope.

Letter, Aug. 21, 1869
To: Lance Morgan, MacDuff Ranch, Terwilliger, Tex
From: Omaha, Nebraska
Deere friend Lance,

This day I have forwarded a draft for $32,600 to your credit at the Terwilliger Bank. This is what remains from the sale of 1232 hd after the Boys was paid off and advance from bank was settled. We was lucky to find a feeder from Illinois who wants to hold the cows over winter on corn and hay. I had hoped to get a little more for the herd, but knowing of your need for cash I went ahead on.

Most of the Boys find Omaha a little to tame for there taste and are lighting out for Abilene to spend there wages. I have resolved to spend a couple more days here to find a buyer with good money for the remuda and waggin. Been several fellers liked the looks of our horses which well they should. They done a good job on the trail.

I hope all is well at the ranch. I will see you on my return with a complete account of monies spent and all. Give my regards to the Boys at home.

Yrs truly
Guy Madden

Lance pulled the high-stepping grey to a halt in a box canyon ringed with dozens of small cave openings. He unlocked the false bottom of the buggy and raised the door. Pulling out a couple of old, worn saddlebags, he slung them over his shoulder, slumping under the weight of them.

"Back into hiding you go. Hope I don't ever have to tote you out for anything again."

CHAPTER 23

The morning was still, and the high altitude and low humidity gave the air an almost tangible crispness. George watched Cliff ride in from the end of the meadow with the horses, riding one bareback and leading the other. The saddles, blankets, bridles, and ropes waited at George's feet where he'd dropped them. He had an idea it was going to be another long, hard day. The trouble with a good calf crop was that it created a lot of work come fall. Still, it was good to see a growing herd of cattle carrying the Big-G brand on their left flanks.

With Henry lending a hand, the work was going smoothly. Every calf should be marked in a couple of days. Not that Henry was much of a hand with a rope, but he kept the fires going and the irons hot while George and Cliff handled the roping and heavier work.

Besides, George purely enjoyed the man's company. Obviously well educated, he never seemed to be aware that George wasn't. George had the native intelligence to know that he'd learned an awful lot from Henry without the man ever assuming the role of tutor.

Helen was the perfect helpmate for Henry. Strong and resourceful when required, she was also graciously feminine with a natural poise that would do credit to anyone that George could imagine.

Together they had George's undying affection. In his adversity-filled life, George had few meaningful attachments, Lance Morgan and maybe young Cliff. He could see a lot of himself in the young towheaded orphan who had attached himself to George for better or worse.

Cliff brought the horses up and slipped to the ground. "I caught your horse for you, George. Okay?"

"Yeah. Thanks, Cliff."

They saddled and mounted. Cliff watched the eastern horizon for a moment. "Wasn't Henry comin' today?"

"Yeah, I 'spect he'll be here. Let's get some of 'em

174

rounded up."

Just as he spoke, they heard the heavy bark of Henry's .50 buffalo gun and several shots from lighter weapons.

George set spurs to the big dun. "Let's go, Cliff."

The two men thundered over the short grassed prairie toward the Porter home. Long before they came in sight, they could hear the high-pitched yelps of an attacking force. George slowed and motioned Cliff to do the same. "Let's see what we're ridin' into 'fore we go flyin' over that hill."

The older man dismounted and tossed Cliff the reins to his horse. Slipping down on all fours, he edged his way to the top of the ridge, took a quick look, and hustled back to the waiting Cliff. "Comanches. Must be ten or twelve of 'em."

"The Porters?"

George spat on the ground. "They're holdin' 'em off."

Just then, the Sharps roared its defiance.

George swung into the saddle. "Let's give those devils the surprise of their lives."

Both unbooted their rifles and, at George's signal, they tore over the hill at a full gallop.

The Indians rode around the house firing at openings as they passed. Five or six were armed with breech- loading carbines, the remainder with bows and arrows. Three with rifles had dismounted to facilitate reloading. George rode straight at those on foot. His first shot dropped one, and before the Comanches realized what was happening, the big horse crashed into another, sending him sprawling. George smashed the third across the head with the rifle butt.

Cliff's rifle shot knocked a mount from under one of the savages, and he crashed heavily to the ground. The young man booted his rifle and dragged a six-shooter from his belt. With a loud whoop, one of the warriors rushed at this new threat, twirling his tomahawk over his head. Cliff fired twice, and he crumpled off the side of his pony.

Swinging toward the house, Cliff spurred forward at a hard run. George also turned toward the house still brandishing the rifle over his head. He knew their best chance was to get out of the open to reinforce the defenders inside the house. Cliff was in a beeline toward the door.

He just pulled up by the hitching post when an arrow thudded into the center of his back. He fell on his face.

Roaring with anger, George slid the dun to a stop and ran toward the still body of the youngster. Before he got there an Indian hurled himself off the roof of the soddy, landing with his knees in George's chest. The impact took him flat on his back. The Comanche stood over him with his war club upraised. Then, there was a sharp bark, and the Indian jerked over backward. George rolled over to see Cliff, raised on one elbow lowering his revolver. The boy had a grin on his face.

George leaped to his feet, scooped the boy up in his arms, and fell through the suddenly opened door into the semi-darkness of the soddy.

George's eyes swept the interior quickly. Propped up in a chair adjacent to the shuttered window was an ashen-faced Henry Porter. His left leg stuck out at an odd angle and hung limply from just below the knee, but his eyes were riveted on the sights of his old buffalo gun protruding through the loophole.

Helen stood at a slot on the other side of the window with a long-barreled revolver. The buffalo gun bucked with an ear-shattering roar. Helen immediately grabbed the weapon, reloaded, and placed it back in Henry's hands. Back of the room, wide-eyed but perfectly still, young Phillip Porter crouched behind the piano.

George gently placed young Cliff face down on the hard-packed dirt floor.

Henry, without taking his eyes away from the loophole, spoke quietly. "Morning, George. Don't guess I can help with the branding this morning. Something came up."

George loaded his own rifle. "I mighta known you'd figger some way of gettin' out of it."

Cliff raised his head off the floor. "I'm gonna hafta lay out on that job myself, George. Guess, you gonna hafta do it all yourself."

The Indians had quit circling and shooting and gathered in a group away from the house.

George whispered. "What're them devils up to now?"

The answer was not long in coming. A scratching noise coming from overhead. "On the roof," he said.

The scratching turned into chopping as the attackers worked on the heavy timbers of the roof. George leaned his rifle against the wall and drew his revolver. "Cover me, Helen, I'm goin' out there."

He sprinted through the door into the front yard and looked up at two surprised warriors wielding their tomahawks on the battered roof. He shot the nearest one under his upraised arm. The other tried to make it to the back edge, but George's next shot cut through his backbone. He collapsed instantly.

The mounted Indians recovered quickly and charged toward George at a gallop. Taking no chances on misses, Helen fired at the larger targets of the Indian ponies, and the charge was disrupted by the thrashing pile of wounded and dying horses. George whirled and added his own firepower to that coming from the house and watched two of the unhorsed warriors drop to the ground. Amid a hail of bullets and arrows, he dashed back to shelter.

The Indians retired out of range of the six-guns to regroup. As they started their council, Henry said, "I think I see which one is their war chief – the big fellow with the black feather in his hair."

Henry braced the rifle on the padded back of his chair and fired. As the echo of Henry's shot bounced across the plains, the Comanche was blasted from his pony. The Indians pulled him back on the horse and held him in place as they turned and rode away from the soddy.

The silence could almost be felt. Helen lowered her revolver. "Is it over?" she asked.

George took a long breath. "I think so. That was the War Chief, Henry. Bad medicine, gettin' killed like that."

Henry twisted in his chair with a groan. "I think you're right, George. They're going after what they came for."

George nodded. "Yep. As of right now, I figger we're both outa the cow business. They're probably whoopin' my herd away right now. The comancheros'll give 'em a barrel of whiskey for the lot."

He turned and knelt by Cliff lying on the floor. "You hurtin' much, Cliff?"

"Naw, not too bad. But I'm kinda cold."

Helen stripped a blanket off the bed and put it over him.

"Brace yourself, boy," George said. "I'm gonna give that arrow a try."

He took a firm grip on the shaft and gave it a brisk tug. Fresh blood spurted from the wound, but the arrow held firm. "Nope. I can't do it."

Cliff raised his head. "You gotta do it, George. Don't give up on me now."

Beads of sweat stood out on George's forehead. "I can't do it. It just starts more bleedin'."

The youngster's voice grew raspy. "You know — and I know — that I'll die if you don't get that arrow out."

Back in the corner, Phillip Porter started crying. Helen led him to a chair at the kitchen table. "Hush. Cliff's been hurt, but we're going to fix him up. Sit here and be still."

Henry painfully turned in his chair. "Looks like you'll have to cut it out, George, cauterizing it as you go. He's right; he won't last the night with that arrow in his back."

George walked to the stove and poked at the glowing coals. He tossed a couple of sticks on top and plunged an iron poker into the glowing embers. He fumbled through the kitchen utensils and selected a thin-bladed boning knife which he passed through the fire several times. "You got any whiskey in the house?"

Helen stepped quickly to the cupboard. "We've got about a half bottle."

"See if you can dull him a little. This is gonna hurt."

Cliff raised his head to watch. "I can take it, George. Just don't let me die. I'm not ready -- I just can't die yet. I'm just sixteen."

"Stop that kinda talk," George said. "I'm gonna have you helpin' me with the chores again in a coupla weeks."

"I ain't got any folks," Cliff murmured, "and not much else neither. You gave me the only home I've had since I was nine. If things don't work out, I want you to have my saddle and rig – and my gun. That's all I got."

George bit down hard on his upper lip. "I said to stop that kinda talk. You ain't gonna get outa work that easy."

Helen knelt by the boy and took his hand. "George is right. You'll feel a lot better when we get that arrow out."

Cliff smiled weakly and lay his head back down.

George tested the knife on his thumb and went to one knee. He pulled back the blanket and took a deep breath. Helen placed a hand on his. He looked up startled at the gesture. She shook her head slowly, tears streaming down her face. "He's gone, George."

George lurched to his feet, letting the knife slip from his nerveless fingers. He stood for a moment looking down at the boy who'd shared his life the past several months and had saved his life not an hour ago. He turned his face to the wall and his shoulders heaved.

Henry Porter slipped slowly out of his chair, face grimacing with pain. His face was pale and bloodless, yet blazed with anger. "Stinkin' savages."

Henry's voice turned George around. "Can't do nothin' for Cliff. I'll see what I can do for Henry."

Stretching the man on his back, George examined the wound. A bullet had smashed through the leg just below the knee. Jagged bone ends stuck out through the skin. With Helen holding Henry's shoulders, George stretched the leg out and slipped the bone back into place as Henry screamed in agony. Through the process of strapping a bed slat tightly to his leg for a splint, Henry was mercifully unconscious.

George looked up into Helen's face. "We gotta get him outa here. He needs a doctor bad. Cover him up real good, and I'll see what the redskins left us."

George found the body of Cliff's mount bristling with arrows not far from the front door. But his own dun he found grazing behind the house. George led him to the Porter's wagon. "I know you never done nothin' like this before, hoss, but we're gonna see if you can pull a wagon."

Nervously, the animal allowed himself to be hitched to the wagon. He pranced sideways as he was rigged into the unfamiliar harness. But he was a good cowhorse, used to feeling the pull of a thousand-pound animal tied hard and fast to his saddle horn. After the first skittishness passed, he learned quickly what his job was and settled into it.

Padded with all the bedding they could find, Henry was made as comfortable as possible in the wagon bed, and they rolled toward Fort Griffin some hundred miles to the east.

Lance felt good. The new pasture was cleared of stray cattle. Some of the neighbors had been a little huffy about removing cattle from range they'd used for years, but it was MacDuff land now, and they had little choice but to comply.

Demand continued for the fine MacDuff horses, and lately the Mexican bandits had done their raiding elsewhere. His relationship with Bain and Mike had been a little cool of late, but they just didn't understand that right now he was preoccupied with ranch business. He'd straighten that all out later when he had a little more time.

He walked over to where Colleen rocked the sleepy-eyed Brent. "Why don't we turn in a little early tonight, dear?" He glanced toward the stairs and their own private suite.

"Shhh," she whispered. "You go ahead. I want to get Brent to sleep, then I'll come up."

Half an hour later, in the bedroom he shared with his wife, Lance paced over to the window, glanced out, and stalked back to his large overstuffed chair. He dropped into it and lit a cigar. He took a few puffs, walked again to the window, and impatiently threw it out into the night. He undressed quickly and went to bed. Somewhat later, Colleen slipped quietly in beside him – being careful to not disturb his sleep.

The little hostel at Fort Griffin had only one room which George shared with the Porters. The kindly owner apologized for having no other accommodations available.

Henry was asleep and burning with fever, but the army doctor was optimistic. "It's a bad break, but it seems to be set all right. He might have a slight limp, but other than that – he should recover nicely."

Helen continued to frown. "But doctor, he feels so hot."

"Only natural after what he's been through. We just need to give him time. I'll be around to see him in a few days -- just as a precaution."

179

Next day, Henry was feelin' chipper. George fed him a good breakfast, then sat down to talk. "Henry, you think you're gonna be all right for a while?"

"Sure I am, George. What you have in mind?"

"Well, I kinda thought I'd go get my cows back -- if you're all right."

Helen looked surprised. "How do you intend to do that, George Gibson? Just walk up and ask the Comanches to please hand back your cattle?"

"Well, I intend to ask the army for help. The Comanches won't have the cattle by now. The comancheros will be heading' 'em to New Mexico. Anyhow, I just can't afford to let everything I own go without tryin' to get it back."

"I'll tell you exactly how it is, Mr. Gibson." The major put both hands on the desk and leaned forward. "We can't go traipsing' all over the country after a bunch of cattle lost by some fool Reb that homesteaded right in the Comanche's war path. Your cattle are gone -- accept it."

George slammed his fist down on the major's desk. "If you're not here to protect people from the Comanches, just what the hell are you doin' here, Major?"

George glared at the major for a full minute. "Well, you can sit here and go to hell, but them is my cows, and I'm goin' after 'em."

Thirty three days later George Gibson returned to Fort Griffin, face haggard under a scraggly beard, his clothing caked with sweat and dust. The ribs of his horse were visible under the briar-scarred hide. He swung to the ground in front of the hostel and creaked his way inside.

Helen opened the door at his knock. Her hair was pulled back severely in a bun at the back of her head, accentuating her hollowed cheeks and sunken eyes that seemed dull and lifeless. "Oh, George, you're back."

She stepped out to him, buried her face in his dirty jacket, and began to sob. Little Phillip clung to her skirt, looking up at the adults in bewilderment.

"What's happened, Helen?" George felt awkward and helpless in the face of the woman's tears.

Between sobs, the story came out. For a while, Henry had done well, then gangrene set in. The doctor insisted that all was well until too late. The infection spread rapidly and Henry had died in delirium eight days ago.

George bathed and shaved. He was dressed in new

180

clothing from top to bottom. Helen and Phillip sat with him at the hostel's modest dining facility.

"No, I didn't get all my cows back. But I got the money for 'em. Ran into three comancheros just this side of the New Mexico line. They was herdin' an even dozen of my Big-G cows. Reckon they'd sold the rest.

"Well, I took back my cows and the money they'd got for the rest of 'em, dropped off the cows at my place on the way back, and hustled back here hopin' to find you and Henry fit."

Helen was amazed. "You mean they just gave you back your property?"

"Well, no ma'am. I kinda had to take it away from 'em."

"And the men?"

"I figger they're tryin' to deal the devil outa his pitchfork by now. Anyhow, I got the money to buy you and the boy a ticket back east if that's what you want. Or wherever you're minded to go."

Helen pushed a strand of loose hair back in place. "Go?"

"Of course. You have to go somewhere."

"What are you going to do, George?"

"Me?" George was surprised by the question. "I'll go back to my ranch. Get started again."

"So am I, George. Home is where I lived with Henry for the past six years – where my son was born. I'm going home, George."

"But you can't live there by yourself. You just can't."

"I can, and I am. You do what you want, George, but I'm going home. I never considered doing anything else."

181

CHAPTER 24

Telegram, March 20, 1875
From: Department of Texas
To: Sec'y of War Belknap

THE COUNTRY BETWEEN CORPUS CHRISTI AND THE
RIO GRANDE IS IN A STATE OF CONFUSION AND WAR
AND IS FULL OF ARMED BANDS OF MEXICANS ROBBING
AND DEVASTATING THE WHOLE SECTION (STOP)
FIVE RANCHES HAVE BEEN BURNED AND PEOPLE
KILLED AND WOUNDED (STOP)
WIRES CUT BETWEEN CORPUS CHRISTI AND
BROWNSVILLE (STOP)
-- *Gen. W. T. Sherman*

The small town of Terwilliger was host to an eventful gathering. Singly, in pairs, and small groups they straggled in. Some rode more than a hundred miles around brush and through arroyos to converge on the tiny town's hotel. They were tall and short, slender and stocky, old and young, but each had the bowed legs and wind-squinted eyes of a Texas cowman.

Thorny as a tassajillo branch and edgy as a green-broke mustang, they gathered in the early dawn in the diminutive lobby. While no mesquite wood blazed in the small pot bellied stove in the pleasant April weather, it still served as the focal point around which they gathered.

The spurs clinked a musical counterpoint to the clump of high-heeled boots on the bare wooden floor. Chair legs scraped as they were pulled out from the wall and tilted back for comfort. Charlie Griffin was there, having ridden in from his spread near Carrizo Springs. Nathan and Hugh Herndon from Bandera, Carlos Montera from Fort Clark to the north. Andrew Thomas and his brother Victor came from Fort Ewell on the Nueces and a dozen or so smaller operators from

Laredo, Castroville, and the upper reaches of the Medina River.

They strolled in casually, exchanging greetings and comments on the weather. Among them were local ranchers, Lance Morgan, Bain MacDuff, Amos Carter, and Elgin Thompson. Their voices were low and bantering, but no one joshed about the subject that had brought them together. There was no talk of rustling -- nor of the raiders who had put the country in a virtual state of siege.

They sat and waited, leaning back in their chairs and hooking bootheels over the wooden rungs. Some lit up rimfire cigars, others bit off big chunks of strong, black plug tobacco. Some applied knives to straight grained white pine, taking off long, clean shavings, making up their shapes and designs as they went along.

Finally, the clip clop of a trotting horse brought an air of expectation to the room. In the silence, they heard the leather creak as the rider swung from the saddle. Heels clicked against the wooden walkway. Then, the door swung open, and every eye watched old Zeb Marlin enter the room. Long, lean and grizzled, with a shock of white hair protruding from his sweaty brown beaver hat, he looked like what he was -- the patriarch of South Texas ranchers.

Piercing blue eyes gazed from under bushy white eyebrows. His thin, slightly hooked nose stuck through a full white beard. A veteran of San Jacinto, he was a genuine, mossy-horned Texian.

The roomful of eyes suddenly shifted their interest to the back of the room where Lance Morgan sat quietly. Old Zeb had been a heavy user of the country that Lance had acquired and cleared of all cattle except those of the M-Bar brand. There was a general feeling among those present that Zeb harbored little regard for the whippersnapper who had such a penchant for taking actual title and exclusive use of land which had long been considered open range. His Long-Z brand had been quite active on the *Rincón de Laguna* which Lance had closed to all but his own cattle.

Amos Carter stopped his whittling. "How'd do, Zeb?"

The man nodded. "Amos."

He looked slowly around the room. How you doin', Charlie? Andrew?

Lance tilted his chair down from the wall.

"That you, Morgan? Glad to see you can work on some things together with your neighbors."

Almost visibly, the room relaxed.

Elgin Thompson spoke. "Boys, we know why we're here. Let's get at it."

Victor Thomas, down from Fort Ewell, lifted his chin off his chest. "Reckon we'll need a chairman – or something. Anybody got any suggestions?"

Lance rose from his chair. "I figger there ain't but one man for the job. I nominate Zeb Marlin."

Charlie Griffin leaned forward. "He's at least got enough sense for that."

A wave of appreciative chuckles went around the room, and Zeb Marlin was elected by acclamation. After all, as one rancher put it, "Zeb was pioneerin' this area while the rest of us was strugglin' with the alphabet."

Zeb stood to speak. "If you boys want me to ramrod this meeting, I got one idea right off. I don't feel rightly comfortable talkin' inside these walls. I'd a heap rather see whoever's gonna be hearin' what we say."

Amid murmurs of assent, he led the group out of the hotel lobby to the town square. There, under the spreading branches of an overgrown mesquite tree, the Southwest Texas Association of Cattlemen was formed with rules and regulations enforceable by hardy riders and quick guns to be hired by the STAC members.

Alternately standing and squatting on the heels of their well-worn boots, the men laid out rules by which the cattle business in the area would be conducted. Rules on which they quickly agreed called for all cattle to be branded fall and spring. Such brands were to be registered with the association. One resolution called for the formation of an intelligence network to collect information on the bandits' activities. The network would pay informers from a war chest maintained by the association. STAC would be financed by an assessment on each member according to the estimated size of his herd.

On other questions, agreement did not come easily for these tough-minded and independent mavericks. Each was too accustomed to running things in his own domain. There was an attempt to bar anyone from membership who enclosed ten acres or more with a fence.

The attempt brewed instant disagreement. Zeb Marlin put the question to rest. "Nobody hates a fence more'n I do," he rumbled, "but the one thing I hate more is somebody tryin' to tell another man what to do with his own property."

In spite of the bickering over other questions, there was unanimous agreement that raiding from across the border had to be stopped. Accordingly the "spy" network received top priority. Carlos Montera, Amos Carter, and Zeb Marlin were selected to organize the system.

Hugh Herndon of Bandera brought the most hopeful news. Governor Richard Coke, the first governor actually elected by the people of Texas since the war, had reestablished the Texas Rangers and had appointed one Leander H. McNelly to enlist a company for special service along the Rio Grande. The announcement was greeted with cheers from the assembled cattlemen. McNelly was not unknown to this crowd. He had served his country well during the war and was one of the few Texas State Police who did a creditable job during the carpetbagger reign. On that note, the meeting was adjourned, and the cowmen nosed their ponies homeward.

Lance and Bain rode up the well-marked trail between ranch headquarters and Terwilliger. They rode in silence, each engrossed in his own thoughts on the new association. Finally, Bain broke the silence.

"Lance, what do you know about McNelly?"

"Not much really. Good record so far as I know. Governor Coke must be high on him -- and I hope the hell he's right. We need somebody who knows what they're doin' to stop these raids. What did you have in mind, Bain? You're not just curious."

"I'm thinkin' about joinin' up with McNelly."

Lance frowned slightly. "What about the ranch?"

"Hell, Lance, we got plenty of hands who can do what I do around there. You run the ranch -- we both know that. I'm not needed there."

Lance rode a while in silence. Bain was right. He was a good hand when he needed to be -- but so were several others. He showed no interest in the details of ranch management. And there was no denying, Bain was an ideal recruit for McNelly -- fast and accurate with all firearms, a superb horseman, just a bit reckless, and with unflinching courage. Hell, Lance thought, I just wish McNelly had a hundred just like him.

Lance said, "Bain, if you're determined to go, you sure don't need my permission. I wish you luck, but I do hope you'll discuss it with Erin first -- you know -- just so she'll know you considered her feelings."

"Sure, Lance. I wouldn't just take off without saying anything. I'll talk to her about it first thing in the morning."

Telegram, April 18, 1875
From: Courthouse, Nueces County
To: Gov. Richard Coke, Austin, Texas
IS CAPT MCNELLY COMING (STOP)   WE ARE IN TROUBLE (STOP)
FIVE RANCHES BURNED NEAR LA PARRA LAST WEEK (STOP)
ANSWER (STOP)   Signed Sheriff John McClane

Erin accepted the news calmly if reluctantly. "As you know, son, I've never approved of wars or killing. But if there ever was a good reason for fighting, I suppose these murderous bandits have given it to us. I know you'll do your duty; just take care of yourself while you do it."

Colleen had mixed emotions. She enjoyed her brother's company and was concerned for his safety, but she also remembered his longing to enlist during the war and understood it. Bain would finally have a chance at adventurous service to his country.

"Will you stay around until tomorrow?" she asked. "It's Brent's birthday, you know."

Bain chuckled. "I wouldn't miss it. Lance and I have something special planned for that little rascal."

"Nothing extravagant I hope," she replied lightly. "He has a younger sister, remember? She could feel left out."

"Ann will have hers next month on her own birthday."

This time, the cake was adorned with seven blazing candles as Erin carried it proudly into the room. Brent had grown into a handsome youngster, well-groomed, sandy hair brushed to a gleaming patina. He had his mother's soft green eyes. A light dusting of freckles spread across the bridge of his nose.

Erin clapped her hands for silence. "Before we have cake and punch, Brent would like to show you his progress in reading," she said, ignoring his frantically shaking head. "Wouldn't you, Brent?"

He bowed to the inevitable. "Yes, ma'am."

He effortlessly skimmed through a passage from his primer and a stanza of *Paradise Lost*.

Everyone gave him an enthusiastic round of applause -- especially the cowboys who were always duly impressed with reading skills.

"I can say my ABC's," young Ann piped up. But her hopeful words were lost in the applause for Brent's reading.

Brent tore into his birthday packages with gusto. After each gift was examined, the giver was thanked. Unnoticed by anyone, Bain quietly left the room.

As Brent came to the end of his packages, he looked around the room, disappointment in his eyes. There had been no package from his father.

Lance stood up with a big grin on his face. "If you're looking for a present from me, young man, you're gonna hafta look outside."

Brent made a dash for the door. As he reached the front

porch, he slid to a surprised stop. Bain was coming up the walk leading a pony -- but no ordinary pony. This was no squat, short-legged, long-haired converted draft animal. This pony, standing about thirteen hands, was sleek and shiny with long rippling muscles, an equine aristocrat through whose veins flowed the blood of the Spanish Barb. Deep chestnut in body color, the animal minced along on four white-stockinged feet, and his slightly dished face was blazed with white. Tiny ears, alert to every sound, were in constant motion.

The boy let out a little gasp of delight and raced down the path. Bain cupped his hands at the pony's side. Brent put a foot into his uncle's hand and vaulted to the pony's back.

The animal, a little unsure of what to make of Brent's exuberant approach, shied slightly but quickly steadied under the boy's confident hand on the reins. Secretly schooled for months by Bain, the pony responded instantly to every signal. After a short run outside the yard with turns and sliding stops, Brent guided him back into the yard.

He slipped off the pony and ran to his father, eyes expressing his appreciation more accurately than his stumbling words. Little Ann's eyes were wide with wonder at all the unexpected commotion, and she clung tightly to her mother's skirts in uncertainty.

Bain's hard muscled grey leaned into the bit wanting to run, but Bain checked him gently. "Save yourself, feller," he murmured. "You'll get your fill of runnin' a little later."

Bain looked around with approval at his fellow riders, twenty-two of McNelly's Rangers. His eyes turned toward the man who rode slightly ahead of the group, L. H. McNelly, thirty-one years old, had already fought in a major war, served with distinction in the state police, had recently cleaned out the trash around LaParra, making the country again safe for honest citizens, and had disbanded local vigilante groups who seemed bent on outdoing the raiders in cruel atrocities performed on innocent citizens.

Bain had no idea where they were going. He had heard that a Mexican ship, bound for Cuba, was waiting for a beef contract to be filled and that rustlers were gathering Texas cattle to fill that contract. He strongly suspected that contract and the Rangers' movements were connected. At any rate, where McNelly went, he was going to follow. And right now, he seemed to be headed right into Brownsville.

The early June weather was turning hot, and Bain wiped a sleeve across his eyes to clear his vision. A small cloud of dust rose from the prairie ahead. McNelly threw up his arm in a signal, sending the group on an interception course.

As they cut across the prairie, a band of men took shape out of the dust cloud, driving some three hundred head of cattle. At McNelly's signal, the Rangers slackened their reins and thundered down on them.

Bain MacDuff arrived home on a short leave. Erin prepared a special meal -- the kind that seems to nourish a body just in anticipation. The savory aroma of roasting beef mingled with the fresh, yeasty scent of baking bread.

Both Brent and Ann hung on their uncle as though they could assure his continued presence by physical force. After the evening meal, the children were peeled off and hustled away to bed. As Erin and Colleen cleaned the table, Lance and Bain retired to the parlor and fired up their cigars.

"Well, Bain," Lance started as he took several quick puffs, "tell me about McNelly's Rangers. I understand you created quite a stir down at Brownsville."

"Yeah – on both sides of the river. The meskin officials were madder'n hell – but not a damn thing could they say."

"Exactly what happened? The story I got was kinda sketchy."

"Well, we were about fourteen miles north of Brownsville when we came on about a dozen meskins drivin' cattle toward the border. When we started toward them, they fired on us. So, I jerked out my Winchester and threw down on one cuttin' for the brush and knocked him rollin'.

"We cut 'em off from the river, and McNelly hollered for 'em to surrender. But they acted plumb crazy — runnin' like hell when they could — and fightin' like hell ever' time we caught 'em. Anyhow, we lost one man, but we killed ever' one of them meskins.

"McNelly had us catch their horses and packed them dead rustlers into Brownsville. We lined their bodies up there on the square and put out the word that their relatives could come claim 'em if they wanted to."

Lance chuckled low. "That's a damn switch. About time that bunch got a dose of their own medicine. Any chance that there was any of Santiago's men among 'em?"

Bain scowled. "I don't think so, Lance. Several of 'em was identified as Cortina's. I don't think Santiago works that far south. Wish it hadda been."

Lance sat his horse watching the workers move across the flats below. One crew dug small round holes in the rocky ground – slamming a heavy steel crowbar into the rocks then cleaning out the rubble. Another set eight-inch diameter

188

cedar posts into those holes. The third crew strung shining strands of barbed wire between the posts.

Behind them, as far as Lance could see, four strands of barbed wire barred the passage of livestock on or off MacDuff land. His long time dream of fencing his property was becoming reality. He'd seen a demonstration in San Antonio in which semi-wild Texas Longhorns had been penned in the middle of town by barely visible strands.

He'd heard "Bet-A-Million" Bates extol the virtues of barbed wire as "light as air, strong as whiskey, and cheap as dirt." He'd immediately recognized the significance of economical and effective fencing to the future of the ranching industry. Now, when he put his livestock somewhere, they would stay put. He could control his range, control his cattle and horses, and so manage the business of ranching.

He turned to his dark-skinned companion sitting a short distance behind him. "Keep 'em at it, Pedro. I want the entire ranch enclosed before winter."

"Yes, *patrón*. It will be done."

The August sun climbed toward noon as Lance reached home. He detoured by the yard well to wash up for lunch. As he turned toward the house, he heard approaching riders. Not wanting to be caught in the open by unknown men, he broke into an easy run to the shelter of the large pecan tree near the front door.

He watched silently as eight well-armed men with large *sombreros* rode up to the spring trickling across their path. They paused uncertainly, then four crossed and stopped. The others rode back about a hundred yards and waited. An old-fashioned but exquisitely built coach, drawn by four matched palomino horses, came over the ridge. Flanked by four other riders, the coach rolled up to the yard.

Lance held his shotgun ready but relaxed a little. If these were bandits it had to be the strangest group in the world. He stepped out from behind the tree and walked toward them.

One of the horsemen reined in between him and the coach. Sweeping off his hat, he revealed slicked-down silver hair above a dark lined face. A close-clipped mustache adorned his upper lip. "We seek the *estancia de Señor* Lance Morgan," he said.

"You've found it, sir; I'm Lance Morgan."

The man dismounted gracefully and bowed from the waist. "Don Miguel de la Garza, at your service, *señor*."

Lance stepped forward and offered his hand which the man shook warmly. For the first time, the Mexican seemed hesitant. His eyes swept the vicinity as though to assure

189

himself no one else was present. "I have a matter of some delicacy to discuss with you, *señor*."

"Of course. However, it appears you've had a long ride. There is room at the bunkhouse for your men to rest and refresh themselves."

"Thank you for your hospitality, *señor*, but my men will be quite comfortable under the shade of your magnificent trees. However, if you would permit, the occupants of my coach would be grateful for the shelter of your bunkhouse."

"Of course, Don Miguel. I'll see to it."

Lance turned to see Cisco Red, Booger Jim, and Mike had carefully approached the house, Winchesters in hand. "Mike," Lance said, "Would you help *Señor* de la Garza's party to the bunkhouse?"

"Yassuh, Mistah Lance. I'll settle 'em in."

Don Miguel cleared his throat nervously. "*Señor* Morgan, it is my understanding that some ten years ago, you had an unfortunate encounter in my country with a scoundrel named Santiago."

"Yes sir. A matter of Confederate cotton," Lance said.

"Yes, of course. Perhaps you recall a — uh — a lady who assisted you at that time – one Arabela Cruz."

Lance sat forward in his chair. "Yes, I believe she was later killed by this Santiago."

Don Miguel shook his head sadly. "Yes, she was — very near my hacienda in fact. I don't know if you knew she had surviving family members."

Lance was surprised. "Why no. I had often wondered about that. She had some property in Pata Chica, and we didn't know . . ."

The Mexican held up his hand. "The property is of no consequence. Under conditions of the past ten years in my unfortunate country, the property has doubtless changed hands many times. My concern is for two human beings who are in great danger right now."

Lance wrinkled his brow in puzzlement. "I see. But how can I be of help to you, Don Miguel?"

Lance saw that his visitor's discomfort had increased. "You may speak freely, Don Miguel. Whatever you say will never pass these walls."

"Thank you. I come to you with great reluctance. My purpose in coming could bring great pain to your life, *señor*, but I have no choice." He took a deep breath.

"Arabela's sister, Juanita Cruz, has been in my service many years."

Lance listened while Don Miguel poured out the entire story. How Arabela had escaped and made her way to Juanita

190

with the young baby, and how she was finally discovered and killed by Santiago and his men.

"I have reared the boy as I would my own grandson. He was the one who was to have carried on the traditions of my family and my ranch, the *Amanda Vista*. But it seems misfortune has struck again.

"In the recent conflicts which have swept across my land, I have taken no active part. I am a rancher – not a politician. But Benito Juarez knew me -- knew of my feeling for my country and its people. Now, Benito is dead, and my enemies have accused me of working for the Emperor Maximilian. To now, only the brave loyalty of my *vaqueros* has saved my land – and my very life. I can no longer afford the protection to Juanita and the young boy that I did one time. I can only appeal to you to offer them the refuge no longer mine to give."

"But surely the authorities . . ."

Don Miguel broke in. "Forgive me, my friend." He smiled bitterly. "In my area, Santiago is the authority. His power is much increased in the past ten years. Yet, he is still a madman who will let nothing prevent him from exacting the vengeance he has sworn on an innocent young boy. No, if you do not take them in, the boy will be surely killed – and in such a way that civilized people can hardly imagine."

Lance sputtered. "I'm sorry, Don Miguel, but this has taken me completely by surprise. The boy and woman will be protected of course. How it will be done is the only matter to be considered. Obviously, explanations will be required. I have a wife who must be told."

Don Miguel inclined his head forward. "I understand, and I'm not unmindful of the difficult situation into which I've been forced to put you, *Señor* Morgan. But now it is in your hands. Only you can decide the best way to proceed. Whatever you do — may God go with you. As for me — I return to live or die on my own land."

CHAPTER 25

Colleen sat with hands folded in her lap.

"There's no room for doubt?" she asked, the words coming out with a rasping quality. Then, as Lance sat silently, she answered her own question. "No, of course not."

Lance cleared his throat. "I've told Don Miguel that the boy and his aunt would be protected."

Colleen smiled weakly. "Of course. No question about that."

"The question is," Lance said hesitantly, "how do we handle it? What will his status be?"

"Status?" She lifted her eyebrows. "He's your son, Lance; there can be no question as to his status."

Lance's chin jutted stubbornly. "I already have a son."

Colleen started to laugh. "Lance, you're such a damn fool. Now you have two sons – and you and I better both get used to it."

It was the first time Lance had ever heard his wife swear.

Lance didn't really know what he'd expected, but this half grown boy with the serious demeanor wasn't it. Tall for his ten years and slender, he moved with the grace and ease of a *matador*. It was obvious he had his mother's natural poise, but there was no question but that he was his father's son – the same bright blue eyes, strong jaw line, the slight droop at the corners of his mouth.

He was ushered into the parlor by a Mexican woman in her mid-thirties. Dressed in solid black, she had a lace *mantilla* draped over her head. Her olive skin was darker than Arabela's, but she had the same delicacy of features. She pried her hand loose from the boy's tight grip and placed her hands on his shoulders.

"*Gabrièl, es tu papá,*" she said, then she looked from Lance to Colleen, "*y tu . . . y tu mamá.*"

The boy bowed stiffly and spoke in perfect if slightly accented English. "How do you do, *Papá?*" He turned

192

toward Colleen. "I am please to make your acquaintance, *Mamá*."

Lance fidgeted in his chair as if uncertain what to do. He finally spoke. "Welcome to our home, Gabrièl. We'll try to make you comfortable here."

Colleen glanced sideways at her husband with amusement, then back at the boy. "Come here, Gabrièl."

The youngster walked quickly to stand in front of this woman with the gentle voice. She took both his hands in hers. "Welcome to *your* home, Gabrièl. Tell me, how is it you speak English so well?"

The boy's eyes brightened. "Do I do it well?"

Colleen laughed brightly. "You do it perfectly."

"My grandfather has taught me since I was a small boy," the youngster said proudly. "He said that anyone should know the language of a neighbor."

Colleen stood up. "Your grandfather was a wise man, Gabrièl. Come, we will go meet your brother and sister -- while your father makes your room ready." She turned to Lance, "Put his things in the guest room at the head of the stairs. That will now be Gabrièl's room."

Later that week, climbing the hill behind the house, Brent MacDuff confronted a terrifying predicament. Eyes widened with fright, he pressed his back against a large boulder that lay about halfway up the hill. In front of him, on a rock ledge basking in the sun, was a large diamondback rattlesnake.

Slithering into his distinctive coil, he stared malevolently with beady black eyes. His forked tongue flicked, constantly probing the air around him. Gradually, he inched forward while maintaining a striking coil, the buttoned tail starting its blood-chilling whirr.

Brent frantically searched for a way out. The boulder behind him was too steep to climb. The only other passage was barred by that fanged horror swaying close by his feet. A rustling sound from below the ledge caught his attention. His voice cracked in fear. "Help me, somebody."

"Don't move, *hermano*," warned Gabrièl's voice, and a moment later his head appeared over the ledge on which the rattler slithered purposefully forward. Removing his hat, Gabrièl maneuvered into position and slapped the hat down over the furious diamondback.

"Run, Brent! Get out of here!" the boy shouted as he struggled to contain the large reptile under the hat.

Brent needed little urging. He bolted over the ledge, and slipping and sliding down the hillside, he made for the bunkhouse, howling at the top of his voice.

The snake was large and powerful. Enraged, he lashed out again and again. Gabrièl tried to get a grip on him through the hat, but his hand was slipping off.

Then, the snake slithered free. As Gabrièl jumped back, his foot slipped and his head banged against the boulder. He slumped to the ground unconscious as the snake struck again and again at his body.

Cisco and Booger had almost reached the bunkhouse when they saw Brent scrambling over the rocks. They raced up the hill to meet him. The boy was incoherent with panic. He could only point back up the hill and say over and over, "Gabrièl – snake – snake!"

By the time the men reached the ledge, the rattler was slipping back into the rocks. Young Gabrièl lay unconscious, a trickle of blood seeping from the cut on his head and another small seepage showing on his trousers just above the knee. Booger Jim scooped the boy up in his arms as Cisco crushed the head of the snake under the heel of his boot.

Gabrièl slowly opened his eyes, blinking at the light. A dull pain permeated his entire being. He felt dizzy, nauseated and disoriented. As he became aware of his surroundings, he could see he was in his own bed, surrounded by people looking down at him from what seemed to be a great height. Out of the swimming faces, one became recognizable. He licked his dry lips and uttered one word, *"Mamá."*

Darkness came over him, and he lost consciousness again.

Young Doc Freeburg nodded with satisfaction. Lance stood a short distance from the bed with his arm around Colleen who dabbed at her eyes with a handkerchief. Doc pulled the covers up over the boy's legs.

"I think he's gonna be all right, Mr. Morgan. He was bitten once on the thigh, and his leg is swollen. However, the swelling is going down now. I suspect the venom was somewhat depleted by the snake striking the boy's hat several times. Otherwise, I don't think he would have been alive by the time I got here.

"The blow on the head is another thing – very difficult to evaluate. Hopefully, it's a mild concussion. Few days rest and he'll be up and about.

"Mrs. Morgan, if you have the room, I think it would be better if I stayed – at least until tomorrow. Then, we should be able to tell a little better. I'll give the boy something so he'll sleep through the night."

Colleen inclined her head. "Of course. Whatever it takes to make sure the boy recovers as quickly as possible."

Colleen turned to the weeping Juanita and translated the doctor's prognosis. The terrified woman seemed to find a measure of comfort in the words, and her contorted face seemed to relax as Mike led her away to her room.

Brent MacDuff gripped hard at Cisco Red's hand as he gazed in frightened fascination at Gabrièl's still figure lying on the bed.

The natural resilience of his young, healthy body brought about a rapid and complete recovery for Gabrièl. He also found he had acquired a new admirer in his young half brother. Perhaps that admiration was based as much on Gabrièl's survival of the rattler's attack as on the fact that he had saved the younger boy's life.

Gabrièl was now feeling very comfortable as a member of his new family. While he still carried strong feelings for his aunt Juanita, they had made a gradual and subtle shift in emphasis. He now thought of her more as an aunt than as a surrogate mother. More and more it became *mamá* to whom he came with his problems and triumphs. It was she to whom he poured out his innermost thoughts and feelings.

And there was *papá*. He was still *"papá,"* a man to be obeyed and respected, but with the reserve that was proper between two men with women and children to care for. The boy had never known the affectionate love of a father and could not notice its absence.

Lance felt emotionally confused. He held a deep regard for this son of his first love, but Brent had taken such a large part of his paternal affection, there was little room for this small appealing stranger appearing in his life so suddenly.

When he had expressed his appreciation to Gabrièl for "saving my son," he was hurt and confused by Colleen's rejoinder that the boy had saved his own brother – not just "your son." As far as Lance could see, that was a fine point over what he considered the "same thing."

However, Lance did feel his heart tug at the vulnerability in the young face when it lifted up to his – the trusting faith that Lance would tell him what was right and wrong. He'd felt parental anguish at the minor hurts and mishaps that are the lot of any growing boy. And he felt a glow of pride at Gabrièl's growing proficiency at the skills required of a cattleman in the *brasada*.

All these things he kept hidden in his heart as he outwardly maintained a courteous detachment in their relationship.

At the bunkhouse, there was no such ambivalence in the feelings of the cowboys. The snake-fighting episode, his gifted ways with a rope and a horse, his willingness to take on any job and "bust a gut" to get it done, these things stamped him as one of their own. His Mexican heritage almost forgotten, he was considered having the makings of a "man to ride the river with."

Cisco and Booger spent hours of their own time instructing the boy on the intricate skills involved in the handling of wild cattle from horseback. No day was too long, nor the work too arduous, to prevent them taking a little time at the end of the day for their eager student.

Mike had taken to the boy from the first. He went to great pains to make sure both the boy and his aunt were comfortable and secure in their new surroundings. It was Mike who suggested to Erin that Juanita would be happier if allowed to share housekeeping chores at the big house as well as cooking at the bunkhouse. And Juanita returned to her vigorous battle with her old enemy, dust.

George Gibson hunched his back and eased contentedly deeper into his saddle. Gazing ahead he could see cattle – his cattle – silhouetted against the setting sun. These were no Longhorn cattle out of the Texas brush, but sleek, stocky Durhams -- the Teeswater cattle descended from the fine Colling Brothers herds of Darlington, England. Although George invested an average of $100 each for his foundation stock, he never regretted his switch to improved blood.

Far to the north of the fever zone, with his rich sub-irrigated pasture and ample water in close proximity, George was ideally situated to take advantage of the breed's propensity to lay on weight quickly and to yield a quality carcass that brought premium prices at the market. Naturally docile, the cattle were easily handled and showed little tendency to wander far from their home grounds.

By George's estimate, he now had about two hundred head of the improved cattle and close to three hundred Longhorns he was upgrading through the use of his Durham bulls.

He drew within sight of home and watched the darkened frame house suddenly flare with light as a lamp was lit inside. In spite of the day's fatigue, he felt a warm, comfortable glow that coincided with the light streaming through the window.

"Looks like your mother's puttin' out a light for us."

The young man coaxed his mount up beside him. "Sure hope supper's ready. My belt buckle's rubbin' a blister on my backbone."

George nodded. "Well, it's always been ready. I reckon tonight'll be no different."

196

Another move he'd never regretted was his sudden and unexpected marriage to Helen Porter. Her determination to go back to her homestead, plus his own loneliness, made marriage the ideal solution to a difficult problem. Originally based on mutual need and convenience, the marriage had evolved through the years into a relationship of deep and abiding love. And George could have wanted no more in a son than he got in Phillip Porter. He was a bright, mannerly boy who responded to the unpolished but heartfelt affection of the backwoodsman turned cattleman, outwardly so unlike his own cultured and frail natural father. As for George, having his own father and son relationship cut tragically short, he lavished his loving attention on the lad from the first. Only Helen's wise and tactful intervention had prevented a destructive spoiling by the boy's doting stepfather.

After unsaddling and caring for the horses, the pair headed up the path toward the house. The aroma of savory stew wafted in the air. George's happiness was unrestrained. He clapped his arm around the boy's shoulders in an unashamed show of feeling. Although Phillip felt he was much too old to be hugged, he made no move to pull away as they clumped across the porch to the welcoming door.

At the M-Bar Ranch, Mike had just made a startling announcement. Lance jumped to his feet. "You what?"

He paced quickly across the room to stare out the window. "I can't believe this, Mike. You're not serious."

Mike sat uneasily on the edge of his chair in the small room Lance used as an office. "Yassuh, we serious. Me'n Juanita done talked. We in love, and we aim to marry."

Lance whirled toward Mike. "I don't care about that, Mike. You can't get married. Juanita is a white woman."

Mike looked up, his eyes cool and steady. "Not accordin' to most folks she ain't. She's Mexican."

Lance looked exasperated. "According to the law she is -- and what you're aimin' to do is against the law."

"You means that, even if we both wants to get married, the law won't let us?" Mike sounded puzzled.

Lance had calmed somewhat, and the sincere tone in Mike's voice reminded him that the big Negro had shown himself to be a sensitive person who could be hurt worse by unthinking words than by deliberately cruel ones.

"It's not my doin', Mike. That's the law. Tell you what. Think this thing over a few days -- what kind of life you'll have -- and your children. If you're determined to go through with it — well, my daddy said there's always a way to do somethin' if you want to do it bad enough."

197

Mike came slowly to his feet. "It's a funny world, Mistah Lance. First, the law says I'se a free man – do what I want. Then, it says I can't marry the woman I loves – even if we both want to. That kinda law don't make no sense to me."

Lance placed his hand on the black man's shoulder. "I'm really sorry, Mike. That's the law. But think it over, like I said, and maybe we can work somethin' out."

Lance watched his old friend and former slave walk slowly away from the house. He turned back from the window and slammed his fist into his palm. Dammit, Mike is right. That law makes no sense. Mike is free – or he's not. A man ought to be able to marry anyone – as long as she's willing.

Letter, Aug. 30, 1874
From: Wichita, Kansas
To: Lance Morgan, Esq., Terwilliger, Texas
Deere Friend Lance,

The market was not so good here in Wichita just like we figgered. But knowing your need for cash I sold the hole herd at $57.50 a hd. Draft is being forwarded to your account in Terwilliger. Total count was 1,824 hd. We musta lost 53 hd at Red River and had to give 5 hd to the Indians to cross the Territory. It was a pretty good trip though.

Our old friend Col. Mel Rankin was there but didn't offer enough to buy the herd. I told him better luck next time. He advises that the fever scare is getting worse, and we will get more money on the cows if we winter north of the fever line. Also a big demand in Wyoming and Montana for breeding stock and horses. You might want to bring up a herd of horses next time. They should fetch a nice price.

This is a heller of a town. The Boys were out drinking and carousing all night last night. I had to bail six of them out of the hoosegow this a.m. I think some of them have enough of there draw left to go at it one more night, then I think they will be ready to come home. Hope to see you before end of Sept.

Yrs trly
Guy Madden

The dark sky began to lighten in the east. Slowly and quietly, mounted men moved across the prairie, spreading out to take their assigned places around the darkened ranchhouse below. Flanked by two of the riders, the squat form of Santiago raked his spurs across the flanks of his mount, pulling back on the harsh Spanish spade bit at the same time, causing his horse to rear on its hind legs. Then, he sent the animal soft-stepping down the slope, motioning for his men to do the same.

"This is very good," he snarled to one of the riders. "The gringos sleep and dream. *Bueno!* Their dreams will soon turn to nightmares. What is the name of this *estancia?*"

One of the riders answered. "This is the ranch of *Señor* Elgin Thompson. Many of his *vaqueros* are gone on the trail north with a herd. This will be very easy."

"Remember," Santiago rasped, "first we kill the men at the house – take what is valuable and burn the rest. Then, we take the horses and cattle back across the Rio. Do not kill the women yet. We must have our sport first. Go *muchachos!*"

Jabbing spurs to his mount, the Mexican charged out of the brush toward the house in the clearing. More than thirty riders raced toward the house from all sides. Some carried blazing torches to be thrown into barns and outbuildings.

Suddenly, every building at the ranch sparkled with flashing fire. A continuous roar of gunfire came from what had seemed to be a sleeping household. Shouts of exultation turned into screams of pain. Horses and men went down in a tangled melee of death and terror.

High on a rise overlooking the destruction, Bain MacDuff sat at ease in his saddle. With him were six more Rangers. Except for Bain, none was more than twenty-three years of age. In the dim light he saw that their faces had turned pale and their eyes were icy cold. Good sign, he thought, they're ready to fight.

"Now, boys," he muttered. "Let's go get 'em!"

The survivors of the band of raiders had wheeled their horses in furious retreat from the deadly fire flickering at them from the ranch buildings. A few were on foot, struggling up the hill hoping to find a loose horse -- or perhaps a ride on a companion's mount. Bain's patrol struck them like a lightening bolt from a clear sky. At close range, the Rangers' six shooters dealt instant death to the confused and demoralized bandits.

Within ten minutes it was over. Those raiders still able to ride were tearing through the brush at a wild and reckless pace, heading for the border. Bain's patrol herded three raiders, arms upraised, into the ranch yard.

Twelve Rangers on foot joined them, some leading their saddled horses. They looked expectantly toward the two figures standing in conversation on the porch of the main house. One of them stepped down and strolled to where the Rangers were gathered. "Boys," said L. H. McNelly, "you have done finely. Mr. Thompson sends his compliments."

He purposefully strode to where the frightened prisoners stood, hands lifted high. He stepped up to each one and slapped their hats off heads and stared deep into each face.

Then, he turned to the Rangers. "Anybody know any of these men?"

Receiving no answer, he walked to his horse and mounted. He looked around the troop, and not seeing the man for whom he searched, called out, "Casuse!"

A dark-skinned Ranger with hard eyes rode forward. "Over here, Cap'n."

McNelly raised his voice. "Casuse Sandobal will question the prisoners. The rest of you follow me."

A murmur and a few chuckles passed through the band.

One of the new men, a nineteen-year-old from Virginia, moved up close to Bain."What's that all about, Mr. MacDuff?"

Bain was solemn. "Casuse Sandobal was a rancher just south of here. The bandits attacked his place while he was gone. Destroyed the ranch, raped his wife and daughter, then tortured and killed them. When we want information from a captured bandit, Casuse is McNelly's official questioner."

"You mean – you mean he tortures them?"

"We don't watch, so we don't know what he does. But he gets the information we need."

"Is that how we knew about the raid today?"

"Naw. That was from McNelly's spies. He's got tricky meskins in just about ever' band of outlaws on the border. The ranchers pay the spies – and we use 'em."

"But this Sandobal, what does he do with the prisoners after — after the questioning.?"

"*Quien sabe?* Who knows? Probably hangs 'em."

The man's eyes widened. "But that's barbaric."

Bain glared at the youngster. "When you don't know what you're talking about -- don't talk. You think this is some kinda field of honor -- with rules of chivalry? If you live long enough, you'll see what we've seen -- and you'll think the way we think."

The young Ranger asked no more questions.

Casuse Sandobal caught up with them later that night as they made camp. He was alone.

CHAPTER 26

Santiago was in a murderous rage. Once across the river, the seething anger replaced the cold fear that had caused the chilling cold of his insides as the Rangers swept down on his band at the Thompson Ranch. He remembered with horror that he had lost control of his bladder and had welcomed the plunge through the shallow river waters that had obliterated the evidence of his shame.

But he knew that all of his blustering and posturing could not erase the fact that he had lost twenty-one men in that shameful encounter with McNelly's Rangers. Even worse was the knowledge that he had been betrayed by one of his own.

It was painfully obvious that the Rangers had not only known he would attack the Thompson Ranch but when that attack would come. Santiago had his own spy network, and he knew that McNelly had fewer than fifty men to patrol the entire region between the Nueces and the Rio Grande. He would not have stationed so many Rangers at Thompson's Ranch for an indefinite period. No! The *Rinches* had to have known exactly when the attack would come. That information could have come only from his own band.

The men were restless. They were afraid to speak, but the bandit leader could see it in their eyes – in the way they sat silently, scratching at the ground with a stupid stick, or gazing vacantly at an empty sky. They had been promised easy victories, bountiful plunder, and herds of cattle and horses. Instead, many of the newer recruits had seen only the cold faces, felt the hot lead of McNelly's Rangers – and viewed the dead bodies of their companions abandoned in wild flight back across the river.

Now he needed more new recruits. The disastrous encounter with McNelly had badly depleted his ranks. He hadn't lost so many men since the raid on the cotton train detail in Rosita some ten years ago. He had to do something to restore his credibility as a successful general – something with little risk and big reward.

George Gibson heard the whinny of a horse. He raised his hand, and instantly Helen moved to the window dragging a new Winchester repeater while George moved to the door and opened it slightly. Although the Comanche wasn't the threat he had been in the past, this was still not a time nor place for foolhardiness. He peered into the harshness of the noon sun. A rider approached from the east.

George stepped out onto the porch, his Winchester carried lightly across his arm. Out of the corner of his eye, he saw a glint from the south window and smiled. "Put up your gun, Phillip, it's just a boy."

He moved on out to the front gate. "Howdy, young feller. What you doing way out here by yourself?"

The youngster squinted a pug nose against the glare. He appeared to be no more than eleven or twelve years old. Hair the color of straw stuck out from under his floppy hat. "Howdy, mister. My folks'n me are your new neighbors. We homesteadin' 'bout five miles down the holler here."

"Well, get down boy. We got some vittles 'bout ready."

The boy hooked his leg over the saddle and slid to the ground. "Thankee, sir, I'd like a drink of water if tain't too much trouble."

With a little persuasion, the boy took a place at the table and gave Helen's cooking all the attention it deserved. When he finally slowed a bit, George managed to learn that his name was Marvin Jerrod, that his paw's name was Claude, that beans were his favorite food – especially with molasses poured over them, and that they'd moved there from Williamson County.

"Williamson County," George mused. "I hear they grow'em tough and longhorned down there."

The boy looked up briefly from his plate. "We's tough enough I reckon."

"How long you folks been there? I rode by that way last week and wasn't nobody around."

"We jest got here yesterday, mister. My paw and brother got started on a soddy this mornin'." He paused, a startled look on his face. "Cripes! I done forgot what I come for. They give us a letter for you down to Antelope Springs when we come through."

He fished into his back pocket and came out with a crumpled letter with George's name on front. "Dang, I'm sorry. I jest clean forgot."

George laughed. "That's all right, boy. After all the time that letter's been on the road, a few minutes more ain't gonna hurt much."

He walked over to the better light by the window and

laboriously read the letter as Helen waited impatiently.

"Doggone!" he exclaimed. "Mike's gettin' married."

Helen smiled. "Mike? The colored man who was with you when you first came by here?"

"That's the one. Doggone, I'd like to see Mike and Lance and Bain and them again."

Helen smiled knowingly. "Well, why not?"

George threw his arms around his wife and kissed her on the mouth while the two young boys chuckled nervously.

The social life that prevailed at the MacDuff Ranch revolved around the stately figure of Lance's mother-in-law. She was social director, dietitian, arbiter of disputes, and sole dictator of codes of conduct for all who entered her domain. Lance Morgan may have built the new headquarters into a veritable mansion, and Colleen had instilled the joy and laughter of new life into it, but it was Erin MacDuff who ran it. Quietly but firmly, she assumed the role as one born to it.

Erin MacDuff didn't just sit at the head of the table, she presided over it. Her question, "Do you prefer white or brown gravy on your potatoes?" deftly precluded the possibility that the visitor might want neither. She carved the roasts, ladled the soups and watchfully supervised the eating habits of anyone under eighteen years of age who sat at the table.

Erin was also very much in charge of all children's activity around the ranch. By talent, training, and preference, she was an exceptional teacher of young people. Steeped in the tradition of the demanding schedule of Scottish schools, she insisted on early and certain mastery of basic reading skills as an essential foundation of a classical education. Social graces she taught by precept and example, and any hint of boorishness in behavior was grounds for appropriate correction, applied promptly and without discrimination.

A steadily growing number of neighbors within reasonable riding distance, plus the solid reputation of the household's effusive hospitality, made the entertainment of visitors a frequent occurrence. Often the visitors were youngsters invited to spend a day or two with the Morgan children.

As youngest of the tribe at five years of age, Ann Marie Morgan was the object of fewer visits than were her older brothers. Yet no one enjoyed the visits more. She had a remarkable talent for insinuating herself into just about any activity the older children might plan for themselves.

Gabrièl exhibited remarkable patience with his half-sister, playing games with her, and helping her with her studies. Brent, however, considered her an unadulterated pest, and except for times when there was no one else to play with, tried his best to ignore her completely.

Erin pursued the continuing education and training of her small charges with loving impartiality. Gabrièl had been instantly accepted as another "grandchild" and was initiated into his own study times in which horsemanship, roping, and other ways of the brush had no part. No outside activity, no matter how exciting, unusual, or important to the ranch, was allowed to interfere with study times.

The rule was put to its sternest test when one of the *vaqueros* from Pedro's crew rode in from Terwilliger with a telegram for Lance. Within minutes, the word was spread throughout the ranch: George Gibson was coming.

Lance was pleased to know his old friend was coming to visit. However, no one knew to what extent he was struggling just to keep his spreading cattle empire alive. The summer had been one of searing drought. His far-flung herds ranged back and forth across his fenced property, searching eagerly for any hardy sprigs that dared to show a slender stem or budding leaf. Little puffs of dust arose where each hoof touched the dry, crusty ground.

The mesquite and other browse was picked clean of leaves as high as a mortgaged Longhorn could reach. Big Frog Spring, which had always been a dependable source of water for almost one hundred thousand acres of pastureland, was reduced to a muddy trickle. The bank held a mortgage on his cattle, his horse herd, and all land other than the small original holdings of Scotty MacDuff.

His herds were finding it harder and harder to get through to an uncertain northern market. The Chisholm Trail was almost completely closed by angry farmers north of Indian Territory. Fields of crops now grew where, just a couple of years ago, drover's fires flickered like fireflies on the grass-covered prairie. Hundreds of thousands of migrating Longhorn cattle were pushed farther and farther to the west. Eastern markets were often glutted with beef and prices would tumble crazily, only to recover and soar again shortly thereafter. Finding a market was a crap game – frequently with loaded dice.

Regardless of the problems, the builder of the Bar-M holdings was determined to keep them to himself. In the back of his mind was the knowledge that a half-dozen leather bags, hidden away in a cave, could very easily wipe out his debt. But he was also aware that he could never use it for that purpose. Not without giving up title to his soul.

It was almost like Christmas at the ranch. The table

groaned under the feast spread by Erin MacDuff. Lance, although saddened by the news of Henry's death, was pleased to see his old friend's obvious happiness with his wife and stepson. Erin was especially pleased to have a person of such obvious culture as Helen as a house guest.

Mike just grinned quietly while George ribbed him about his upcoming marriage. Juanita was at first uncomfortable in her unaccustomed role as guest at the big house but soon warmed under Colleen's still considerable charm.

The group had barely tasted the soup when there was a commotion, the door swung open, and a dusty figure rushed into the room. "Have I missed supper yet?"

Bain MacDuff was home for the wedding.

Lance ushered the diminutive black man into the MacDuff parlor. Dressed in worn black broadcloth, white shirt and wide black scarf knotted around his neck, the man eased cautiously into the proffered chair. Eyes that appeared too large for his head peered over half-rim spectacles, giving him the appearance of a flat-beaked owl.

Lance took a chair next to the man. "We appreciate your coming way out here from San Antonio, Reverend Parks."

"Wal, suh, I figgers I goes where the Lord has work for me. Besides," he chuckled lightly, "my flock is snake-pore, Mistah Morgan. Them twenty-dollar gold pieces don't show up much in our collection plates."

He squirmed a little in his chair. "Uh, where's the happy bride and groom?"

Lance heard the outside door open. "I think they're here right now."

When Lance introduced them to the preacher, he noticed the man's eyes grew wide at the sight of Juanita. He rose from his chair, obviously agitated. "Mistah Morgan, scuse me, but I can't do this here marriage."

"Why not, Reverend Parks? Mike has the proper license."

"You tryin' to get me hung, Mistah Morgan. Dat's a white woman. And, if I marry her to dis nigger here, I gonna be in big trouble."

"Oh no," Lance replied. "There's no problem here. The woman has colored blood."

"I don't know, sah," the man protested, "she look mighty white to me."

"Tell you what, Reverend, I'll take full blame if any trouble comes of it." Lance folded a five-dollar bill and tucked it into the preacher's vest pocket.

The man patted the pocket appreciatively. "Now you mention it, I believes I does see some nigger features in dat

205

woman. If you say she colored — I ain't goin' to dispute no white man's word."

"Goshamighty, Mistah Lance," Mike said later when they were alone, "I had a hard enough time talkin' Juanita outa a priest. Never figgered on no trouble from my own kind."

As Mike went on his way, Lance spoke to himself. "I'm afraid you haven't seen the real trouble yet, my friend."

The wedding was simple. Erin and Colleen decorated the parlor in a fall motif with pumpkins and corn from the garden. Sunflowers and cattails made attractive arrangements on either side of the bride and groom. Immediately after the ceremony, Mike and Juanita climbed into Lance's old, but still fancy, buggy to leave for a honeymoon in San Antonio.

Lance and George strolled toward the corral after an inspection of the ranch's new facilities. George was impressed with the prosperous air of the MacDuff spread.

Lance put a hand on his shoulder. "I've been thinkin' of somethin', George, that might benefit us both."

George laughed. "You still wanta drag out that gold. That it, Lance?"

"No, that's over. This is cattle business. You know about the granger quarantine in Kansas?"

"Yeah, I know about it. Don't affect me much, but I know about it,"

"That's the point. You're above the fever line, right?"

"That's right. Get a nice premium for my cattle too."

Lance grinned and slapped him on the arm. "But just a few cattle, right?"

"Well, I've got nearly five hundred head -- lots of 'em improved."

Lance looked solemn. "You market what? — maybe two hundred head a year? I could bring two thousand or three thousand head every fall, winter 'em at your place, beat ever'body to market the next year with certified clean stock. Top the market for sure."

George furrowed his brow. "How would I keep your Longhorn bulls away from my improved cows?"

Lance caught his arm. "You gotta fence your place. That's gonna be the future of ranchin'. Do it, George, whether you take my deal or not."

The man squinted. "You've turned into a real crusader on this thing, Lance. No wonder I hear you ain't too popular with some of your neighbors."

Lance's face was grim. "They don't like fences, but sooner or later, they'll all fence their land."

After their return from the honeymoon, the newlyweds settled down in the small cabin Juanita had been using since her arrival at the ranch. Lance took Mike over to the *Rincón de Laguna* and showed him a herd of cows being worked.

"Know what they're doin' down there, Mike?"

Mike frowned at his former master. "I ain't been away that long. They brandin' cattle."

"Do you know what brand they puttin' on 'em, Mike?"

Mike was puzzled. "I reckon the M-Bar same as always."

"Nope," Lance said smugly. "It's the Double M -- registered with STAC in the name of Mike Morgan. It's a little wedding present, Mike."

"I don't know what to say, Mistah Lance." His eyes brimmed with tears.

"No need to say anything. I haven't showed it much lately – and I've done some things that hurt you – but I know I owe you plenty, Mike.

"You've given me somethin' I couldn't have bought anywhere -- loyalty. Now, I figger it's time you quit doin' ever'thing for me and started doin' somethin' for yourself -- and your new family. I'm gonna help you get some land too. We'll start lookin' right away."

Mike looked at the ground. "Mistah Lance, I appreciates you givin' me these cows. It's more'n I ever figgered to have. But I'll have to pass on the land, thanky very much. I been talkin' to Mistah George. I likes the sound of that country where he lives. Guess I'll be goin' up there this spring."

Lance was stunned. "Doggone, Mike, I ain't never thought about you leavin' this country. We ain't ever been separated very long 'cept when I was in the army. You been with me as long as I can remember."

"Yassuh. But I guess maybe it's time. I sure don't gotta watch over you no more – and like you say – I guess it's time for me to go on my own."

Lance sat for a moment in quiet thought. That was a new country George and Mike would be going to – less tied to custom and tradition – and old ideas.

"Maybe you're right, Mike. It might be for the best."

CHAPTER 27

Lance glanced out the window. "Colleen, have you seen Gabrièl? Erin was looking for him. It's time for his lessons."

Colleen wrinkled her brow. "Not since earlier. He went for a ride this morning. I think he was supposed to eat lunch at the bunkhouse. Maybe he's still over there."

"I'd better go see. Wanta go along, George?"

"No thanks, Lance. I can hardly move. I'll wait here."

Lance wasn't really concerned although it wasn't like the boy to be late for lessons. He saw Cisco coming out of the bunkhouse. "Hey, Cisco. Is Gabrièl in there?"

"No, I haven't seen him since early mornin'."

Lance frowned. "Didn't he have lunch here?"

"No. He was supposed to, but he never showed up. We thought he decided to eat at the big house."

Lance hurried toward the stables. He shouted over his shoulder, "Cisco, get ever'body out. We gotta find that boy."

They found Gabrièl's horse about three miles from headquarters, lathered with sweat, laced with cactus thorns, and the saddle had slipped under his belly. Cisco caught the animal and turned him over to one of the younger hands to take back to the stables.

Pedro moved out in the lead, backtracking the animal through a wide flat and around a large whitebrush motte. There, they found the answer. The ground was scarred with many hoof prints. There had been at least three other horses whose tracks blended with those of Gabrièl's mount.

Pedro read the story quickly. "Here's where they caught him. Then, the tracks lead to the west. *Patrón*, I'm afraid our Gabrièlito has been taken by the *bandidos*."

Lance's sunbrowned face drained of all its color. "We gotta catch 'em. Let's get goin'."

The others exchanged glances. Finally, Booger Jim spoke. "You ain't thinkin' right, bossman. Them tracks is at least three hours old. They'll be right at the river by now."

"I don't care," Lance exploded. "I'm goin' after 'em."

He lunged his horse forward, but Cisco reached out and caught the horse by the headstall, bringing him to a spinning stop. "Booger's right, bossman. You know we'd all ride into hell and fight the devil over his pitchfork if that'd get your boy back. But what you're aimin' to do won't help none."

Lance knew if they'd planned to kill the boy, they would have already done so. If not, they had some other purpose. Lance was sure he would not be long in learning what it was.

He had only to wait until morning. A lone Mexican rider approached the ranch with a white rag tied to a stick. Lance, flanked by George and Bain, rode out to meet him.

"*Buenos dias, señores,*" the Mexican chirped. "I bring you greetings from my great leader, General Santiago."

Lance growled, "You mean from that cutthroat scum. Whatta you want?"

The man held out both hands, palms outward. "I want nothing, *señor*. It is you who have kidnapped a young Mexican boy – whom we rescued – who want something. You want him back. General Santiago is a reasonable man. He is willing to bargain."

Lance, with an effort, controlled his anger. "What kind of bargain does Santiago have in mind?"

The Mexican laughed, showing a mouthful of dirty and crooked teeth. "Gold, *señor* – $140,000 in gold."

Lance's face didn't change expression. "What makes your leader think I have that kind of gold?"

"Ha! He knows you had the gold. He knows you never used it. Therefore, you still have it, *no es verdad?*"

"And if I do?"

"You will bring it to the Rio Bravo, Carrizo Crossing, day after tomorrow, and you will exchange it for the boy. If you do not, the boy dies."

"Day after tomorrow? He will let the boy go?"

"Of course, *señor*. At midday – *en punto!*" The Mexican turned his horse away and looked over his shoulder. "Santiago sends you this little present to make certain you understand his intentions, *señor*."

The Mexican tossed a small leather bag at the feet of Lance's horse, jabbing spurs to his mount at the same time and headed west at a dead run.

Lance stepped off his horse and picked up the bag. He opened the drawstring and emptied an object into his hand. With a roar of horror, he dropped it to the ground, leaped into his saddle and spurred the animal into a lung blowing race after the disappearing rider.

George started after them but was restrained by Bain's hand. "No George. He won't catch him. See what it is."

George dismounted and reached down into the clump of grass and picked it up – leathery and crusted with dried blood. "It's an ear, Bain."

His face hardened. "Why would the bastard do something like that?"

"He was gettin' our attention, George."

Next day, Lance, George, Mike, and Bain took the buggy into the hills. When they returned, six dusty bags of gold were tucked into the secret compartment in the buggy's bed. It was decided to take Booger, Cisco, Pedro, and three of Pedro's most trusted *vaqueros* to the exchange in case of treachery.

Colleen turned her face up to Lance as he sat on his most dependable horse in the dawning light. "Bring him back to us, Lance, no matter what it takes. Nothing else matters — your damned land — cattle — your stupid pride — none of it. Just bring our boy back."

Erin turned from her tasks. "And if you can't, Lance, make them pay for what they've done. There are times when violence is our only protection against such scum."

Lance, pale faced and solemn spoke quietly. "You can count on it, Erin."

The trip to Carrizo Crossing took the entire morning. The horsemen, accompanied by the buggy, pulled up to the river's edge at midday. Both banks appeared to be deserted.

George rode down beyond the brushy edge. "Lance, they ain't showed up."

Lance pointed to a thin, double line of rope stretching across the water. It was looped around a scraggly mesquite tree on the near bank and tied to the bow of a small boat. "They've been here," Lance said.

Across the river, another boat was tied by its bow to the other strands of rope. As one boat was pulled to the near bank, the other boat would be pulled across in the opposite direction. A dozen Mexicans topped the rim and rode down to the far edge of the water. The boy, hands tied behind his back, was with them. One rode to the front.

"I am General Santiago," he shouted across the water. "Do you have the gold, gringo?"

Lance shouted back, "Yes. Give us the boy."

The bandit roared with laughter. "Not so fast, gringo. Put the gold into the boat on your side, and we will put the boy into this boat. As we pull the gold to us — the boy will be drawn to you. Could anything be more fair than that?"

Lance checked. It appeared to be as Santiago said.

He gave the signal, and the men began carrying the bags to the skiff.

Lance, still suspicious, instructed the men to keep a firm hold on the boat so it could not be pulled across prematurely.

"All right, it's loaded. Put the boy in the boat."

At a signal from the Mexican, one of the bandits pulled the young boy off the horse, and pushing him roughly down the bank, threw him into the boat.

Slowly, they began to pull on the rope. The boat with Gabrièl aboard slipped into the stream and swung broadside to the current but was held firmly by the rope at its bow. The pitiful figure, a dirty and stained bandage around his head, hunched his thin shoulders against the cold wind and turned a yearning face toward the near bank.

"*Papá! Papá!* Help me, please!"

Lance felt pressure against his heart at the forlorn cry, and his eyes watered.

As the boats neared the halfway point where they would pass one another, there was a sudden stir on the Mexican side. Two of the horsemen grabbed both strands of the rope and wrapped them quickly around their saddle horns. Another rushed up to his knees into the water and cut one of the ropes.

"Watch it, Lance. It's a trick," Bain rushed to the water.

Lance made a grab for the loose rope as it slithered through the water, but it was jerked from his burning hands by the now running horses on the other side.

The boat with the screaming boy swung rapidly downstream to crash into a bank where a waiting Mexican snatched him up and dragged him back into the heavy growth along the river bottom.

Lance struggled to his feet in waist deep water and screamed at the bandit. "You'll pay for this, Santiago."

The Mexican sat calmly on his horse watching the American flounder in the water. "*Oh no, amigo*, you will pay. You will do exactly as I say or the boy will surely die."

Lance fought for control of himself. "What could you want now? I have no more gold."

The bandit laughed. "Gold? I have no need for more gold. I have plenty already." His eyes narrowed, and he pointed a finger at Lance. "I want you ruined, gringo dog. You will bring me five thousand head of cattle one week from today -- and I will give you back your bastard. Bring the cattle here to this crossing. If you are one day late - you will get back the boy's other ear. Another day late - and you get a finger. How long this can go on I leave for you to imagine."

"You scum! You rotten sunuvabitch!" Bain and George had to wade out where Lance was and pull him back. It took their combined strength to overpower him. In the distance they could hear Gabrièl call, "Help me, *Papá!*"

A short distance from the river, the men made a rough camp. Lance sat silently by a small fire. George and Mike moved in close. "What you gonna do now, Mistah Lance?"

Lance turned blank eyes toward Mike. "Huh? Oh, I don't know yet. Gotta think of somethin'."

George bit off a chew. "I expect you'll think better back home, Lance. We'll regroup and come up with somethin'."

Lance looked surprised. "I'm not goin' home. I don't dare show my face at home until I bring that boy with me."

Bain asked, "You gonna give him the cattle, Lance?"

Lance's mouth hardened. "I ain't givin' that meskin one lumpy-jawed head. He won't turn Gabrièl loose no matter what I do. We're gonna hafta take him back."

Bain squatted on his heels. "Don't do anything 'til I get back, Lance. I'm gonna report this to McNelly."

Lance looked up in surprise. "McNelly's got no authority to go into Mexico, Bain."

"True," Bain muttered, "but I know McNelly. He'll know somethin' to do."

Lance looked interested. "How long'll it take, Bain?"

"Day to get there – a day back."

Lance nodded. "Get gone, Bain. I'll wait two days."

Lance jumped to his feet. "Cisco!" he called, "I want you and Booger to go down there by the river. Kill anything that tries to cross in either direction. Santiago don't need to know where we are or what we're doin'.

"Pedro!" The Mexican stepped out of the darkness. "Pedro, I want you to take your three *vaqueros* back to the ranch. Get the rest of your men out and start gathering cattle. Make a big show of it – kick up plenty of dust."

"*Si, patrón.* I leave immediately."

Next day at mid-morning, Lance was surprised to see a cloud of dust signaling a band of riders coming in – not from the west and Mexico – but from the east. Taking defensive positions in the surrounding brushland, Lance and the others waited to see what new threat might be coming down on them.

When the riders were a hundred yards away, Lance stepped out in plain view. At least fifteen riders strung out behind a leader, who threw up his hand at the sight of Lance. The riders slowed to a stop, and the leader approached at a walk. Lance recognized the white beard and shaggy mane.

"Zeb Marlin? That you, Zeb?"

The man rode up slowly. "Understand you got some trouble, Morgan."

"You're right about that," Lance responded.

As the riders dismounted, Lance explained what had happened and how they had been tricked. "But what're you doing over here, Zeb? Ain't this outa your territory?"

The man tilted his head. "Not when a neighbor's in trouble it ain't."

Lance felt confused. "But how did you know about it?"

Zeb grinned causing the mustache points to stick out at a rakish angle. "Your woman come ridin' into my place last night like a wild Comanche. Told me what happened. I sent a couple of hands over to fetch Amos and Elgin. Figgered you could use some help."

"You ain't wrong about that, Zeb."

Zeb nodded. "And we had quite a few volunteers from our hands. Couldna' kept 'em from comin' with a shotgun."

"We can sure use ever'one of 'em, Zeb. If you don't mind invadin' Mexico with a handful of people."

"Whooee. You're bitin' off a mouthful, boy. You know where them meskins are hidin' out?"

"Nope. Guess we'll have to track 'em down."

"Not a chance, boy," the rancher said. "You cross that river, you need to know exactly where you goin'."

"But I don't know where he is," Lance protested.

The rancher winked. "I do."

"How could you know?"

"Boy, that's what you pay dues for. I know where he keeps his stolen livestock. I know where he hides when things get too hot for him. I could find out what he ate for breakfast if I gave a damn."

"I owe you, Zeb. More'n I could ever pay back."

"That's what neighbors are for." He chuckled. "Even them as builds bobwire fences across God's own rangeland."

"Zeb," Lance said, "if you ever wanta go somewhere and one of my fences is in your way – just cut that sonuvabitch!"

Sundown the next evening, Bain rode into the camp with six riders. L. H. McNelly had not been at Ranger headquarters as he had taken the bulk of the company into Brownsville where Cortina was threatening trouble from across the river. However, Bain was able to contact him by wire. While he could give no orders for Rangers to cross the Rio Grande, he gave all Rangers remaining at headquarters a week leave of absence. They were free to go where they pleased. Six

213

Rangers were at headquarters. Six came with Bain.

Lance calculated the odds. "Looks like he'll have us outnumbered about two to one. We should have surprise on our side, but I don't want anything to happen to the boy . . ." he hesitated, ". . . my son."

The men swam their horses across the river by the light of a half moon. Within an hour, they were crouched in the brush that surrounded a Mexican ranch with several adobe and log corrals, an adobe main house and a carrizo-roofed bunkhouse that was little more than an open shed. A large adobe wall encircled the *hacienda* and featured a gate of wood reinforced with iron straps and bolts.

"I'll go in first," Lance said. "I want to get to the boy as soon as the fight starts. Give me ten minutes, Bain, then you and the Rangers open the gate. The rest of you ride in and shoot anything that moves -- except for women or children. God be with you all."

Lance slipped away into the darkness along the wall. A little later, they saw him ease over the top and drop out of sight on the other side.

CHAPTER 28

When Lance dropped to the ground, he quickly moved toward the main building. With a cursory glance toward the fires burning in front of the long open wall of the bunkhouse, he decided that, for security reasons, the boy would not be there. He slipped along the side of the main building until he came to a small, barred window.

Carefully moving to get a look inside, he saw a long table in what appeared to be the main room. Santiago was sitting at the head of the table. Seated along each side were several of the bandit's *bravos*. Food and drink covered the table, and the men were sloppily shoveling it down. Lance searched the room carefully, but Gabrièl was not to be seen. He ducked low and bypassed the window to another one through which no light gleamed. He was running out of time.

He removed his hat and exposed as little of himself as possible as he strained to see into the darkened room. He soon gave up on sight and listened carefully, ear pressed to the barred window. Then, he heard a movement and a short outcry. He had to take the chance.

"Gabrièl!" He whispered. He heard movement inside.

"Quien es?" No mistake, it was the voice of his son. He scratched lightly on the window.

"Gabrièl, *es tu papá*. Be very quiet."

"I will, *Papá. Cuidado* — be careful."

Lance fingered his shotgun and looked frantically for a way in. There was none – other than through the room where the bandits were eating. He withdrew his watch and held it to the light. In three minutes the fighting would start. Lance had the feeling that Santiago would kill the boy at once rather than take a chance on a rescue.

There was no longer time for caution. He walked to the door, opened it slowly, and stepped inside. His manner was so matter of fact that he was well into the room before the bandits noticed he wasn't one of them.

The man to the left of Santiago opened his mouth to shout

215

a warning. Lance tilted his shotgun. The roar masked the scream as he died in his seat. Another was on his feet, kicking back his chair. The load from the second barrel blasted him backward. Lance sprinted through the door leading into the hallway slamming it against the hail of bullets thudding into the other side. He looked at the row of doors. Which was the one in which Gabrièl was being held captive? He picked the most likely and kicked it off its hinges. A cry of alarm rose from the guard at the gate. It was cut off by the sounds of gunfire and galloping horses.

As he entered the room, he felt the slight form of Gabrièl fasten itself to his legs. *"Papá,* you came for me."

Lance quickly fished two shells out of his pocket and reloaded the shotgun. He heard the barking of rifle fire as the attackers raked the bunkhouse. He heard the hall door being opened very slowly. He pushed Gabrièl back into a corner and riveted his eyes on the doorway. A figure, a revolver in each hand. The man fired quickly -- too quickly without finding his target – and the left barrel of the shotgun blew him against the opposite wall.

Lance risked breaking the gun's action open to load another round. Santiago urged his men to rush the room. They hesitated, none too anxious to face the deadly blasts from the shotgun.

The gunfire outside had almost stopped. Only the sporadic bark of an occasional Winchester cut the night air. Zeb Marlin called out. "You, in the house, surrender right now – or die where you stand."

Lance listened to a murmur of voices from the main room. A voice shouted. "No shoot! We surrender, *señor.* The outer door squeaked open and footsteps shuffled as the bandits marched out.

Edging up against the window, he watched the Mexicans filing out, hands upraised. He put an arm around the shivering boy. "It's all right, Gabrièl. You're safe "

He led the boy into the bullet-ridden main room.

"So, *amigo!* You are looking well."

He whirled and looked down the bore of a .45 caliber revolver. The bandit chief sat cross legged under the table.

"But not for long. Here you will die, gringo -- you and the bastard boy." The bandit rose gracefully for one of his bulk and thumbed back the hammer, then hesitated. "First, give me the shotgun. I have need of such a weapon."

Pushing the boy behind him, Lance stepped forward.

"Wait," the Mexican muttered. "Turn it around."

Lance reversed the weapon, and holding it by the barrel, offered it stock first. As the man reached for the weapon,

Lance thrust the butt hard into his face, at the same time striking at the revolver with his left hand.

The pistol bucked with a deafening blast as Lance brought the heavy shotgun down in an arc to land solidly across the bandit's forearm. Through the ringing in his ears, Lance heard both weapons clatter heavily across the floor. A searing pain immobilized the entire left side of his body. He staggered toward the fallen shotgun, but his path was blocked by the bulk of his adversary.

"So, it comes to this, eh gringo? *Mano a mano.* Perhaps this is better – as it should be between men – agreed?"

Santiago lashed out a booted foot against Lance's kneecap that sent him crashing backward to the floor. Light-headed with pain, Lance rolled frantically to avoid the impact of another powerful kick. He was only partially successful, as the heel of the Mexican's boot raked sharply across his hip joint.

Brutal hands closed on his throat. In his pain-distorted vision, the bandit's face loomed unnaturally huge like a giant Halloween pumpkin, bloated and distorted by a killing lust. Bloodshot eyes became mere slits and flecks of spittle formed on the thin lips.

As Lance felt himself lifted from the floor, his remaining vitality ebbed away, leaving behind an inert shell to be pushed against the wall by Santiago who was squeezing out the last drop of life from his body.

The Mexican's face blurred out of focus. The hands loosened their grip, and Lance slid down the wall. The snarling bandit turned from Lance to deal with a form attacking with a flurry of small fists. With a smash from one hand, Gabrièl was sent flying across the room to lie senseless in the corner.

He turned back. "I deal with the *cabronito* later. First, we finish here."

Hands flexed, coming for his throat. He seemed unable to act. Santiago was going to kill him, and the young boy who had trusted him would now die at the hands of this madman.

He had to do something to survive – to save Gabrièl. He couldn't just die here doing nothing – but that seemed to be exactly what he was going to do.

"No-o-o!" The sound wrenched up from his gut with a strength that surprised both men. Startled, Santiago fell backward. Lance lurched forward, bringing his knee up into the bandit's groin with all the force he could muster.

As the man doubled up with a groan of pain, Lance fell across his neck and shoulders. They both crashed to the floor. Deadly hands again groped for his throat. Instinctively, ignoring everything else, he seized one of the wrists with both

217

hands and sank his teeth into the flesh of the forearm. Clamping down tightly, he twisted his head from side to side, tearing at the wound like a predatory animal.

A satisfying scream of agony ripped from the bandit's throat. Fighting in a desperate frenzy, Lance slammed his head into the bloated face in front of him. Cartilage cracked under the impact. He was beyond pain – beyond feeling. He gouged with his thumbs at the little pig eyes now wide open in terror. A red haze blurred his vision and all consciousness fled his mind.

"Lance — Lance Morgan!" The voice seemed to come to him from the bottom of a well.

He could feel a cool wetness on his forehead, but the rest of his body seemed to have no feeling at all.

"Can you hear me, Lance?"

Lance opened his eyes and fought to clear his vision. Several figures materialized, faded, then came together again. He could make out the familiar faces of Bain and Mike peering down on him. Just behind them, Jeb Marlin. George was holding his head up.

He tried to raise himself farther, and the pain asserted itself. A sharp, burning pain streaked down his left side, his throat ached, and his head felt ready to split.

"Wha — what happened?" His voice croaked like a frog.

Bain smiled slightly. "It's all over. We got 'em."

"Gabrièl?" Lance struggled to his feet. My son?"

Mike broke in. "Don't worry. He's fine. Mistah Thompson took him on home. Said this wasn't gonna be no place for a young boy."

"And Santiago?"

George grinned. "Well, he was still alive when we pulled you off of him. But just barely. We had to pry your fingers from around his neck."

Lance pulled himself to a sitting position. He was in the courtyard of the main house. The first rays of sunlight were breaking over the bunkhouse and probing the far end of the *hacienda* enclosure. "How many of us . . ?"

Mike shook his head. "One of Mistah Thompson's boys is dead, and a Ranger got shot in the hand. And, Cisco – he hurt pretty bad, Mistah Lance."

Lance struggled to his feet, fighting a stitch in his side. He touched the area of pain and found it tightly bandaged.

Zeb Marlin stooped and helped him to his feet. "You took a bullet in that side, boy. Creased a rib and came on through. You're gonna be stiff and sore."

"Where are the bandits?"

Zeb stroked his beard. "Boys got about fourteen in the stable."

"Santiago with 'em?"

"Yep. Though he may not know it yet. He was still out cold when we dumped him in there."

"What you gonna do with 'em, Zeb?"

"Hell, we reckoned that'd be up to you, boy. But I sent a couple of boys to string up some ropes in the cottonwoods down by the creek. Figgered we might need 'em."

Pulling himself erect with all his strength, Lance picked up his shotgun and walked slowly toward the stables.

The bandits sat motionless in the dirt under the watchful eyes of two Rangers. There was the sprawled figure of Santiago painfully pulling himself up on his elbows.

Lance cut his eyes toward the stern figure of Zeb Marlin. "Don't guess you'd wanta take 'em back to Texas for trial?"

The man snorted. "Think they'd get tried – or us?"

Lance chuckled. "You got any spies among 'em?"

"Yep. But I thought I'd better see what you was gonna do with the rest of them bandits before I pointed him out."

"Call him out, Zeb."

Zeb called out, "Morado! Come out here."

One of the prisoners leaped to his feet and trotted up to the rancher. *"Si, señor."*

Zeb leaned close to the man. "Get your butt outa here, Morado. But if I ever hear of you raidin' into Texas again, you're one dead meskin, understand?"

"Si, señor." He headed for the gate at a trot.

Zeb raised his voice. "Let this one go. He's one of ours."

Lance looked over the prisoners who stared back with sullen eyes. "Anyone here called *El Cojo?*"

One of the men in back raised himself hesitantly. *"Si."*

Lance beckoned him. "Come here, *El Cojo.*"

Lance asked, "You speak English?"

"Si. A little."

"You helped the woman, Arabela, one time?"

"How do you know this, *señor?*"

Lance sighed. "It's enough that I know. Go home. *El Cojo.* You're not cut out to be a bandit."

The man shook his head. "It's all I know, *señor.*"

Lance looked at him incredulously. "Then, stay the hell outa Texas. Now go on home."

"Thank you, *señor,*" The man limped toward the gate.

Zeb called again. "Let this one go too."

Lance checked his shotgun. "Santiago!"

The bandit leader dragged himself to his feet. His swollen

face took on a crooked smile. "Now," he croaked, "now we strike the bargain."

"I will make no bargain with you, Santiago."

The bandit came closer, glancing to see that the others were out of hearing range. "I will tell you where the gold is hidden. You will let me go. Could anything be more fair?"

"Santiago . . . for the crime of murder . . ."

"Only I know where the gold is hidden, *hombre!*"

"For the crime of rape and kidnapping . . ."

"It is a fair exchange."

"For the crime of arson and robbery . . ."

"You'll never find the gold if I don't tell you!"

"For rustling and extortion . . ."

"You would lose nothing. We would both win."

"I sentence you to die."

"You would have the gold – all of it! I ask only to live!"

"You tortured my son – and killed his mother – you will not live. There can be no bargain."

Santiago, who had been edging closer, lunged at Lance, a small dirk clutched in his fist. The shotgun bucked in Lance's hands, slamming Santiago to the ground. He raised his head disbelievingly. "But the gold . . ."

His eyes clouded over and his head sagged into the dirt.

Lance turned wearily to the surprised Zeb Marlin and said, "There's another one you won't have to hang, Zeb."

Lance stood on the front porch in the early morning sun. Mike and Juanita's wagon was packed and ready to roll. Lance clasped his hand.

"Mistah Lance," Mike said, "that gold was your ace in the hole."

Lance smiled ruefully. Mike would never know how badly Lance needed that ace right now. "Maybe I didn't do the smart thing, Mike. But it was all I could do. No way I could have let Santiago live."

Mike grasped the hand tighter. "I reckon you did the right thing, Mistah Lance. I'd never believe you wouldn't. But I reckon that gold's gone for good."

Lance nodded. "I reckon it is."

Juanita ran the gauntlet of hugs before climbing up beside Mike.

Lance watched until the wagon disappeared from sight, then looked all around him. Good friends were leaving, but they were still good friends. Gabrièl, head freshly bandaged, was playing with Ann and Brent down by the corral. The doctor said the boy would be fine, and Cisco would make a complete recovery from his wound.

Most of his new cattle and his new land would go to the bank, and the familiar figure of Drought still paced across the land. But Guy had come in yesterday saying that cattle were bringing premium prices in the silver fields of Colorado. He had a deal with George to winter cattle above the fever line, and cattlemen in Montana and Wyoming were crying for good Texas seed stock. The dry, but securely fenced, pastures of the original MacDuff Ranch were teeming with cattle ready for the long trail north.

The beautiful woman clinging to his arm raised an adoring face as his mother-in-law watched proudly. Life was good, and there remained an empire to build. He sniffed the breeze and laughed out loud. He could smell rain in the air.

* * * * *

Drugs and dealers infest a small Georgia town, determined to destroy three generations of a family—except they underestimated a battle-scarred old man. . . a fast moving tale by Jack P. Jones

The Third Season

With determination, the old man slowly forced a path deeper into the swamp. In the distance, wild dogs gathered for a killing hunt. He knew dangerous men were trailing him, and he left clear signs for them to follow. It was all part of his feeble plan. Elmer Goodhand shifted the bags of angry rattlesnakes, hoping he could save the life of the five-year-old granddaughter he raised from a baby. If he were lucky, he might even save himself.

This is the story of one man's devotion for a child and her worship of the one who is her world. Hauntingly and brilliantly, it portrays in a unique tenderness, the best of us and the worst of us.

You may purchase copies of *The Third Season* at a 20% discount, postage prepaid. Complete the coupon below and mail to the publisher.

Name_____(2-7)

Address_____

City_____State_____ZIP_____

I am enclosing ($17.56) per copy $_____
GA residents add 6% sales tax ($1.05) $_____
Total amount closed $_____

Valid in U.S. only. All orders subject to availability

Credit card purchases: Toll Free 877-282-7586

Use your___Visa___MasterCard #_____

Exp. date_____Signature_____

GoldenIsle Publishers, Inc.
2395 Hawkinsville Hwy
Eastman, GA 31023

A note to our readers

Thank you for spending time with us. We hope your visit has been an enjoyable one.

The staff of GoldenIsle Publishers, Inc. is committed to bringing you some of the best in contemporary, adventure, and historical romance stories by writers who know their craft and instill deep feelings in the characters that bring life to the pages of a book.

If you have enjoyed sharing the adventure with the people who moved throughout this novel, write to us and let us know. Your comments will be forwarded to the authors who constantly strive to entertain their readers with carefully researched and intricately plotted stories.

GoldenIsle Publishers, Inc.
2395 Hawkinsville Hwy
Eastman, GA 31023